The Silent Minaret

The Silent Minaret

Ishtiyaq Shukri

First published in 2005 by Jacana Media (Pty) Ltd.
10 Orange Street
Sunnyside, 2092
Johannesburg
South Africa

Second edition published in May 2006

ISBN 1-77009-249-8
978-1-77009-249-5

Cover design by Disturbance
Set in Bembo 12/15
Printed by Paarl Print
See a complete list of Jacana titles at www.jacana.co.za

To

Colette

&

the National Missing Persons Helpline, UK.

When Cities Crack

When cities crack, do stories too,
their scaffolding
collapsing?
Then I trawl the fragments lying disarranged,
searching, this side and that.
Emerge, ashen,
fragments limply
dangling
from upturned palms.
When cities crack, do memories too,
like china heirlooms
smashing?
Then I crawl into the folds of memory,
lifting,
calling,
tapping.
Searching for the missing,
never finding.
Brushing, carefully dusting,
only ever finding
skeletons of silence
cobwebs of sound.

When cities crack, do people too,
their lives
disintegrating?
Then they seep slowly through the cracks,
drip drip,
only brittle vessels remaining.
Then I come with upturned palms of stained
– scraps and chips of –
glass,
bits and
– collage –
pieces,
mosaic pictures hobbled together from fragments.
Here, I say, I've salvaged what I could,
your stories,
and then capsize ashen palms into cracked vessels,
everything together
lumping.
"I'm sorry it's so disarranged, like ravaged cities
cracking."

Contents

I

The Room

Prayer Beads and Cigarettes 13
Black and White 23
Summer of 2003 31
Homelands 35

ﷴ

Disappeared 41
The Karoo 47
Violent Night 61

II

The Bookshelf

The Silent Minaret 75
Remembering Hide and Seek 80
Purple Rain 81
jím, ayn, káf, mím, há´ 83
"I just don't give a – " 84

ﷴ

'A road map into our past' 91
The Monster's Name 105
The Sanctuary 115
Russell Square 131

ﷴ

alif, dál, dhal… 156
The Verses 157
Missing Persons 163
Finsbury Park Mosque 170
sifir wahed athnaan 175

III

The Café

Vasinthe's Letter 179
Another Brick in Another Wall 185
Baghdad Café 189
London N4 195

ꕥ

Vasinthe and Gloria 199
Somewhere and Nowhere 205
The Last Night 219
Closed Chapters 225
`The summer is over, Theresa´ 237
Katinka's Text Message 239

ꕥ

Acknowledgements 243

ꕥ

Thanks 248

I
The Room

'History includes the present.'
Eric Auerbach

Prayer Beads and Cigarettes

"NOW, AND AT THE HOUR of our death. Amen." When she has finished her prayers, she struggles out of her armchair and shuffles across the room. In just a few months she has begun to feel her age. She opens the window at the other end of the room and peeps out over the early-morning clamour of the station and bus terminus below.

Another hot day has been forecast and news images from France have unsettled her; old people who have succumbed to the heat are being kept in refrigerated trucks till awayonholiday relatives return to claim them for burial. Some have already been placed in temporary graves. She draws the curtains against the bright light. Unless she shuts out the sun now, the room will soon become unbearably hot and she will have to retreat to her tiny bedroom at the back of the building for respite. She settles back into her armchair and pours her rosary beads, like precious grains of amber, from a cupped palm into a red satin pouch in which she also keeps the tasbeeh he gave her.

❧

"Ah!" she exclaimed when he casually dropped the beads into her lap, then proceeded to explore the string with curious fingers. "Issa, this is exquisite. I can't possibly accept it."

Yes, you can.

"But your friend brought them fro –"

Tradition. He knows I'd never use them.

"Then that was not why he gave them." She held out her hand. "I think you should keep them. To remind you of your friend and his pilgrimage."

Issa leaned forward and folded her fingers gently around the beads. *My friend also gave me a lewd T-shirt he'd picked up in Amsterdam on his way back. I'd rather remember him by that. I want you to have the beads.*

She squeezed his hand and smiled mischievously. "Can I see the T-shirt before I decide?"

He didn't laugh often. But that cracked him up.

It was she who first realised that he had gone missing. They had creaked around each other's lives between cheap paper-thin walls for nearly three years, during which time she had come to rely on his routine.

She wasn't too keen when she first realised that a student would be moving in downstairs. Sat anxiously in her armchair while he dumped boxes, waiting for the music, the endless cycle of noisy friends to start and never stop. But she was needlessly concerned and sat up, startled, when she heard the rare sound of footsteps ascend the staircase and land outside her door.

Knock knock.

She knew it must be him, so she pressed her palms gently to her hair and opened the door without interrogation.

Good morning, he greeted. *I've come to introduce myself. I'm Issa. I've just moved in downstairs.* He extended his hand.

"How do you do?" she responded. "I'm Frances," and put her hand in his, the old and fragile enfolded in the young and strong. She hurriedly unpacked a smile when he unexpectedly accepted her hopeful invitation to a cup of tea.

"...You must be thirsty?"

That would be very nice, thank you.

Her anxieties proved premature; his movements downstairs soon became a comforting, harmonious accompaniment to her own lonely life.

Like her, he woke early. At six o'clock, as she started to recite her first prayer of the day – "The angel of the Lord declared unto Mary..." – she would hear his radio alarm click on to the serious political breakfast programme he always listened to in the mornings. She puzzled at how one so young could take the world so seriously. *We southerners have to*, he responded curtly to an enquiring comment she once passed.

The only quality of life most of us dare to hope for is after death.

The response resonated and for a few mornings after that she also tuned in, but the sound of all those politicians lying and bickering first thing in the morning didn't appeal to her.

ꕥ

She slips the red satin pouch into the pocket of her cotton house gown. Satin pouch cotton pocket, satin pouch cotton pocket. She does not withdraw her hand immediately but waves it gently around inside her pocket. Satinpouchcottonpocket, satin cot an pocket. She enjoys the feeling of cool cotton brushing against her skin and the muffled jingling mingling of the beads, like the sugar crystals reserved for special guests, that she used to sneak into her pocket from her grandmother's silver sugar bowl when she was a little girl. The two strings of prayer beads always get tangled in the pouch – a trosebery, she thinks – so that she has to peel the beads apart, like seeds from a pomegranate, when she sits down to pray. Sometimes, her gnarled fingers struggle and when the light is bad, she has to start with the cross to help her identify which of the almost identical beads belong to which string. She doesn't mind; the ritual helps settle her mind – rosary tasbeeh, rosary tasbeeh – and evokes a scene he once described of a mosque in the shadow of a cathedral. She looks up to imagine the sight: a cathemosdraquel, she thinks – to match her trosebery.

ꕥ

"He washed a lot," she recalled to his mother during her brief visit to London immediately after his disappearance. "Extraordinary the amount of times that boy washed during the course of a day. He had a shower every morning at six thirty – just as the sports news was starting, you see – and again every night at ten which, I must admit, rather baffled me."

"Well, that's not unusual back home," Vasinthe said, defensively. "In fact, bathing has always been central to our daily routine."

"Yes, I understand that, except he also washed several times during the course of a day."

Vasinthe frowned.

"Oh yes. He was always washing. I'm surprised he had any skin left on him at all. Do you know, he washed every time he came in from outside. Yes, I could tell because I would hear the key in the door, then the sound of him kicking off his shoes and walking to the bathroom which is directly under mine, turning on the hot water tap – I could hear the boiler come on – and then washing for several minutes. He would do that every single time he came in from outside, without fail."

ꕥ

The cross, she thinks as she handles it – a barbaric execution on a plank, the main difference between the two faiths. She hadn't realised that that was all. In recent weeks she has not been able to make the short walk to Mass and resolves to share this with Father Jerome during his next Communion visit.

"It's a rather crucial difference," the priest responds in his heavy French accent.

"But even the immaculate conception and the virgin birth! Did you know that, Father?" She passes him a slip of paper from her bedside on which she has copied a quote in her neat, careful hand. "Have a look at this."

The priest takes the quote, but sets it aside.

She watches him blow out the candle and slot it into place in the black leather bag, his portable altar, she thinks, like a doctor's bag is his portable surgery. Portable altars, portable surgeries, portable meals.

"And don't you think it peculiar, Father, how one religion remembers things another doesn't?"

The priest picks up the quote:

> Behold! The angels said:
> "O Mary! God hath chosen thee
> And purified thee – chosen thee
> Above the women of all nations…

Behold! The angels said:
"O Mary! God giveth thee
Glad tidings of the Word
From Him: his name
Will be Christ Jesus,
The son of Mary, held in honour
In this world and the Hereafter
And of (the company of) those
Nearest to God.

Qur'an S.iii. 42-45

"You mean like Christ, *God incarnate* – remember – having died on *the cross* to redeem our sins?" Father Jerome lays down the quote and secures the buckles on his black satchel. Done. Next, Mr Anderson on Stroud Green Road.

She smiles slowly. "I was thinking about the name of the Virgin's father."

The priest is hot. He wants nothing more than to snap the white strip from his collar and undo the tight button underneath. He lifts his satchel from the chair and tugs ineffectually at the neckline of his black shirt instead.

"Imran," she says, picturing him, as she always does, standing on a bridge.

"Pardon?"

"Christ's grandfather on earth. He was called Imran."

The priest frowns.

"Yes, Father, he was. And the Wife of Bath, she was an Arab woman. Did you know that, Father?"

ﷴ

By seven he would be scratching around in the kitchen. So far as I could tell, he didn't eat very much. I never saw him coming and going with big bags of shopping or garbage. But the recycling bin downstairs was always full of newspapers, often with articles cut out. He used to get them everyday from the newsagents on the corner, and some milk for me if I needed it. On his way back, he'd hand the sports section to the fruit vendor outside the station who always gave him a piece of fruit in return.

At about ten past eight the volume would go up on the radio for the main interview of the day – some big wig, who, for some or other reason had made it into the news that morning. At nine the radio would go off. This was my favourite time of the morning because then there would follow the most beautiful piece of music I've ever heard. A gentle, lilting, slightly sorrowful tune – just beautiful.

As nine o'clock approached, I knew that tune was coming, and as I got my rosary out to say my morning prayers, I would try to hum it in anticipation, but I would never get it quite right.

And so every morning at nine, I would smile with recognition when it came rising up through the floorboards, and I sat down to pray: In the name of the Father, and of the Son and of the Holy Spirit...

I knew then that he would be at his computer, surrounded by all those books, writing for hours, all through the morning, with the same piece of music playing over and over again in the background. He said it blocked out the noise from the street below and helped him concentrate.

She doesn't know how to use the tasbeeh. He didn't really know either, but said it was simple, that you just rolled the beads through your hands during prayer rather than pause at every individual one. Sometimes, when she hasn't been attentive, she's found herself saying the rosary with his tasbeeh.

When this happens, she doesn't stop to swap prayer beads, she just continues by counting the decades on her fingers, the tasbeeh dangling from her old bent hands:

> Hail Mary,
> Full of grace,
> The Lord is with thee;
> Blessed art thou amongst women,
> And blessed is the fruit of thy womb,
> Jesus.

At around noon he'd nip out to the local shops on the other side of the station. It's very vibrant down there, lots of Algerian, Ethiopian and Caribbean stores. You can buy almost anything you can think of – so different from when I first moved here. You couldn't find an onion then. Bananas. And satsumas! Good heavens, back then they were a treat rare enough for Christmas stockings.

He always knocked on the ceiling to see if I wanted anything. I would knock back, once for no or twice for yes. If I knocked twice, he'd come scaling up the steps, three or four at a time as he used to, to see what he could get me.

He didn't have a TV, so he'd call by most evenings to watch the news at seven. We'd usually have a bite to eat together, bread and soup, beans on toast, simple fare – like me, he wasn't one given to excess, though I always got the impression that for him, simplicity was a choice rather than a necessity. Sometimes, when he was feeling homesick, he'd cook his favourite, lentils and rice, for which I soon developed a taste, but which he always ate with a faraway look, only ever having a couple of mouthfuls, moving the food around his mouth slowly, as if it hurt, before giving up and setting his plate aside.

After dinner, he'd stay for a while and chat about this and that – what he'd heard on the radio or read in the papers that day. Sometimes he'd bring clippings from the day's newspapers to show me. I always pretended to understand them, but to be honest, the issues that interested him were a bit too advanced for me. He must have known I was none the wiser really, but he never lost interest or patience and was always very polite.

Occasionally, he'd even talk about his writing. He'd get carried away and very animated about it all and I would watch with interest, not because I understood very much about what he was saying, but because I enjoyed seeing the excitement his work brought to the face of someone usually so serious.

But more often than not, it was me who did all the talking, especially, you know, towards the end. He didn't seem to mind listening to all my ramblings, about the war and that. Very unusual, I thought, for such a young lad to be interested in an old lady's memories. But then again, perhaps that's not so surprising. After all, he did spend his days writing about history.

Then he'd go back down there, and that piece of music would start up again for a couple of hours. He'd have another shower at ten and at eleven his light switch would click off.

And there you have it. That was how Issa spent his days. Well, at least till everything changed. Occasionally his friend Katinka would call round and sometimes he would go to see her. But otherwise he was here, downstairs, at that computer – day in, day out. Doesn't sound like much, does it? Boring even, some might say. But they'd be wrong. I spent too much of my life being dazzled by peacocks, learnt too late that it's the quiet ones, the ones who make themselves invisible, God's abstemious creatures, who often hold the trick.

❧

She looks up at the clock. Half past nine. A long hot day full of desolate sighs yawns ahead. She wishes it were evening so she could step out onto the roof to take in the cool air. It will be two hours before her newspaper is delivered. Her newspaper and her portable meal. And then? What next? Portable toilets? Portable black bags? Zip. Portable refrigerated French –

She stops herself. Reaches for the packet of cigarettes from the table next to her chair.

Katinka had forgotten a packet during one of her visits some weeks back. At first it lay there for days. She'd look at the packet, wishing for Katinka to call by for them. She almost picked up the phone once to remind her about them, but she stopped herself. Don't be silly, you old bird. Why would someone want to come half way across London to collect a packet of cigarettes? She smoked them instead.

"A bit late to be starting new habits, Frances," the woman from Social Services remarked while she laid out her portable meal on a portable tray in her lap.

"Helps pass the time," Frances responded indifferently.

"But you want to be looking after your health, especially at your age."

"It's my age that needs the health warning," Frances said. "It will see me off long before these do."

"Don't be so silly," the woman chided, slinging her bag over her shoulder. "Now eat up. I'll be back with your tea at five," and then she vanished through the door.

Portable altars, portable surgeries, portable meals. Come and go. Come and sorry, can't stop, go.

Black and White

"LADIES AND GENTLEMEN, we have commenced our descent for London's Heathrow airport. In preparation for the landing, please make sure that your seats are in the upright position and your seatbelts fastened, that your tray tables are folded away and that your hand luggage has been safely stowed."

The announcement wakes Kagiso. Sleepily he moves his journal into his lap and folds away his table. He does not crane, like the woman next to him, eager to catch a glimpse through the tiny window of the enormous city below; he'd rather not be doing this. Instead, while the aeroplane bides its time, swooping and tilting and dipping in the skies above the sprawling city, waiting for its moment, he closes his eyes again and tries to chase the dreamlike memories that have been scattered by the announcement.

When he was a little boy and already captivated by the moving image, a grainy black and white sequence, an amalgam of the SABC propaganda films of their childhood constituted Kagiso's mental picture of what that spring morning in September 1970 must have been like. No dialogue accompanied the images, only the imagined rattle of an antiquated projector. He knew very little about what actually happened on that day, so his mind film was very short.

In it, she is walking down a road in an affluent Johannesburg suburb. A two-month-old bundle is strapped in a blanket to her back. She is in search of work. She knocks on another front door. A heavily pregnant woman opens. They have a brief exchange, which he cannot hear above the rattle of his imaginary projector. The pregnant woman smiles and invites her in. She closes the door.

That is it. The end.

The pregnant woman has her baby, a boy, later that same day. But he only knows that in these few words. That is all there is to know. He never imagined the birth. For a long time it never occurred to him to do so.

He has spent most of the overnight flight from Johannesburg scratching in the journal cradled in his lap, at first repeating, as has become his custom, his opening affirmation as soon as they were fully airborne:

SA 238 Johannesburg – London

Thursday 7th August 2003

I am Kagiso Mayoyo. I grew up in Johannesburg, but I was born in Taung. Taungs as the old people say, the place of lions…

Taung, a small village hardly ever featured on the map. Approximately half way between its more famous neighbours: to the south, Kimberley, city of diamonds and, consequently, home to the largest man-made excavation on earth; and to the north, Mafikeng, besieged by 6 000 Afrikaners under the leadership of Generals Snyman and Cronje at the start of the South African War in 1899 and defended by Colonel Robert Baden-Powell for 217 brave days.

Yes, the very same and very honourable Colonel Robert Baden-Powell, founder of the Boy Scouts, brave defender of Mafikeng and arguably the determiner of Issa's fate. But has anyone ever heard of heard of the Black Watch? And does anyone even know that, were it not for them, Mafikeng would have fallen to Snyman and Cronje because, during the siege, Baden-Powell relied heavily on the Barolong, the Black Watch, *my* people, to defend the town?

History was not intended to capture this part of the story; Baden-Powell went to great lengths to omit it from his reports and from his diaries. He also omitted to mention that my people were forced to survive on less rations during the siege than their British counterparts. Yet, at the end of the siege, which had turned Baden-Powell into a national hero in England, not one of my people so much as saw the glint of a medal. But while the Colonel was able to contrive his written submissions of the siege to London, he had less control over the version of events that passed from the mouths of my forefathers into the ears of their descendents. My grandmother would gather Issa and I at her feet on the mud floor of her dark shack that smelt of fire wood and into which daylight sparkled through holes in the corrugated iron like stars in the canopy of night.

"Forget about medals," she'd roar in a big voice imitating the elders in the kgotla. "Land will be our true reward for aiding the British in this war. The honourable Baden-Powell has promised it to us in abundance." But then my grandmother would lower her head and look to the mud floor between her feet. "They received," she would start, letting her pointing hand rise and fall three times, once for each word that followed, "not one inch. African land – Baden-Powell's to give, Baden-Powell's to withhold."

My grandmother would lean forward, her elbows resting on her knees. "'Forget about medals,' the elders urged, 'and land takes long to allocate. But money, money is easy to give and we hear that the good people of Britain have raised money, a lot of it, £30 000 for the reconstruction of our town. The generosity of the good people of Britain, that will be our true reward.'"

At this point I would look to the forefinger on my grandmother's limp hand as it dangled between her knees, and when it started to unfurl as it always did, I knew what was to come. "Not one penny. The only reward our people received for their sacrifice, was more death – more than, 1 000 of our people died of starvation. So, your Boy Scouts' Baden-Powell may be a national hero in Jo'burg and London, but here, among our people, he's a lying thief." And then my grandmother would disappear into the even darker darkness behind the thick curtain that divided the shack in half and into which we never assumed we could follow.

Surprised?

I was too. And angry. Exactly how, I started to wonder, could one people's hero be another's villain? And how, I wanted to know, would my people have been any worse off if the demonic Boers had been victorious?

But what has all this past got to do with me, now, here hurtling northwards towards Issa-less London, the African sun setting dramatically to my left? Well, everything. Ma Vasinthe received an e-mail from Issa some months before he went missing. It contained only one line: 'The past is eternally with us.' It may have contained more. Ma Vasinthe may have deleted the rest before she forwarded the e-mail to me, but I doubt it. Issa was very good at one-line summations. 'The past is eternally with us.' That is very Issa.

So yes, even as we approach the equator at an altitude of 36 000 feet and travelling at an awesome 840 kilometres per hour (Taung not even a speck on the global co-ordinates of our flight path), the past gives easy chase because of Issa. It was he who first challenged the official version of events we were taught in school, though I must confess that I shook my head in dismay when he called Baden-Powell a 'lying thief' in our history class. This caused an outrage that unsettled sensibilities at our private school for months – Mr Thompson, our history teacher, being leader of the northern suburbs branch of the Scouts and a long-time admirer of the Colonel.

But Issa remained resolute, even as he became the butt of snide comments from Maths to Phys Ed: 'Dreamer, schemer, history's cleaner.' Eventually, Ma Vasinthe, who usually let us fight our own battles, intervened. She put Issa in touch with a research student at the university, who helped him compile a bibliography of recent revisionist research into the South African War. It took weeks and Issa read every entry before presenting it to Mr Thompson.

"Conjecture!" he exclaimed dismissively, throwing the bibliography to one side. "Mere conjecture. Speculation by a bunch of new age leftists at Wits. And woe betide that university for encouraging it. History cannot be re-written," he confirmed. "History *is*, and at St Stephen's we accept only the thorough, rigorous and sanctioned historical versions outlined in the syllabus, in which, let me remind you, the conflict of 1899 to 1902 is referred to as the Anglo-Boer War. I would advise you to remember that, Shamsuddin, when you take your examinations."

But Issa didn't heed the warning. As I read the question in the mid-year exam asking to explain Baden-Powell's role in the siege of Mafikeng, I knew that not only would he ignore the alternative question on the Jameson Raid, but also that he would present Mr Thompson with his view of Baden-Powell as a lying thief. Even though the final examination of that year was externally marked, the fact that Issa had compromised his mid-year scores meant that in the end he got five A grades and a B for matric, rather than the six A grades he would almost certainly otherwise have attained. It was a defining moment. Issa was never given to excessive displays of emotion, but in the end he lost the struggle to fight back the tears as a huge drop fell, plop, on the official advice of results.

Issa took to his room for three days playing 'We don't need no education' at full volume, over and over again. During that time, only Ma Gloria was allowed in. We never knew what they spoke about. When he eventually emerged, it was to pick up the phone to turn down his place at the prestigious white liberal University of Cape Town where we had both, to Ma Vasinthe's delight, been accepted.

I'm going to UWC, he declared to our shocked assembly when he put down the phone, and then spent the next few days rushing in a late application to the University of the Western Cape, the intellectual home of the left and the most radical university in the country.

I should perhaps also mention that Taung has its own claim to fame, unearthed as it were, by my great-uncle, my grandfather's brother, while he and his fellow labourers were toiling away in a lime pit in 1925. My grandmother still keeps the article from *The Star* announcing the discovery. I took a copy of it for my journal the last time I saw her:

Tuesday, February 3, 1925

THE MISSING LINK?

FOSSIL SKULL MIDWAY BETWEEN
MAN AND THE APE

LIME CLIFF FIND NEAR TAUNGS

IMMENSE IMPORTANCE OF
DISCOVERY
BY PROFESSOR DART

> A scientific discovery of the very first importance has been made in the Union and developed by investigation from Johannesburg. So far as its nature can be put into a sequence, it is the discovery of a fossil skull representing something really midway between man and the great apes.
>
> The expression "the missing link" – loose and unscientific as it is – most clearly covers the nature of the owner of the skull in question, which is that of an individual about six years of age...

I remember Issa asking me from the corner of his mouth where my forefather's name was when my grandmother brought out the article during one of our visits to Taung. I shrugged my shoulders.

Missing, he whispered. *Just like the Black Watch. Missing from history. Missing from archaeology. Like a missing link.*

❧

When the aeroplane finally slams onto the runway, his head falls forward, once again spilling his rekindled dreams. He presses back into the seat to steady himself against the forwardbackward thrusting of the craft as it rushes down the runway, wings distorted like a mating mantis, straining desperately to bring its trans-global propulsion to a halt.

"Ladies and gentlemen, welcome to London Heathrow. Please remain seated until the aircraft has come to a complete stop. We trust that you've enjoyed your flight with us. On behalf of the captain and all the crew, we wish you a pleasant stay and look forward to seeing you again in the future. Thank you for flying South African Airways and goodbye."

In the arrivals hall, Katinka walks up to the monitor of flight arrivals: SAA 238 Johannesburg landed 06:25. She smiles at the safe arrival of her saviour, her knight in student banger. It was Kagiso who insisted that Issa stop to give her a ride through the scorching Karoo all those Februarys ago, poised as they were, at the dawn of a new world. They have spoken on the phone several times since Issa went missing in April, but this will be their first reunion in many years.

Summer of 2003

THEY HAVE BEEN STATIONARY ON the motorway for nearly ten minutes, though, for Kagiso, after all the speed and motion, it seems like much longer. An overhead electronic road sign flashes a warning: 'Congestion ahead. Slow down.'

"Has there been an accident?" he asks, moving around awkwardly in his seat.

Katinka shakes her head. "Nope, just the rush hour into central London."

"Sjoe!" he exhales before unbuckling his seat belt to remove his jacket. "You were right. It is hot." He leans forward, shaking his arms behind him to shed the unwanted garment. "The pilot warned of a scorcher on the plane."

Katinka adjusts her sunglasses. "I know. Can you believe it? There's been great excitement about it on the radio as well. But I'm not complaining. I like this transformation." She pulls up the handbrake and reaches down to a cavity by the gear stick for a packet of cigarettes. "Fag?"

ꕥ

Summertime in London. Coats and boots, low grey skies and bare trees, long dark nights and long miserable faces, have all been rolled up like winter rugs and stuffed into the cupboard under the stairs – the control switch on the central heating panel finally flicked, with the victorious sigh of a survivor, from constant to off. However brief its forecast stay, however disappointing its outlook, spirits are high: anything is better than the winter.

Now, dragonflies dart around to the buzz of lawnmowers. Garden furniture has been dusted, huge sun-deck umbrellas unfurled, and cookers abandoned for barbecues. Flat roofs, however precarious, have become terraces. Long carefree dinners are enjoyed outside. At nine thirty when it is still light, it is hard to imagine the long winter nights when it is dark by four. Trees are lush and green.

The sky, especially down by the river, is big, blue and high, Katinka thinks. Issa used to love it down there.

'London ceases to be London.' Pubs are covered in hanging baskets bursting with brightly coloured blooms and by midday, skiving punters flow over onto the pavements like the white froth from their chilled glasses. Flesh is everywhere; shirtless men, wispy-frocked women, translucently pale at first, painfully red as the season progresses, celebrate their liberation from the confines of coats and jackets. Parks, like temples of Akhenaten, burst with sun worshippers; the animated movement of skate-boarders, roller-bladers, kite flyers, Frisbee throwers, contrasts acrobatically with the horizontal inertia of the religious proceedings. The annual traditions of tennis at Wimbledon, cricket at Lords, racing at Ascot, the jubilation of carnival, long queues at tourist attractions and nightly classical music concerts at the Royal Albert Hall all confirm that, even though it might not look like summer, it definitely is not winter.

Inching their way through the city, Katinka turns up the volume on the radio, then turns to smile at Kagiso:

"Su time / ving

mmer And li is

the ee

zee..."

There is nothing ambiguous about this summer, she thinks. It will surely be remembered for generations to come, earning its place in the national memory of climatic abnormalities, along with the storm of '87, the summer of '76, the floods of '53, the gales of...

She remembers walking the streets of the sun-baked capital in July, desperately dishing out 'Missing' leaflets of Issa to anybody who would take one.

At the time she found it hard to imagine that earlier in the year they were grid-locked for hours when a few inches of snow had brought the city to a standstill. Once again Britain's fragile infrastructure stood by the roadside, helpless hands on flabby hips, jeering at stranded commuters. Trains, also capable of being rendered immobile by leaves, ground to a halt on icy tracks and motorists forced to spend the night in their cars stuck on frozen motorways, snowed in ahead of the snow ploughs and gritters who got caught up in the gridlock having left their depots too late.

How *do* they manage in Russia?

But then, as cloudless day succeeded the novelty of cloudless day, a feeling of disbelieving excitement took hold of the city: the wish that 'if only it could be like this every day' supplanted by the glorious reality of it being like this everyday.

"Today London was hotter than Nairobi!"

"Keep your homes well ventilated." (Houses built for the cold can become murderous furnaces in the heat.)

"Drink plenty of liquids."

"More sangria, anyone?"

"Strawberries?"

The tube became even more unbearable than usual. "Ladies and gentlemen, this train will no longer be stopping at Cockfosters. In your own interest, we have been redirected to the Caribbean instead. Ladies and gentlemen, this train is for the Caribbean. Please stand clear of the closing doors." Smiles became broader, skins darker, office hours shorter.

While bookmakers braced themselves for the biggest weather-induced betting spree since the summer of '76, leaf-fearing trains ground to a halt on temperamental railway tracks – in the heat they had buckled – and motorists were once again stranded on constantly worked-on but eternally inadequate road surfaces – in the heat they had melted.

How *do* they manage in India?

On the 10th of August the unprecedented was confirmed: the mercury reached 37.9°C at Heathrow, 38.5 in Kent, the highest since records began in 1875, the highest, in fact, since the thermometer that contained it, was invented. Paradise had come to London. And before the year was over, heaven arrived too, in the form of a big gold cup brought back from a rugby pitch in Australia. Everybody wanted a photo-op, especially the 'Things can only get better' Prime Minister, who was, by now, gagging for a bit of good news, perhaps making constant invocation to his name-sake saint, the finder of elusive things.

And now Kagiso, who also understands something of the frustration of a futile search, has arrived to a city transformed. Fountains have become swimming pools and the sandy enclaves on the riverbank at low tide, venues for impromptu beach-like parties: "Do you really like it? / Is it is it wicked? / We're loving it loving it loving it / We're loving it like that."

When Katinka tells him that they're approaching Issa's flat, he looks intently at the throng, the crowded pavements, the busy roads, the well-stocked shops already trading briskly, but all he can see in the teaming multitude of normality is what has gone from it, what is not there, skulking, a haunting absence everywhere he looks – the missing link, he thinks, between him and the city.

He wants to leap out of the car and shout, "Stop! Please, don't anybody move. Everybody just stand still." That will make finding him a lot easier. But who would take any notice? People would just walk through him, around him, like they're doing right now, paying no attention to the cavity in their midst.

"I can't park here until after six thirty this evening," Katinka explains when they eventually pull up outside the flat. "I'll have to drop you here, if that's okay?"

A few seconds lapse before Kagiso registers that she is talking to him. "Sure! That's fine, thanks."

"I'll pick you up for dinner at six thirty. Say hi to Frances if you see her. Tell her I'll pop in this evening. And get some rest. You look completely fucked."

Homelands

KAGISO IS IN LONDON TO PACK and clean Issa's flat, but apart from the bookcase, there isn't actually much to pack; apart from a thin layer of dust that has slipped in through the gap under the door, like the angel of death, he imagines, to cover everything. There isn't really much to clean.

Katinka had warned him of the heat on the phone, but he was dismissive – I'm from South Africa. How hot can London get? When he returns to Issa's abandoned flat after dinner, he opens the only window in the room. In Johannesburg, he would be able to step through it onto his balcony overlooking the pool. Here, there is only this tiny window, a droning bus terminus and an entrance to a station into which people flow like miners into the tunnelled baking bowels of the earth.

He turns away from the window and moves towards his open journal on Issa's desk. He writes the date, Friday, 8th August 2003. And then he writes two words: disappear disappearance. But that is all he can manage, so he starts doodling instead. He turns the F of Friday into an E, which he then forces into the number 8. He extends the tail of the y into a squiggly circle all around the date. Encouraged, he moves his nib over to the two words. He slashes them into syllables. He colours in the loopy letters, except the p's. These, he turns into two sets of searching eyes with bushy eyebrows. Their tails become noses. He adds two sad mouths, then a loop around each word transforms them into faces. The words now seem to wrap around the faces across the eyes, like blindfolds. He doesn't like the image so he blots out the negative prefixes and tries to invert the sad mouths into happy smiles. This only achieves sinister grins. Frustrated, he draws an angry line through the sketches, clambers out of his clothes and walks into the shower.

On the eastern side of the city, Katinka is seated at her kitchen table, pen poised at the top right-hand corner of the page (she'd positioned the pen instinctively on the left at first but moved it quickly to the other side when she realised her mistake) eyes on the alphabet stuck on the wall in front of her, another of Karim's little gifts.

Karim.

Whom she does not want to share.

Karim.

About whom she speaks to no one.

Karim.

Her secret.

Karim.

Now behind the wall.

She has pledged to learn the alphabet during the summer vacation. "If I do nothing else this summer," she told a colleague, "then at least I will have learned a whole new code, turned the key to literacy in a whole new language."

Now she is seated at her kitchen table, pen poised at the top right-hand corner of the page, eyes on the alphabet stuck on the wall in front of her, another of Karim's little gifts. Karim. Whom she does not want to share. Karim. About whom she speaks to no one. Karim. Her secret.

Karim.

Now behind the wall.

She says the first letter out loud – aa – and simultaneously pulls a downward stroke on the paper: ا. She sits back to evaluate her effort then repeats the letter a few times before moving on to the next, bá': ب

ﷺ

Kagiso steps out of the shower knowing what to write, the words forcing at his fingertips, making them twitch. He does not shave as he had intended, does not dry himself, does not get dressed, but immediately returns to his journal to write, not like

Katinka is doing, slowly, deliberately, letter for letter, but swiftly, his fingers responding nimbly, dishing out words and phrases that have stewed for decades through a keen and agile pen, beads of London water, like teardrops, weeping from his skin.

I am Kagiso Mayoyo. I grew up in Johannesburg, but I was born in Taung, Taungs as the old people say, the place of lions. I found myself thinking again tonight, far away and on the other side of the world, about my place of birth while I was in, of all places, the men's toilet in a restaurant in Brick Lane, East London.

"East London?" I checked, confused, when Katinka announced our destination. "But I've only just arrived."

"Not *that* East London! East London here, where I live, in the East End, mate."

Of course, I'd realised my mistake as soon as I opened my mouth, but I went with it. It felt good to laugh again.

"And here we are, Brick Lane!" Katinka declared, introducing me to the vibrant colourful cobbled street by gesturing up it with a theatrically extended arm. "Like the Meghna River flowing through East London."

I was amazed. Here was a London you won't find in the postcard shops. Like the time I accompanied Issa on his illicit trip to Durban. It was as though we had arrived, not in Zululand, but somewhere on the sub-continent. In Brick Lane, where Katinka took me to eat dhal, even the street signs are in another language.

"Welcome to Londonistan," the waiter joked when he heard we were South African and then, looking at Katinka and then at me, smiled an approving smile, "So nice to see you getting on these days, so nice to see."

When we had placed our order, I went to the toilet. Inside the cubicle was a long chain of graffiti. It started with: Bangladesh used to be East Pakistan. To this had been added: Pakistan used to be India. The chain rolled on: Israel used to be Palestine / Lebanon used to be Syria / Eritrea used to be Ethiopia / Alsace used to be France then Germany then France / America used to be England / England used to be France. Alongside this main chain ran a parallel chain, around which someone had drawn a huge bracket which pointed to the heading, insha'allah: One day Basque will have been Spain / Northern Ireland, Wales and Scotland will have been Britain / Tibet will have been China / Palestine will have been Israel / Chechnya will have been Russia. Under all of this was a somewhat unrelated contribution thrown in for good measure. It read: St George had never been to England. And in red, right at the bottom, somebody had made a final addition, which made me laugh: And what about Kashmir? Self-rule never contemplated, not even in the bog.

This bit of graffiti reminded me of Taung, my place of birth, because it used to be in the Republic of South Africa, but in 1977 it became part of the newly created Republic of Bophuthatswana under the leadership of His Excellency, President Lucas Mangope. Bophuthatswana was one of the more bizarre homelands because it had no territorial integrity. Instead, it consisted of seven different entities, pockets of Setswana-speaking islands scattered all over the central and northern regions of South Africa.

My mother and I were already living with Ma Vasinthe in Johannesburg by the time it was created, but to a child, it felt as though the whole world had changed, as though my grandmother had been packed up and moved to another planet. Despite Ma Vasinthe's best efforts to explain, I couldn't understand how a whole town could become part of another country just like that, and although I hardly knew her at that time, I cried for days about what had become of my grandmother.

My grandmother never acknowledged the change, or Mr Mangope's puppet presidency, and she didn't care who knew it. "Idiots and stooges," she called all those who insisted on their Bophuthatswanan nationality. "The place of lions has been thrown into the puppet's den. I'll have nothing to do with it."

For her dissent, she regularly had her electricity cut and her miniscule state pension withheld. When, seventeen years later, Mangope eventually fell and Bophuthatswana was reincorporated into the new South Africa, my grandmother rejoiced for days, not because she was a patriot, but because she was a democrat and the collapse of the 'imaginary homeland' meant that she could now vote in the first democratic elections of April 1994. "I have waited a long time to see this day," she said as she proudly took up her place in the queue that stretched for miles and miles, "and now it has finally arrived."

Of course, literally speaking, my grandmother could not see at all, her cataracts having become inoperable.

"It's because of my political views, isn't it, doctor," she confronted the young medic.

"No, not –"

My grandmother cut him short. "But let me tell you something," she said, waving a foreboding finger. "Opinions are expressed with this," she pointed at her mouth, "and as you can hear, it's in tip-top shape. Do with my eyes what you like, but we know it's my mouth you're really after."

My grandmother was right to be suspicious. She had had medical treatment punitively withheld, but in this instance, her politics weren't the reason. Even a supporter of the new republic would have been told the same: "Mrs Moyoyo, in Bophuthatswana we can't do cataracts."

Ma Vasinthe had offered that she come to Johannesburg to have them removed privately, but my grandmother would hear nothing of it. "Hayikhona!" she exclaimed. "Me, in Jo'burg? That crazy town! I don't need my eyes that much."

Ma Vasinthe did not insist. "The operation would have made little difference," she told me. "After all the years of obscured vision, her brain will almost certainly have forgotten its ability to see."

This memory made me want to add: 'Bophuthatswana, Venda, Transkei, Ciskei, Lebowa, Gazankulu, KwaZulu, KwaNdebele, KaNgwane *all* used to be South Africa', to the graffiti chain, but I didn't have a pen on me.

After Katinka and I had left the restaurant and were walking back to the car, taking in the cool air, I recalled the graffiti chain and was glad I had not added to it. Apart from the fact that most of its readers would probably never have heard about the homelands or the immense suffering they contained, I thought it rather pointless to insert a now-settled dispute alongside so many contemporary and unresolved ones.

Disappeared

KAGISO LOOKS UP FROM THE PAPER. In front of him, stuck to the wall above the desk, is a quotation, one of many placed in various locations around the room. This one kindles a nostalgic melancholy, a fetid brooding, like a swampy afternoon, a hot night. He can't stop himself reading it again:

> I consume the day (and myself) brooding, and making phrases and reading and thinking again, galloping mentally down twenty divergent roads at once, as apart and alone as in Barton Street in my attic. I sleep less than ever, for the quietness of night imposes thinking on me: I eat breakfast only, and refuse every possible distraction and employment and exercise.
>
> *TE Lawrence*

He turns to look around the cell-like room. To someone who didn't know him, it would seem stripped, cleared of all personal belongings, and abandoned. But to him, the room is full of Issa. It is spartan, monastic; a desk, at which he is seated, a mattress on the floor. The kitchen is a cupboard at one end of the room, the bathroom a tiny cubicle. The only thing of excess is a neat but overflowing bookcase, behind which is concealed the bedstead. The room is sweltering now, but according to Frances, it is a very cold room in the winter, "having only storage heating." He didn't really understand what that meant.

On the bookcase is a postcard of home, the skyline at night, taken during a thunderstorm. It rests above the five volumes of the TRC Report, a city of gold balanced on a catalogue of crimes. He remembers sending the card, in the early days, soon after Issa first came to London. He likes the picture. It captures something of the city, he thinks – its drama, its ambitions. People often mistake it for a picture of New York.

He repositions himself at the desk. Earlier that afternoon, he'd come across another picture, one he'd almost forgotten about. It disconcerted him. After having forced himself to look at it for a while, he laid it face down on the desk. Now, his eyes move slowly to the down-turned photograph. Cautiously, as if handling a dangerous device, he lifts the photograph.

It is of the two of them as boys. He remembers Ma Vasinthe taking it with her new camera, Ma Gloria watching from behind. It was springtime. She had got them to crouch on the lawn in the front garden.

"Say cheese."

"Cheese," he smiled, self-consciously obedient.

Paneer, Issa said, leaning on his cricket bat. In the picture his mouth is poised for p.

"Why do you *always* have to spoil things, Issa?" Ma Vasinthe complained. "Let's do it again."

But Issa was already halfway up the garden path, eager to return to his cricket match in the street.

Nearly twenty years later, Kagiso has to strain to recognise himself in the shy and withdrawn figure in the picture. But even at that age, Issa's steely confidence, his intense good looks, were already apparent. He turns over the photograph, this time depositing it in the desk drawer before picking up his pen.

ꕥ

I, we, still find it difficult to accept what has happened. We seldom talk about it. What more is there to say? We've given all the statements, answered all the questions. We seldom look at one another for fear of detecting it, lurking, in ever searching eyes. We've done, it seems, what we can, provided all the red-T-shirt descriptions, followed the few ephemeral leads to their nose-breaking dead ends. Nothing. Except a pile of 'Missing' leaflets for distribution, which, like watches, keys, wallets and cell phones, have become part of the baggage that orbits us as we drift like off-course planets searching an endless universe. Issa, difficult, contrary, spoilt to the last, had been, it seems, the centre of our lives, the improbable silent force that held us all together. Now, sitting in his chair, at his desk, surrounded by his simple things, I am trying again to piece together his story, but there is much I don't know; Issa had become a stranger to us during his time here. And in the years before he left, he and I, well...

Yet I have to do something with the little I do know. I can't keep it to myself. I have to let it out. And then, it seems, let it go. For months I have scratched around in this notebook trying to make sense of things, of Issa, of me. But now, sitting in his room in London, his last known address, I am aware that before long I will have packed his scant possessions into boxes for posting back home and cleaned his room ready for its new tenant. By the time I leave London, I will have made his disappearance complete.

ꕥ

He shrinks away from the thought and searches the journal, like a killer returning to the sight of his crime, for the remains of the two words he had mutilated earlier.

When he finds them, he leans forward, trying to draw meaning from their rotting carcasses, like a pathologist, examining these basic components, the two words, just the two, a verb and its noun, that seem to have become a part of his family, it would seem, for good.

He reaches across for the dictionary and copies the definitions:

> **disappear** *v.intr*: **1** cease to be visible; pass from sight. **2** cease to exist or be in circulation or use (*trams had all but disappeared*). **disappearance** *n.* **1** vanish, evaporate, vaporize, fade (away or out), evanesce. **2** die (out *or* off), become extinct, cease (to exist), perish (without a trace).

What to make of them? They seem a bit... far-fetched? The noun especially sounds scientific, clinical. Improbable. I can relate them to lost wallets, errant socks, missing pets, the Marie Celeste and planes over the Bermuda Triangle. Until now, I've only ever had to use them in that sort of context, and in relation to the disappearance of others: Steve Biko, Victor Jara, Phakamile Mabija, Ché. But that was the sort of stuff Issa used to talk about.

We can match his name with other verbs and other nouns. For instance, we can say that Issa has gone to London. Even though he and I had drifted apart by then, that was still a hard sentence to get used to at first. And saying goodbye was an inner wrench, because, for a long time, there hadn't been very many hellos. We missed him terribly during those first months. Funny how one misses the presence of a silent person. But after a while, we could say it. Issa has gone to London. Issa now lives in London. Issa is studying in London. Issa is doing a PhD in London. We never had difficulty with that one, especially Ma Vasinthe. Issa is doing a PhD in London. It made her proud. It made us all proud.

In the same way, we can attribute nouns to Issa: Issa's intensity, Issa's integrity, Issa's intelligence, Issa's temper, Issa's good looks.

But, nearly four months later, we cannot reconcile Issa's name with this verb, to disappear, and its noun, disappearance. We can't say, "Issa has disappeared." We can't talk about Issa's disappearance. To us, they are incompatible, irreconcilable; like oil and water, they just don't mix. Like red next to green, they just don't match, can make you sick, and if you look at them juxtaposed for long enough, can drive you crazy.

Of course, when it first became apparent that that was what had happened, we had to. We, or rather, I, had to report the event to others. So I had to make his name the subject of that dreadful verb: Issa has disappeared. I had to match it to that unlikely noun: Ma Gloria is devastated by Issa's disappearance; Ma Gloria rarely talks, following Issa's disappearance, or, Ma Vasinthe keeps her cell phone on all the time, following Issa's disappearance. In fact, Ma Vasinthe has taken to clutching her cell phone, like a talisman, waiting, as though the constant contact will make it ring, make him phone. Her assistant once told me that she just apologises at the start of meetings. "But people don't mind," she smiled sympathetically. "They understand."

And in the cinema, which she has developed an increased liking for, she sets it to vibrate and always sits in an aisle seat. She hates flying because then she has to switch it off. I once called her phone when I knew she was on a flight from Cape Town to Johannesburg, just to check. She had switched it off but the message said, "Issa, this is your mother. I had to switch off because I'm flying from Cape Town to Jo'burg. You know that it's only a two-hour flight. I'll switch on again as soon as we have landed. Please leave me a message."

I was waiting for her at the airport when she arrived. I watched as she switched on her phone immediately upon entering the arrivals hall. I saw the expectation that the message signal brought to her face, and then I saw it disappear when she realised that the call was from me.

"You didn't leave a message," she said. "Is everything okay?"

"Everything's fine," I said. "I dialled your number by mistake."

She re-recorded her standard message in the car on the way home: "You have reached the voicemail of Dr Vasinthe Kumar. For urgent medical enquiries, please call 011 776 9132 or 011 776 9133. For urgent academic enquiries, please call 011 761 7595. Otherwise, please leave a message here. Thank you."

ꕥ

As a final act of the day, Kagiso stretches, as if trying to span a continent, towards the postcard of home on the bookshelf. He transfers it carefully to the desk in front of him before falling, knees first, onto the mattress on the floor, asleep before his face touches the pillow.

The Karoo

1989. Slogans resounded across the country.
'We will not forget?'
'Steve Biko!'
'Long live?'
'Nelson Mandela, long live!'
'We Shall Overcome!'
'Liberation before?'
'Education!'
'The People Shall?'
'Govern!'
'We will not forget?'
'Matthew Goniwe!'
'We will not forget?'
'Hector Pieterson!'
'Viva?'
'Oliver Tambo, viva!'
'Long live?'
'Govan Mbeki, long live!'
'Amandla!'
Freedom is taken, never given.
'Awethu!'

IN DECEMBER, AT THE END OF THE disrupted academic year, they reverse the summer holiday routine of their childhood and set off once again on the long drive from Cape Town to Johannesburg, a 1 500-kilometre journey north-east along the N1, the main national road that runs for days through the vast, arid centre of the country. You can follow its route on a map, as Kagiso now did, wistfully tracing its path with a slender finger from its starting point at the foot of Table Mountain, distracting himself from Issa's loud ominous silence.

They know the mammoth journey like they do their garden path – Cape Town / Paarl / Worcester / Laingsburg / Beaufort West /

Colesberg / Bloemfontein / Winburg / Ventersburg / Kroonstad / Johannesburg – backwards and forwards, eyes closed; summer school holidays were spent traversing its harsh unending miles to get to the coast. Then Vasinthe would drive, vrou alleen, as men observed admiringly, with the boys in the back and Gloria's constant presence by her side, ready to make conversation, turn cassettes, pour cups of coffee or help keep an eye on the road:

"We need to watch out for kudus now."

Why?

"Because they're dangerous."

But we're in a car. And we're going fast.

"*That's* why they're dangerous. If a kudu jumps into the road, this car will fold like paper."

But there's a fence.

Gloria laughed dismissively. "That fence is for farm animals. It can't keep back a kudu."

Why not?

"Because a kudu is *big* and *wild*."

Wild! The word thrilled him.

"Yes," Gloria continued. "And with its strong hind legs it can stand right next to a fence three times as high as this one and just hop over."

Wow! Kagiso, we have to look out for kudus. You look your side. I'll look mine.

Except to buy petrol, about which they had no choice, they avoided the verkrampte little dorps that occasionally interrupted the otherwise relentless isolation of the journey. Vasinthe always imagined that she would have time, to explain. Gloria agreed that it should come from her, that she should be the one to inform them about the way things were. She knew the dates and the facts and the names. She had them all in her head and at the tips of her fingers; could summon them like she does surgical instruments in an operating theatre. She would be much better at it.

Vasinthe thought constantly about what she would say when the time came. She tried to anticipate how it would arise, how she would phrase things, what questions they might ask. She anguished about not leaving them feeling angry or inferior. These were often among her first thoughts of the day as she tied her sari, while sometimes inadvertently humming her favourite morning bhajan from childhood. She'd rehearse her explanation while she walked the gleaming corridors of Jo'burg General, a time when she also remembered her father. He used the theatre of the hospital to distract her, following the delayed admission of her broken-bodied mother:

"Watch, Sinth!" he said to her when they were expelled from her ward by a cacophony of bleeping machines: "Doctors Laategan, Du Preez and Smidt to ICU! Doctors Laategan, Du Preez and Smidt to ICU!"

"Look," he prodded her, "here they come."

She saw a group of earnest, marching medics come rushing down the corridor towards them, their unflinching sights set on the finishing line, the threshold of her mother's room.

"See their white coats flapping, Sinth. See their stethoscopes."

"What, Baba?"

"Ste tha scopes."

"Ste tha scopes," she repeated.

"Good girl. Come. Step aside now." He pulled her towards him as if from the path of a speeding car. As it rushed down the corridor towards them, the group reshaped itself into a lean line of hierarchy, a white-coated stethoscoped streak, which flashed past them and disappeared into her mother's ward, leaving a foreboding gust of wind in their wake that chilled her father to the bone.

"Did you see that, Sinth?" he asked, summoning the excitement of a spectator at Kyalami.

She nodded. "Yes, Baba. I saw," then threw her arms around his knees.

He crouched and ran his trembling fingers through her windblown hair. "Would you like to be like them one day, Sinth? What could be more important than rushing to save a life?"

And so it was that, as his wife, his 'Mumtaz', lay dying, her 'Shah Jahan', who within a month would die a premature, brokenhearted death, opened a door in their only daughter's mind as they sat huddled in a long, gleaming hospital corridor.

"Yes, Baba," she said.

He lifted her chin and wiped the dust from her cheek with a licked wet thumb. "Good girl," he said. "Very good girl."

Vasinthe would run over her explanation in her mind while she checked their homework before she herself sat down to a long night of study. But whatever her preferred choice of words – it changed from day to day – in the end she always decided to leave it till they were a little older. For the moment, she just wanted them to be children. She had herself known too soon:

"Baba. Why isn't the ambulance taking Ma?"

He didn't look at her. "They're sending another one, Sinth. That one is full," he said as he sat down in the sand to stroke her mother's limp arm.

"But there was no one in it, Baba. I saw."

"Come Sinth, hold Ma's other hand so she can feel you near." He pulled her towards them. "The other ambulance will be here soon."

It wasn't. For nearly two hours they crouched in the heat and dust by the roadside next to their wrecked car before the non-white ambulance arrived.

But when the time for explanations came, Vasinthe was asleep.

December 1977. It is a hot day. When they arrive in Victoria West, Vasinthe stops for a break in the shade of the trees by the white graveyard. She and Gloria watch from the car as Issa leads Kagiso by the hand to the small store just across the road. Though the younger by two months, Issa is by far the more confident of the two.

They have promised to cross the road carefully. They will buy their iced lollies, not forgetting to say please and thank you, and return immediately to perch themselves on the low wall beside the car. They will sit quietly; they are not at home now. They disappear into the store. Vasinthe reclines her seat and shuts her eyes. Gloria rolls down her window and remains vigilant.

The boys re-emerge from the store, empty-handed. They walk hesitantly to a barred window at the side of the building and join the short queue. Gloria looks down at Vasinthe whose lips have quickly started to puff the way they do when she is on the verge of sleep; the early morning delivery of Christmas hampers to Taung followed by a visit to the Open Mine Museum in Kimberley was perhaps too ambitious for one driver, in one day.

Gloria slips quietly out of the car and joins the boys in the queue. Issa relinquishes control and slips his hand into hers.

When Gloria steps to the front of the queue she assesses the dark interior of the store through the black bars. It is a general store, selling basic provisions as well as some cooking utensils, paraffin stoves, toolboxes, a couple of bicycles. She asks for two iced lollies. Asseblief. The shop assistant retrieves the lollies from a noisy refrigerator and lays them down on the dirty wooden plank that serves as a counter.

"Dankie." Gloria lays down R70 on the counter. The assistant is surprised. This is far in excess of the cost of two iced lollies. Gloria adds to the order. "And a bicycle. Asseblief."

Issa looks up questioningly at Gloria but knows not to interrupt. She pats his hand, still clenched in hers, reassuringly on her thigh. Kagiso has started whispering reluctant responses to a dirty little girl in the queue.

"For the bicycle, you can come around the front." The shop assistant reaches for the money. Gloria slaps her hand down on it. The woman looks up at her, startled.

"I'll take it through the window. Asseblief."

The shop assistant is taken aback. A crowd of curiosity has gathered. Somebody quickly whispers an update to the newcomers. "The bicycle is too big to pass through the window. You'll have to come around the front to get it."

Gloria edges the money forward without releasing her grip on the notes. "Then disassemble it. Asseblief." The crowd murmurs incredulity. Issa studies their rough, leathery faces, their toothless smiles, their threadbare, tattered rags, then looks to the woman behind the counter.

"That's impossible. I can't dismantle the bicycle. You'll have to collect it from the front. It's not far. You only have to walk around the corner."

"If you can't dismantle the bicycle, then you'll have to break down these bars."

The assistant splutters in disbelief. "But that's mos malligheid. You expect me to break down these bars because you won't come round the front to fetch the bicycle?"

Gloria lays out another R20 on the counter. The crowd gasps. "You won't break down these bars, but you will break the law by bringing me into the front of your shop." The lollies have started to melt on the grimy counter. A frenzy of flies buzzes erratically around the sweet sticky water.

Kagiso has tired of the little girl who won't believe that they are from Johannesburg, that that is their car, that this is his brother. "Maar hy's 'n coolie en jy's 'n kaffir," she objects. "Hy't dan gladde hare, en joune is kroeser dan myne!" the girl remarks, pointing to the difference in the texture of the boys' hair. Kagiso tries to enlist Issa's support, but is brushed off.

"The law doesn't stop you from coming into the front of the shop."

"What does?"

"My husband. And you'd better stop playing these silly games. He'll be back soon."

"Then I'll wait." The crowd gasps. Gloria tightens her grip on Issa's hand. He watches the sweat trickle from her perspiring palm down his wrist. Soon his hand starts to go numb, but he doesn't attempt to release it. Instead, he shifts his weight to the other leg as a sort of ineffective distraction and, with his left hand, traces the patterns on her printed skirt.

"Then step aside and let me serve the rest of the people in the queue." Gloria turns around and scans the onlookers. Nobody steps forward. She repositions herself at the head.

When her husband arrives, the woman reports the deadlock. The man assesses Gloria and the boys. He looks over to the car parked under the trees. "That your car?"

"Yes."

"Very nice. Jo'burg plates?"

"Yes."

"Going to Cape Town?"

"Yes."

"Where will you put the bike?"

"We'll make space."

"These your boys?"

"Yes."

"Him too?" Issa glares at the man from under a furrowed brow.

"Yes."

Kagiso nudges the dirty girl. "*Now* do you believe me?"

The man looks at Gloria then at the crowd behind her. He steps back from the counter. He looks at his wife, then turns back to face Gloria.

"The bicycles are sold."

The woman looks surprised.

"Yes. I sold them this morning, before you came in, to Jan from Soetfontein. He bought them for his boys, for Christmas. I forgot to tell you."

Vasinthe is woken by the sound of closing doors. "Ready?" she asks sleepily.

"Yes," says Gloria. "Let's go."

On the back seat, Kagiso taps Issa for answers, explanations. But Issa looks past him at the crowd outside the shop. Some start to trail away. Others take up their places obediently in the queue. Issa sees the dirty little girl stoop to pick up the remnants of the molten lollies as the woman in the shop brushes them off the counter and onto the dusty pavement. The girl steps out of the crowd and watches them drive away, holding her salvaged lollies in upturned palms. When they have left the town behind, Ma

Vasinthe taps her thumbs on the steering wheel to initiate another sing-a-long:

"We're all goin' on a summer holiday / No more workin' for a..."

But Issa doesn't join in. He turns away from Kagiso to look out at the dry and barren wilderness that stretches out eternally beyond the windows of their speeding car.

ൠ

Now, more than a decade later with Issa at the wheel, they are able to anticipate every ridge and bend, peak and valley, as the road cuts its dramatic path from Paarl across the Hottentots' Holland Mountains – eventual refuge of the indigenous Khoi expelled from the ever-growing Dutch settlement – and into the picturesque valleys of the hinterland, before eventually reaching up through the Hexrivierberg Pass and out onto the great escarpment. They take the longer route across Du Toit's Kloof Pass, avoiding the new tunnel that cuts through the bowels of the mountain and to which Issa is still not reconciled; a few months earlier he had joined in the demonstrations organised to coincide with President Botha's ceremonial opening of the tunnel. *Why the Huguenot Tunnel? Has nothing happened in the 300 years since their arrival that might also merit remembering? Had they not received enough recognition, enough recompense – a pristine corner of the world's fairest Cape, forever named Franschhoek, on which to start an industry that would make them wealthy beyond their persecuted Protestant dreams? How many refugees get a clean slate, let alone such a fabulous one?*

As they wind their way slowly through history's majestic backdrops, Kagiso stares out of the window at the fertile valleys of pristine vineyards and orchards unfolding below. This is his favourite part of the journey.

He can't imagine anywhere being more beautiful and sighs despondently when they arrive in Laingsburg.

But for Issa, Laingsburg is where the real journey begins. Relieved finally to have left behind all the deceptive liberal prettiness of the Cape – the picturesque wine farms, where labourers are paid by the tot; the plush southern suburbs, whose residents know little of the squalor and violence that afflicts their neighbours in the slums of the Cape Flats. Even the breathtaking panoramas from Table Mountain, which also reveal the black hole in the middle of the bay into which his hero has been sucked. What lies ahead is the harsh, honest isolation of the Great Karoo, where everything is exactly as it appears, unforgiving, dry, vast, desolate. He prefers it. Can position himself in relation to it. Death Run looms ahead. He isn't daunted because it does not conceal what it is, makes no pretences, has no hidden little catches. To him, the desert is an honest landscape.

ঌ

In junior school he does all his geography tasks on deserts: Sahara is the Arabic for desert; Dune 7 in the Namib, biggest dune on earth in the oldest desert on earth – it never changes shape; the Kalahari grows by a phenomenal two centimetres a year. He calculates that, at that rate, it would take ten million years to travel two thousand kilometres to the Cape. The Karoo gets its name from the Khoi word, karo, meaning dry. But it was once an endless lake. Fossils of aquatic life have been found on what was once the bottom of the lake but is now the surface of the desert. It covers one-third of the country's surface. He wishes one day to see its illusive hare. His teacher eventually forces another topic on him:

But I like deserts, Teacher.

"Yes, I know that Issa, but what I don't understand is why you like them so much."

Issa looks at her, deciding whether to trust her with a piece of himself. *Because they're clean, Teacher.*

The class explodes with laughter. Kagiso lowers his head.

"Silence!" the teacher shouts, knocking her ruler on the board. "Silence!" When an uneven quiet has hissed through the class, she returns her attention to Issa. "That is a strange answer, Issa. Tell us, what makes you say so?"

The whole class turns to look at Issa.

"Issa?" the teacher calls out. "Stand up when I'm talking to you."

Issa stands.

"Now," the teacher repeats, "tell us why you think that deserts are clean."

But Issa doesn't respond. He just stares back at the teacher over the heads of his bursting-to-laugh classmates.

Uncomfortable with the silent standoff, the teacher resorts to threat. "If you can't explain yourself, I'll give you another topic."

"Tell her, Issa," Kagiso wills silently. Tell her. Tell them all.

Issa doesn't move.

"It's because of Lawrence, Teacher," Kagiso wants to shout. "We saw the film. It's his favourite. He watches it over and over again." Tell her Issa. Tell Teacher that it's what Lawrence said:

Bentley: … May I put two questions to you, straight?

Lawrence: I'd be interested to hear you put a question straight, Mr Bentley.

Bentley: One. What, in your opinion, do these people hope to gain from this war?

Lawrence: They hope to gain their freedom. Freedom.

Bentley: "They hope to gain their freedom." There's one born every minute.

Lawrence: They're going to get it, Mr Bentley. I'm going to give it to them. The second question?

Bentley: Oh. Well. I was going to ask… erm… What is it, Major Lawrence, that attracts you personally to the desert?

Lawrence: It's clean.

"Well then, Issa," the teacher intones, "if you've nothing to say for yourself, your next task will be on something completely different – oceans." But her decisive nod is undermined by Issa's immediate response.

Oceans are not completely different to deserts.

The teacher stares back at him across a sniggering class.

They're deserts of water. And "the desert is an ocean in which no oar is dipped."

ꕥ

"Don't distract Ma Vasinthe now. Kudu are nocturnal."

Knock?

"Noc tur nal."

Noc tur nal.

"Yes. That means they are most active at night, like leopards and foxes."

And bats and owls.

"Yes. So we have to be especially vigilant when driving in the dark."

Vi gi lant. He turns around and stares out the back window at the road already travelled, counting the white stripes as they flick by in the tail lights. There are no other cars behind them. It feels to him as though they are alone in the world. He tries to imagine what he'd do if he were left behind in this wilderness. Would a black dot appear from a mirage on the shimmering horizon and grow slowly into a Bedouin on a camel with a gun? The prospect fills him with dreadful excitement.

Look, he says.

"What is it?" asks Gloria from the front.

He doesn't respond.

Kagiso turns to follow Issa's gaze. "Ha ka ka!" he exclaims.

Vasinthe peers into the night sky through the rear view mirror. What she glimpses makes her pull over onto the sandy embankment on the side of the road, sending clouds of dust rushing into the beams of the headlights. They get out of the car and watch in silent amazement as it rises serenely over the horizon, the bride of the night, big and full and red behind a veil of desert dust, like another world coming slowly and silently to envelop their own. He wants to run forward a little, but Ma Gloria is running her fingers through his hair, so he stays by her side, slips his hand into hers and with his left forefinger held up to his narrowed eyes, he traces the outline of the man on the moon.

❧

Kagiso traces the path on the map north, past Johannesburg and across the border into Zimbabwe at Messina. Then on to Harare and across the border into Malawi at Nyampanda. Then up to Lilongwe and around the shores of Lake Nyasa. At Mbeya, he traces the route to the right through Iringa and across the border with Tanzania to Dodoma, then Arusha. Still further north, across the border with Ethiopia at Moyele, up through the Great Rift Valley as far as Asmara.

"As ma ra," he says, breaking the silence of rubber on tar.

The interruption pulls Issa back from his own far-off place. He can recall whole paragraphs, entire chapters of what he has read, in minute detail:

> In these pages the history is not of the Arab movement, but of me in it. It is a narrative of daily life, mean happenings, little people. Here are no lessons for the world, no disclosures to shock peoples. It is filled with trivial things, partly that no one mistake for history the bones from which some day a man may make history, and partly for the pleasure it gave me to recall the fellowship of the revolt. We were fond together, because of the sweep of the open places, the taste of the wide winds, the sunlight, and the hopes in which we worked. The morning freshness of the world-to-be intoxicated us. We were wrought up with ideas inexpressible and vaporous, but to be fought for. We lived many lives in those whirling campaigns, never

> sparing ourselves: yet when we achieved and the new world dawned, the old men came out again and took our victory to re-make in the likeness of the former world they knew. Youth could win, but had not learned to keep: and was pitiably weak against age. We stammered that we have worked for a new heaven and a new earth, and they thanked us kindly and made their peace.

What? He asks, as if stirred from sleep.

"Asmara. In Ethiopia."

It's not in Ethiopia.

"It is according to the map."

Forget about maps. They don't show things as they are. Asmara is in Eritrea.

"Eritrea?" He scrutinises the map. "Don't see it."

That's because it's still a dream. Maps don't show dreams either. Only nightmares.

"But in reality, Asmara is still in Ethiopia."

Not to the people of Asmara. Not to those men and women dying on the battlefield for their convictions. To them, Asmara is in Eritrea and will one day be its capital.

From Asmara Kagiso follows the route as it sweeps to the left and across the border into Sudan. At Kasala he pauses, contemplating left to Khartoum or straight ahead to Port Sudan on the Red Sea Coast. He decides on the road to Khartoum, union of the Blue and White Niles. It sounds to him a magical place.

From there, he traces the path up through the Nubian Desert all the way to Wadi Halfa on the shores of Lake Nasser, where his finger leaps across the lake to Abu Simbel and then all along the Nile to places with names, which, like As ma ra, call out to be uttered:

"Aswan
Luxor
Qena
Asyût
Beni Suef
Cairo
Alexandria
A lex an dri a."

Memory house of the world.

"Is that so?"

Issa nods.

"Let's just carry on. Imagine that, if we didn't stop at Jozi but just carried on all the way north, up and up and up. Wouldn't that be amazing? Let's do it sometime. You like driving. You can drive all the way across Africa, all the way to Alexandria, to the world's memory, on the northern edge of Africa."

Violent Night

KATINKA STRIKES A MATCH AND holds it to the nightlight on her bedside table. Slowly, the tiny flame starts to lick away the darkness from the objects in its shaky circle: two photographs; one of Issa, the other of Karim, and the items from the ritual she enacts here every day. Flowers arranged along the base of each picture. Leaves, picked in passing from the same tree, flat and large, on which to stand ornate bottles of unction. Precious, the crushed essence from a thousand flowers – jessamine, violet, rose – their fragrance so concentrated, it endures a bath. But only ever used here to anoint the cherished photographs.

She reclines and lets the flame lull her back into the violent night when she searched the smoky room, looking left, looking right, over and under, for her friend among the dazed onlookers...

Eventually, she catches sight of his red T-shirt, but it retreats from her when she tries to focus on it. So she stops, rubs her eyes, and tries again, this time not looking directly at him, only approximately, so as to keep the blurred T-shirt in view. But then there is a flash and a thunderous noise. She looks towards it – explosion – and in its intense rays, she glimpses a vision of him, not face to face, almost; he has his back turned towards her, slightly, so that she only catches his profile, askance, as he sits, chin to chest, in an opulent room, smoking a water pipe. He doesn't notice her. From underneath a furrowed brow, he stares ahead in disbelief at the giant screen, which fills the wall at one end of the room.

His shoulder-length black hair is tied back from his face with a black and white kefiya in the manner of the lead singer in one of his favourite bands, Fun-da-mental; one of the first gigs he went to after coming to London. On the front of his red T-shirt is emblazoned an inscription: 'I am a standing civil war', and the letters MK. On the back, just below the neckline, the logo of the South African Communist Party and its motto: 'Simply Revolutionary'.

He is fastidious, but not to the unobservant: notice his used serviette, folded neatly on the saucer beside his empty glass, not crumpled into a ball and thrown aside; that would irk him. And in his left trouser pocket is a handkerchief, but not for his nose; he keeps that one in the right pocket. Careful never to touch anything in the public domain with his bare hands, he uses this one, inconspicuously, as a protective shield between himself and the city's contaminated door handles and handrails. The handle of the water pipe is a rare exception; despite his ascetic preferences, he likes the feeling of the rich, velvet casing in the palm of his gently squeezing hand.

She stayed with him for part of his vigil, but only for an hour or so before leaving – she had to teach the next morning – a move she now regrets and for which she constantly reproaches herself: You should have stayed with him. He was clearly disoriented. You should not have left him alone…

ﻚ

On the bedside table the flame has settled quickly into a steady, perfectly still glow. The more she returns to the violent night, the more she remembers. On the table in front of him are the dismembered remains of the day's broadsheets and an open folder. She knows it well, but has not seen it for some time. She'd proofed its contents, his near-complete thesis. For several weeks, months, he had to drag himself away from the news, the thesis untouched, set aside.

"Haven't seen this for a while," she recalls saying. "What prompted its exhumation?"

The headlines, he replied, not looking at her. *Here.* He slid the manuscript in front of her: *Read.* Then, with a direct translation from Arabic, handed her the mouthpiece: *Drink.* She was so at home in this world now turned upside down that the imperative didn't sound strange to her. There must certainly have been a time when it would have, but she can't remember it. At a glance, she spots the changes, the redrafted sentences, the adapted opening, which now starts with a quote:

> History is the science of reality that affects us most immediately, stirs us most deeply and compels us most forcibly to a consciousness of ourselves. It is the only science in which human beings step before us in their totality. Under the rubric of history one is to understand not only the past, but the progression of events in general; history therefore includes the present.[1]

The history of early European exploration and settlement at the Cape of Good Hope remains universally and eternally pertinent. The procedures of dispossession and domination implemented here in the fifteenth century would be repeated around the globe for the rest of the millennium, and then again at the start of this new millennium.

To declare these events over is the recourse of perpetrators, collaborators, benefactors and perpetuators. While Europeans and latterly North Americans have achieved the economic gain, which was the ultimate aim of their economic migrancy, the majority whose indigenous systems and futures were adversely shaped, experience the political, economic, cultural and mnemonic consequences of this flooding as present and perpetual catastrophes: what exactly, to begin with, do the Khoi of southern Africa, the aboriginals of Australia, the natives of North America, have to 'move on' to? Another barren, ever-shrinking reserve? The past is eternally with them.

And us.

Detailed records remain of the early years of the Dutch settlement at the Cape as well as of the voyages of discovery – or, rather, as the accrual of geographical knowledge was, after all, a bogus veneer for a less scholarly motive – the pursuit of pathways to plunder, hacked by the Portuguese and Dutch, followed by the French and eventually the eternally wait-and-see British. It is therefore possible to access an almost day-to-day account of life in the early settlement.

In this thesis, I would like to focus on this initial phase of European/African contact at the Cape, in particular, the first fifty years leading up to the establishment of a permanent Dutch settlement there, 1652-1702.

My interest is in the hybrid dynamic, the complex trans-cultural exchange and fusion that, though fragile and uneven, nevertheless formed an integral feature of the early settlement and ensured its development; the heterogonous bartering, which, by the time of the disaster of 1948, had been almost entirely obliterated from memory.

Whatever shards of the bastard truth remained by that stage, would, over the next four decades, be ruthlessly revised, edited and suppressed as racist nationalists in South Africa – and their counterparts around the post-war world – embarked upon the simplification, the very literal whitewashing, of history. They commenced their collision path with the intricate fabric of diversity by substituting the reality of global cross-pollination and intermingling with the sanitised invention of 'man's most dangerous myth: the fallacy of race', and the synthetic fabrication of inviolate national identity.

❧

She hands him back the mouthpiece and turns to look around the room. Whole sections of the thesis were refined here, in this café, in the middle of the night, under this ornate ceiling in which little lights twinkle in embossed brass panels – the Smoky Way, they call it. Written and rewritten on these tables with mother-of-pearl laid into intricate geometric designs – though not at this particular table – at his favourite, the one in the corner behind the mashrabeya screen. But it is a busy night and that seat was already taken by the time he arrived. She strains to see who is seated in their seat on the other side of the screen. He observes her futile attempt – a mashrabeya shields the privacy of those who want to see without themselves being seen – then looks down to the voluminous manuscript under her tapping hand.

He knows it virtually, by heart, not just because he wrote it, painstakingly, word for meticulous word, but also because it is his nature: his eyes move over the pages of a book like the beam of light in a copier; every detail of the written word is captured, and pleasure is deferred. Later, far away, he will turn the pages again slowly in his mind. At school, the habit of reading books that hovered in front of his seemingly vacant, distant stare got him dismissed as a distracted daydreamer: 'Dreamer schemer, history's cleaner'.

When coverage on the screen is interrupted – the prime minister is about to make a statement – they scramble for distraction. He feels around under his T-shirt for the control switch of his most extravagant possession, a portable music player, a gift from Kagiso, then inserts one of the earphones while passing her the other. When the mournful tune he has selected starts up, lilting, gently, she watches him lean forward and sink his eyes into his palms. She starts again to read:

On 6th April 1652, three ships belonging to the Dutch East India Company, *de Drommedaris, de Goede Hoop* and *de Reiger,* dropped anchor in a beautiful bay on the southwest tip of the African continent. On board the flagship, *de Drommedaris,* were Jan van Riebeeck, the commander of the mission, his wife, Maria de la Quellière, and their young son, Lambertus. They had just completed the three-month voyage from Amsterdam; their charge, to set up a refreshment station at the Cape, the Cape which Van Riebeeck would name after the second ship in his fleet, Kaap de Goede Hoop, the Cape of Good Hope.

From the shore, their arrival would have been keenly observed by the Goringhaicona, a small group of around fifty Khoikhoi who first appear in the logbooks of passing ships as early as 1608 and who "had survived for many years by hunting and gathering, and by being alert when Dutch, French and English merchantmen put into port."[2] In this group were three individuals; Autshumao, their self-serving leader, Krotoa, his young, impressionable niece, and the militant, Doman, "the first indigenous South African resistance leader"[3]. History had arrived on their beach. Forced by it into a new consciousness of themselves, each would respond to it differently. All would be forever changed by it.

Van Riebeeck's instructions from the Company were immediately to start the construction of a fort and the cultivation of a garden, which would provide passing Company ships with fresh produce. On April 7, he went ashore and, without consultation, chose a piece of land at the foot of Table Mountain – where Cape Town's Grand Parade is today – for this purpose. Building work commenced promptly, on April 9. Within three days of arriving at the Cape, Van Riebeeck had set in motion "a process whereby the landscape used not only by the Goringhaicona but by thousands of transhumant pastoralists was adversely and irrevocably changed." The Dutch had not chanced upon an empty, abandoned landscape: the site chosen was in the middle of the most fertile seasonal grazing pastures of cattle-rich Khoikhoi who had retreated with their herds into the interior for the winter.[4]

ﷺ

He glances up at the screen. The prime minister has said his bit, handing them back to the horror of shock and awe. She takes a final puff. "Yalla?" she suggests, laying down the mouthpiece. "I'll give you a ride. We can chat about your revisions in the car if you like?"

No. Thanks. I'll stay here a while longer.

"You sure? It's late. The tube will be closed."

I'll be fine. Thanks for coming.

She lays her hand on his shoulder. "I'm sorry it's turned out like this, Issa. But try not to let it get you down."

He didn't rise to see her off as usual, so she bent down to kiss him on the cheek. Stubble – but not like Karim's, wispy and sparse, no – more dense and prickly. When her lips touched his jaw she felt it tense as he clenched his teeth. Did he sniff? Was he crying? She couldn't be sure, didn't want to intrude, so withdrew and started for the door.

The thesis had, till recently, been his only constant companion, its characters, centuries old, more real to him than anybody, more actual than the affluent family from which he had become estranged, cut asunder, more compelling than the successful career-minded comrades back home, paralysed by self-congratulatory nostalgia for their part in an amicably settled dispute. His characters' 17th century dilemmas were more vexing than the mundane popular preoccupations of his adopted city. Then time buckled, history flipped and the 17th century became indistinguishable from the 21st. He found it impossible to drag himself from the present and into the past. He was no longer able to distinguish between the two.

"Why not take a break?" his supervisor had advised some months earlier. "You're way ahead of schedule, so you can spare the time. Go away, maybe South Africa, the weather will be great. Get away from this dark war-mongering winter. It will do you good. You'll return refreshed."

I don't know, he shrugged. *A thesis that started off as history now reads like current affairs. How will a holiday change that?*

At the door, she glanced over her shoulder for a final wave, but he didn't turn around, just stared ahead at the screen. She dithered for a moment, but then she left.

ﷺ

He rose to leave not long after she had gone, but was detained by new footage on the screen – a horrendously maimed boy. Like many in the room, he flinched and looked away, but then sat down again and forced himself to take in the horror, holding the long velvet-covered stem of the mouthpiece upright, like a crook, in his tightly squeezing hand.

ﷺ

When the café had emptied, leaving only the regular late-night patrons, he asked to be relocated to his usual seat, in the corner behind the mashrabeya screen. He gathered his papers while the sabby obligingly lifted the elegant pipe with its elongated blue glass base high above his head to ensure its safe passage to the other side of the room. Issa settled in his new position, a vantage point from which he could see without himself being seen. When the sabby had stoked his pipe, Issa offered him the mouthpiece discreetly. The young man accepted it with a smile and drank deeply, pretending only to be getting the pipe going again, making a show of rearranging the fresh, already well-placed, coals. A waiter approached with a clinking tray of glasses and fresh mint tea. The sabby drank one last time, his cheeks sucked right in, then handed the mouthpiece back, picked up his basket of coals from the brass floor and rushed off to attend to other pipes, fragrant smoke funnelling from his flared nostrils.

The waiter aimed the crescent spout at the gold-rimmed glass and Issa watched as he poured, lifting the teapot higher and higher into the air with a gracefully draped wrist, so that the tea bubbled and frothed in the glass below. But when the glass had filled, the waiter did not stop. Issa looked up and followed the waiter's gaze. Blurred pictures on the giant screen of heavily shackled men in orange overalls behind high-security fences, their arms chained behind their backs to their feet, sent an ominous hush through the room.

Issa's eyes flashed between screen and glass. *Shukran!* he exclaimed to prevent a spillage. And then, in fluent Arabic, added, *My cup over-floweth.*

"Afwan," the waiter responded, not really aware of the flood he'd almost caused, one eye still on the screen. He set down the pot absent-mindedly and drifted back to his post, never looking away from the footage on which the camera had now settled: a notice on the fence – 'Honour bound to defend freedom'.

Issa leaned back into his seat and watched as history rose up from the open manuscript on his table and came to hover between him and the images on the screen:

In 1694, Abadin Tadia Tjoessoep, a member of the Macassarese royal family and the nephew of King Bisei of Goa, arrived at the Cape Colony shackled in chains that belonged to what was then "the world's greatest trading corporation"[5], the Dutch East India Company. It is impossible to overstate the impact his detention at the Cape would have on the culture and political ethos of the colony and that of the country into which it would eventually develop.

Dutch interest in the Cape was, at first, specific and the role of their settlement there, narrowly defined: because of its strategic position approximately half-way between the Netherlands and its empire in southeast Asia, the settlement was to be no more than a refreshment station where merchant vessels of the Company could be replenished with fresh produce. Investment was minimal and the settlement was by and large expected to be self-sufficient.

For this reason, Company directors decided to import slave labour – already illegal in the Netherlands – to the Cape; in a global corporation that was, in effect, "a state outside the state"[6], the attainment of economic profit and the power to pursue it, unchecked, superseded any obligation to an already acknowledged and adopted ethical policy. Slaves were brought in from Mozambique and Madagascar, but most were shipped to Table Bay from Dutch colonial territory in their eastern empire: India, Malaysia, Indonesia, Ceylon. The majority were Muslim who, at the Cape, became known collectively as Cape Malay. Initially, their influence was minimal and their religious practices curtailed, but within just a few decades, their contribution, as even the most fleeting visit to modern-day Cape Town will reveal, would be definitive.

❧

Katinka readjusts her pillow. The movement of air causes the candle to flicker beside her and shadows to scurry across the faces in the photographs. The flame struggles to regain its composure, rising and falling, bowing and twisting. She holds her breath, not wanting to hamper its efforts. She watches the flame gather its layers, like a poised woman rising, adjusting her scarf, straightening her jacket, arranging her charms, until everything is properly displayed – the blue glow at the base, the translucent clove in the centre where the bright tip of the black wick burns like a jewel, the whole arrangement rounded off with the golden yellow crown.

ꕥ

During the second half of the seventeenth century, resistance to Dutch Colonial rule in southeast Asia lead the Company to make a more sinister reassessment of its remote settlement at the Cape. Faced with the threat of increasingly militant opposition to its lucrative enterprise in the East, the Company now saw the colony as more than just a one-stop-shop; because of its geographical isolation, Company directors identified it as a place, far removed, suitable for the incarceration of political prisoners and exiles from the Eastern Batavian Empire.

In 1667, the first banished exiles landed at the Cape. Men of high social standing, all of them were prominent Muslim leaders. Their arrival would be formative; with it, fierce opposition to colonial subjugation on the one hand with political exile, banishment and incarceration as its punishment on the other, became defining traits of the fledgling colony just fifteen years after its establishment. The arrival of these exiles rekindled a new spirit of political resistance – the Khoi, now virtually decimated, no longer posed any serious threat to Dutch rule – and brought a new momentum to the struggle of the dispossessed and subjugated against colonial domination, a struggle, which, for the next three centuries, would be the hallmark of the country into which the Dutch settlement at the southern tip of Africa would eventually evolve.

Although nearly seventy years old by the time he arrived at the Cape, Tjoessoep was the most influential of these exiles, remembered as Sheikh Yusuf of Macassar, the father of Islam in South Africa. During his brief five-year incarceration at the Cape – he died in captivity there on 23 May 1699 – "Skeikh Yusuf established the first Muslim community in South Africa, attracted runaway slaves who converted to Islam, and represented a symbol of resistance to European colonialism."[7] Throughout his imprisonment, Yusuf continued to agitate against Dutch colonial rule so that the history of Islam in South Africa is therefore synonymous with the struggle against oppression. Three centuries later, as South Africa was preparing for its first democratic election of April 1994 under the leadership of another insurgent septuagenarian, Muslims were also celebrating the tri-centenary of Islam in the country. "The high point of the celebration was a mass encampment around Sheikh Yusuf's tomb. It was a significant indication of how Sheikh Yusuf had been adopted as a symbol of Muslim presence in the country and Islamic resistance to colonialism and apartheid."[8]

He shuts the manuscript. On the screen, an ancient city now lies decimated, smouldering. How, he thinks, will a holiday change that? History has arrived at his table with its intricate geometric pattern and mother-of-pearl inlay. When he has wound the mouthpiece neatly around the stem of the pipe and tucked the mutilated broadsheet into his rear pocket, he leaves his payment on the table and moves towards the door, forced into a new consciousness of himself. On his way, he brushes past the waiter, almost touching, a handkerchief already concealed in his left hand. But the waiter, staring at his ruined home town, does not notice the silent departure; only closes his welling eyes and inhales, trying to decipher the sudden, delicate fragrance – jessamine, violet, rose – which has started to snake its way through the columns of apple scented smoke. By the time the waiter turns around, sniffing left, sniffing right, searching for its source, his eyes settling on the empty seat in the corner behind the mashrabeya screen, the wound-up pipe, the serviette, folded neatly next to the empty glass the abandoned manuscript,

Issa has already slipped through the door into a dawn that is beginning to illuminate the devastation wrought by the violent night.

ꚛ

When she wakes in the middle of the night, the candle is spent. It has given itself entirely to the struggle against darkness. She watches as the flame clings desperately to the burnt out wick, fluttering, like sleepy eyelids almost shutting, then flaring back to life again with optimistic determination: flutter and flair, flutter and flair. She once received a greeting card in which the inscription read: 'There is not enough darkness in all the world to put out the light of one small candle.' But there is, she thinks. The flame stumbles, like a flogged princess, tries one last time to lift itself against the night before it collapses, exhausted, under the crushing, all consuming darkness. You should have stayed with him. He was clearly disoriented. You should not have left him alone… She never saw him again.

1 Eric Auerbach; "Philology and *Weltlierature*," trans. M. Said and E. Said, *Centennial Review*, (Winter 1969): 4-5.
2 VC Malherbe; *Krotoa, called Eva: A woman between*; 1990:4.
3 Freda Troup; *South Africa: An Historical Introduction*; 1972: 130.
4 Ibid.; 5.
5 Leonard Thompson; *A History of South Africa*; Yale University Press; 1995:33.
6 Ibid.
7 Abdulkader Tayob; *Islam in South Africa Mosques, Imams, and Sermons*; University of Florida Press; 1999:22.
8 Ibid.

II
The Bookshelf

'All a long summer holiday I kept my secret, as I believed: I did not want anybody to know that I could read. I suppose I half consciously realised even then that this was the dangerous moment. I was safe, so long as I could not read – the wheels had not begun to turn, but now the future stood around on bookshelves everywhere.'

Graham Greene
The Lost Childhood
1951

The Silent Minaret

AFTER DINNER, FRANCES INVITES KAGISO to sit out on the roof for a while. "It's only a makeshift affair out there," she confesses, as she leads the way through the open window, "but in this heat, it provides a pleasant enough escape from a stuffy London flat."

Once outside, Kagiso walks over to the low wall at the front end of the building and leans out over the bustling street below: a constant stream of commuters still pouring out of the station; the increasingly animated revellers who have spilled out of the pub on the corner and taken over the pavement; a group of kids on skateboards practising routines under a giant, brightly coloured mural across the road; the incongruous bird-like couple outside the station – she in a high-necked frilly white blouse, he sporting a comb-over and black dinner jacket with velvet lapel – anxiously expecting their lift. And all the while the continuous coming and going of buses in the terminus.

He turns around. The image of Frances sitting in the front seat of a sports car, the letters GTi in neon green on the headrest, makes him chuckle.

"Where's the rest of it?" he asks.

She laughs too. "Issa dragged this up here last summer. He'd ripped it out of an abandoned car that had been down there for weeks. He intended going back for the other seat the next night, but by then the car had been towed. So he got that deck chair instead."

Kagiso unfolds the chair next to the upturned crate on which Frances has balanced their glasses. He leans back into the chair and throws his head up to the sky. Not the mass of stars he'd been expecting. Not the chirping of crickets, which as a boy he took for the sound of twinkling stars.

"Light pollution," Frances explains. "In a big city like this, only the brightest ones shine through."

It occurs to him that he is now in the northern hemisphere once more. "Which is the North Star? Do you know?" he asks, while making a mental note to check the direction in which water spins down the drainpipe. He forgot to do so during a brief visit to DC.

"I'm afraid I don't and isn't that shameful? Issa asked me that very question when we were out here once. He was reading about the first European explorations down the west coast of Africa. For centuries, European sailors were terrified at the thought of crossing the equator because they'd lose sight of the North Star if they did. I didn't understand why that was such a terrifying prospect until he explained that they used to navigate by it and so would have wanted it constantly in their sights.

"Anyway, I expect you probably know all this stuff, but I found it very interesting and we pledged to locate it but never did. In my case," she shrugs reaching for her glass, "too much sitting around to do."

Kagiso smiles as he watches her recline. She must be the same age as his grandmother, he thinks, yet she seems so much younger. Though more frail and with none of that big African sturdiness about her, her eyes retain a mischievous and enthusiastic sparkle.

"I remember the first time I brought him up here. It was to see the minaret," she recalls, tilting her head towards it.

Minaret? Kagiso puzzles, then quickly scans the skyline for clues. I haven't heard a mosque.

Then, suddenly, there it is, right in front of him, as though it had just stepped out from the shadows.

'The Silent Minaret,' he used to call it.

At home, minarets declare God's greatness five times a day, but here they stand silent, like blacked-out lighthouses.

Kagiso returns to the low wall. From here he can only see the small domed enclosure at the top of the minaret with its windowless pointed arched openings from where traditionally the muezzin would call azaan:

Allah-u-akbar, Allah-u-akbar
Allah-u-akbar, Allah-u-akbar

Ashadu an la illaha illAllah
Ashadu an la illaha illAllah

Ashadu anna Muhammad ar Rasool Allah
Ashadu anna Muhammad ar Rasool Allah

Hayya alas Salat...

The railway bridge and a criss-cross of overhead electricity cables obscure the rest of the building.

"Another night, he told me about mosques and minarets: the one at the bottom of your road in Johannesburg, the one you grew up under, as he so quaintly put it. And the white mosque in the city centre reflected in the glass building across the road. The mosque in Durban sounded impressive too."

"I only have vague memories of Durban," Kagiso interrupts with a faraway stare. "I remember the journey more than I do the place." He turns to face her, leaning with his back against the wall. She doesn't seem to mind the interruption, so he continues. "Issa and I went there secretly one weekend. We'd told our mothers we were going hiking with friends in the Eastern Transvaal as it was called then, but we jumped into a taxi to Durban instead."

"Were you found out?"

"No. But that was down to Issa's cunning."

"Why Durban?"

"Oh," he sighs, "One of his quests. I just tagged along to lend authenticity to the lie."

"Did he find what he was searching for?"

He shakes his head. "No."

"Did you see the mosque?"

"May have," he shrugs. "We went to so many places, I really can't recall. Wish I'd paid more attention... Why? What did he say about it?"

"That it was the largest mosque in the southern hemisphere. That it stands so close to the Catholic cathedral that from certain angles the two buildings almost seem one. I rather liked the sound of that."

Yes Frances, imagine that, a sky that echoes simultaneously with azaan and the Angelus.

She tried:

Allah-u-akbar, Allah-u-akbar
The angel of the Lord declared unto Mary
Allah-u-akbar, Allah-u-akbar
And she conceived of the Holy Spirit
Ashadu an la illaha illAllah
Hail Mary, full of grace
The Lord is with thee;
Ashadu an la illaha illAllah
Blessed art thou amongst women
And blessed is the fruit of thy womb,
Jesus

Ashadu anna Muhammad ar Rasool Allah
Ashadu anna Muhammad ar Rasool Allah
Holy Mary!
Mother of God,
Pray for us sinners, now,
And at the hour of our death.
Amen

"It all suggested such pictures to my mind, such sounds to my ears. I can't think of such a place or imagine such a mingling of sounds here. That would need to be nurtured with love and respect, not battering rams and riot gear...

"He spoke of the gigantic minaret of the Great Mosque at Samara, for centuries the world's largest, with its staircase that winds around the outside. He brought me up a picture of that one a few days later. Huge, it was. I'd never seen anything like it.

"The highest minaret in Casablanca. That *was* impressive too. It has a laser at the top that beams across the Sahara in the direction of Mecca. I often sit here at night and try to imagine what that must look like – a green laser beaming across a clear desert sky.

"And my favourite, the Issa Minaret, like his name, in Damascus, where the faithful expect the Messiah to appear on the Day of Judgement."

The church-like mosque used to be the Roman temple of Jupiter, then the Basilica of St John. It's where the head of John the Baptist is buried, a holy place for both Muslims and Christians.

"I've thought about that one often since. I'd never heard of it. I wouldn't have minded seeing it. Such a link." A *real* cathemosdraquel, she thinks.

"The oldest minaret in the world is in Tunisia, and the oldest mosque in Britain is in Woking, would you believe," she says, rising from her seat to join him at the wall. "And the largest mosque in north London is in Finsbury Park. Look at it! I'm certain it used to be lit up before. You can't see the building itself from up here, but it's all boarded up now. Shut down, like a shipyard, because of the threat it poses." She shakes her head. "Shameful. Just shameful, while all the time we are the ones fighting our *second* war."

Remembering Hide and Seek

TONIGHT, SLEEP DOES NOT BESTOW herself freely. From the mattress, he looks across to where the shiny knob of the desk drawer plays with light from the street. He crawls two paces on his knees across the floor, takes the yellowing childhood photograph from the drawer and returns to the mattress to study it. Lying awake, his eyes have adjusted to the darkness and there is no need to turn on the light.

When they were little boys there was sometimes the novelty of playing hide and seek indoors, with their mothers. With each game, their hiding places grew more and more elaborate: in Ma Vasinthe's secret bathroom behind the built-in wardrobes in her bedroom; behind the geyser in the roof. Once Ma Gloria even took them to hide in the neighbour's kitchen, where they ate cakes and biscuits while they waited for Ma Vasinthe to find them. Ma Gloria had thrown them over the back wall, before jumping over the wall herself and spraining her ankle.

Wherever they hid, Ma Vasinthe would always find them. As she approached their hiding place she would say, "Fee fie foe fum, I smell the blood of three South Africuns!" And then she would open the door and they would cling, squealing and laughing, to Gloria's skirt, while their mothers nodded reassuringly at each other.

The game would start with a knock at the door. Ma Vasinthe would look at Gloria who would rush the boys into hiding, while Ma Vasinthe counted slowly and went to answer the door. But the charade soon turned sinister. Once, when they didn't have enough time to find a good hiding place, they scrambled under Ma Vasinthe's bed and waited. That was an eerie round and they didn't enjoy it very much. It frightened them and, even though Ma Vasinthe said that they were imagining things, they knew that from under the bed they had seen the boots of the dreaded Black Jacks come to drag Kagiso and Ma Gloria away. After that, they enjoyed the game less and less.

Purple Rain

SEPTEMBER 2ND 1989 WAS A SATURDAY. When he wakes, still holding their childhood photograph in his hands, that is the day he remembers. Then, as now, his waking thoughts were of Issa, Issa with boyhood lips eternally poised for p. P is for paneer, p is for purple… They hadn't seen each other for months, not since his birthday in July, in fact, when Sophie, drunk, tripped Issa up and broke his leg. During their years at university, he at the 'Ivory Tower' on the slopes of the mountain, Issa at 'Bush College' out on the Cape Flats, they had grown apart. But when he opened his eyes on that Saturday morning, he knew Issa well enough to know he would be involved.

The whole country knew about it. He did too. For weeks, the activists in Jan Smuts House had spent their days falling over one another and their nights in long meetings behind closed doors, followed by dinners of hushed whispers, and Tracy Chapman 'Talkin' Bout A Revolution' in the common room, now reserved by unspoken agreement for their exclusive late-night use:

Don't you know
They're talkin' about a revolution
It sounds like a whisper
Don't you know
They're talkin' about a revolution

Their efforts paid off, as thousands took to the streets of Cape Town on that spring day to take part in the biggest demonstration in South African history.

But he wasn't there, having opted instead for a matinee screening of *Dangerous Liaisons* in Rosebank with Sophie, Richard and the other bright young things from Upper Campus. Richard Mc Kenna, he thinks. Sophie Scott-Harris. What became of them all?

After the film, they went back to Jan Smuts House; it would be quiet, it wasn't far and it had started to rain, and town would surely still be a mess.

They had the place and its panoramic vistas to themselves, a welcome change after the weeks of frantic covert planning it had witnessed. They'd stopped for pizza and some wine on the way – Constantia, as Richard rarely drank anything else – and Sophia had brought some hash that they smoked secretly in Kagiso's room under clouds of incense. The boys agreed that Michelle Pheiffer was gorgeous; the girls did too. Then the girls agreed that John Malkovich was gorgeous, and the boys did too. Everybody agreed that the American accents were distracting. None of them had read the novel and all of them were oblivious to the chaos that had erupted on the other side of the mountain...

The Defence Force, armed with water cannons, had sprayed purple dye on the peaceful protestors as a means of marking participants, and then set about arresting everybody who bore the stains for their involvement in an illegal gathering.

Kagiso and his friends knew nothing of their plight; of the defiant hairdressers who did their bit for the struggle by giving refuge to fleeing demonstrators in their salons, draped them in towels and gave them un-purple rinses; nothing of the desperate crowd who, in vain, sought refuge on holy ground – the police, armed and dressed in full riot gear, raided St George's Cathedral, in the interest of national security. They knew nothing of the 500 demonstrators who had been rounded up by the end of the day and trucked to police stations around the city.

And then, at around ten thirty, just after they'd heard the punch line to Richard's joke, the activists – wet, bedraggled and purple – walked under the archway and into a courtyard that was about to explode with gales of drunken laughter. It was not until the tears of hilarity had been wiped away and Kagiso had caught his breath that he recognised Issa, stained purple, staring at him, from among his purple comrades.

jím, ayn, káf, mím, há'

IN HER SUNNY KITCHEN, she closes her reference book and turns away from Karim's alphabet on the wall. On a clean page, she starts to write down the alphabet from memory – all 29 letters, from alif to hamza, saying each letter out loud as she writes – sound and symbol, sound and symbol. Some letters – bá' ب and nún ن , jím ج and khá' خ – still throw her; like b and d, g and j, they confuse the novice. She has to think carefully whether to place the dot above or below the otherwise identical shapes. Fluency and instant recognition will come with time and practice, she reassures herself.

Her favourite letter is m: mím – م – with its loop and tail, a little like a p. She likes the word moemkin – it contains two míms and her other favourite letter, k: kaf – ك . She likes its look and its sound: m oe m kin. She sometimes talks to herself, making whole sentences with just this word: "Moemkin moemkin moemkin moemkin moemkin!"

Now she writes the word moemkin, remembering that the letter م changes its shape to مـ when it appears at the beginning or in the middle of a word and the letter ك is written ک when it appears in the middle of a word: ممكن . It means possible.

Then she writes his name, Karim: كريم. It means noble.

She smiles. She can read and write her two favourite words. She touches the tip of her forefinger to her lips and then, gently, to the words she has written on the paper, Karim, possible: ممكن كريم.

She opens her eyes, takes a deep breath and moves on to the next phase, memorising the mutations of those letters that change their shape depending on whether they appear at the beginning, middle or end of a word: jím, ʿayn, káf, mím, há' ح م ك ع ج.

"I just don't give a – "

"The anger," Frances remembers through narrowed eyes, "came later. First, there was the despair. On that Sunday night, 26 days later, as we watched the bombs start to fall, he fell silent. But I didn't notice it at first – was too absorbed in what was happening on the screen:

> As you all know from the announcement by President Bush, military action against targets inside Afghanistan has begun. I can confirm that UK forces are engaged in this action. I want to pay tribute at the outset to Britain's armed forces. There is no greater strength for a British prime minister and the British nation at a time like this than to know that the forces we are calling upon are amongst the best in the world.

"The world had lost its moment," Frances sighs, "and Britain was again at war. Never thought I'd see the day. Of course there was the Falklands, but that was Thatcher's doing. Wicked woman. This chap on the other hand. I won't be voting for him again," she declares, grimacing with distaste and slapping her hand on her armrest with the finality of a judge passing sentence. "And so it wasn't until I saw his shoulders shake that I realised he had started to cry. I turned –"

Kagiso leans forward. "Frances?"

She shows him her palm. "I've just remembered something."

"What?"

She starts slowly, like a medium, eyes unmoving, reporting events from another world. "It was a few weeks before he went home for his mother's inaugural lecture, late August, early September, before the world went mad. He'd started reading a novel earlier in the summer, quite a thick one it was. He read snatches of it to me from time to time." She shakes her head, annoyed with herself. "What was it called? Never mind," she says, waving dismissively. "It will come to me later."

"Anyway," she continues, "he wanted to finish it before he went home, so he brought it up to the roof the day before he left for Johannesburg. He sat himself down in the driver's seat while I made some fresh lemonade. When it was ready, I took it out to him and then I let him be.

"Mind you," she confesses, "I kept peeping out from time to time to see how he was doing. It felt so reassuring to have him out there, his nose in a book. All I could see from here were his big feet stretched out on the crate in front of him.

"When I was sure he'd finished, I peeped out again. This time I saw him hunched over his knees, the book cradled in his lap. I went out to see if he was okay. As I got nearer, I heard sobs.

"'Issa,' I whispered. 'Are you alright?'

"He looked up at me, his eyes red and puffy."

"Fine thanks", he said.

"'What's the matter?' I asked.

"*The book*, he said. *It's the saddest thing I've read.* And then he started crying all over again.

"We laughed about it afterwards, but even when he left for the airport the next day, I could tell that the story was still with him, there, in his eyes, when he turned around to wave goodbye one last time before going down into the station.

"What *was* it called?" she asks again, staring hard into the middle distance, a bent finger tapping at her lips. "I can still see the cover. It had a picture of a little girl balancing on a stick... Never mind."

She turns to Kagiso with renewed focus. "But the night the bombs started to fall, that night was a different sort of crying. I turned to him but he seemed not to notice me. I strained to hear the words he kept muttering to himself, over and over again."

There's nothing there to bomb. There's nothing left to bomb.

"That was when he started listening almost constantly to the World Service. Its muffled, crackly transmission reminded me of the dark days of the Blitz when we would gather around to listen to the news on a long wave Bakelite wireless that took five minutes to warm up."

"Welcome to Talking Point on the World Service of the BBC. US forces continue to pound the military installations of Osama bin Laden's al-Qaeda network and its Taliban protectors inside Afghanistan.

"The US has declared the military operations a great success, but President George W Bush has also warned that the campaign is only the start of a war against terrorism that could last for years.

"Violent protests against the US-led air strikes on Afghanistan have taken place in Pakistan, which threaten to further destabilise the region.

"What is your reaction to the US-led attacks in Afghanistan? Are the strikes justified? What are they likely to achieve? And what could be the repercussions for the people of the region and the rest of the world?

"The lines are now open. Let's take our first caller, Raymond in Singapore. Hello, Raymond."

"Yes, I think it unlikely that Osama bin Laden is going to sit and wait for the US forces to capture him in Afghanistan. I assume that if it becomes necessary, he will go underground in some friendly community. Will the US then start bombing other suspects, presumably Islamic countries?"

"And he hardly ever watched the news on TV anymore. He'd still come up here most evenings – more, I think, out of habit and to keep me company – but he always brought a mangled newspaper with him, which he flicked through while I watched the set, or a little transistor radio which he'd take out onto the roof."

"This week in Talking Point: the worst fighting may be over in Afghanistan but aid agencies warn that the refugee crisis will not be solved for years to come.

"There were at least two million refugees in Pakistan alone before the start of the American bombing in October, more than 200 000 are thought to have crossed the border since then.

"Many of these refugees are desperate to return home, but the UNHCR has been urging them not to return immediately, since Afghanistan is not ready to receive them.

"The primary obstacle to large-scale repatriation now is security, as tribal warlords continue to fight over the spoils of war.

"Jobs and food are both in short supply in a country where six to seven million people are reported to remain on the brink of starvation.

"Does the West need to do more to help the Afghan refugees? What should the new government do to help the Afghan people repatriate?

"We'll go immediately to our first caller, Paul in England."

"Here we go, another huge flood of welfare claimers and council house takers heading our way. Isn't it time we told people to go back into their own countries rather than coming in and sucking ours dry – which is the inevitable conclusion if we don't tell these people to go back to their homes?

"I wouldn't mind aiding people if they were willing to help themselves – but people are too ready to cry and whinge. When I saw people dancing in the streets and enjoying themselves in their country, it showed me that it can't all be that bad, and now they're out from being oppressed they have a golden opportunity to make something great of themselves. They'd have the backing of everyone if they didn't send their people over here to claim our money from our welfare system and send it home."

"No. It wasn't till several months later, not until the summer, following that dreadful incident in Lye, that the anger started to set in." Frances slips away again, a pensiveness coming over her. "I can still see him sitting in that very armchair you're in now, circling words in the newspaper article: riot gear, metal battering ram, mosque – children, refuge, deportation. He turned to me, pleading to know…

What sort of society can make sentences out of such disparate words, Frances – casual, matter-of-fact sentences out of such disparate words?

"'Well,' I stumbled for an answer, 'the same sort that only two generations ago displayed signs like: no blacks, no Irish, no dogs. Things have come a long way since then.'"

Yes, Frances, they have – a very long way. Bigoted signs have become battering rams, detention camps and bombs. A very long way, backwards.

"What did happen at Lye?" Kagiso asks.

"Wait a minute," she says. "I still have the article right here. He dropped it into my lap before he stormed out and disappeared for days. You can read it for yourself." She retrieves a white envelope filled with prayer cards and parish leaflets from a folder on the smoking table next to her chair. On the envelope, in her careful, old-fashioned hand, is neatly written, *Issa's article*, and the date, *25th July 2002*. Kagiso opens the envelope:

> **Mosque raid causes anger**
>
> Police yesterday raided the Ghasia Jamia Mosque in Lye in the West Midlands in order to remove an Afghan family that had sought refuge there after the Home Office ruled that they had no right to remain in Britain. The raid caused anger and has been widely condemned by Muslim and human rights organisations.
>
> Police officers dressed in riot gear used a metal battering ram to break down the door of the mosque. The Afghan parents and their two young children have been taken into custody pending their deportation from Britain.
>
> The raid has caused anger and outrage in Britain's Muslim community. A community spokesperson outside the mosque said that they were angered and disgusted by the way in which the police and the Home Office handled

> the situation. "Seeing a destitute family hounded and traumatised and our place of worship violated has left us feeling angry and humiliated."

"*That's* when the anger started," she says resentfully, pointing to the article when he'd finished reading. "After that, there was very little talk of stars or deserts or forgotten histories, no more tears shed over sad books, just an intense, brooding silence. He would come in here, slouch in his chair, and listen with distant glassy eyes as I did all the talking. Not that that was ever a problem, you understand."

Kagiso laughs. But her smile fades quickly.

"Sometimes I think I may have talked too much. If I'd kept silent more, perhaps that would have made him come out with things, get them off his chest a bit. But I didn't want to make him feel unwelcome. Didn't want to shut him out."

"You shouldn't blame yourself, Frances. Issa's always been prone to withdrawal, ever since we were children. He sometimes used to shut himself in his room for days."

"Well, I still wonder whether if I had – Anyway..."

She removes a cigarette from the box and rolls it in the tips of her fingers for a while. When she has lit it, fearful of the flame, she lays it in the ashtray.

"And I don't think he was working very much either."

Kagiso frowns.

"Yes. I came to know when he was writing by a piece of music he used to play. I can hear it now. Oh, it *was* a beautiful piece. I do miss it. I don't even know what it was called. Didn't want to ask. Thought he might think I minded. Didn't want him to turn the volume down. So I never asked. Suppose I'll never know now." She looks up at Kagiso who looks down at his hands.

"Now everything was silent down there, with only the news on the hour, every hour. Beep beep beep, then the announcement of capital cities around the world. If he *did* play music, it was always that terrible shouting stuff that young people listen to these days. And I'm sure one of the songs – he used to play it often – used to go something like, 'I just don't give a – ', you know?" She raises a palm to her mouth, as if to exclude a child, then mimes an F.

Kagiso nods.

"So if he wasn't working, then what did he do all day?"

"Well, he washed a lot."

Kagiso sits up in his chair. "He washed?"

"Yes, his mother reacted to that too. Yes, all the time."

"And was he… seeing people? Getting visitors?"

"Well, he never used to get any visitors, apart from his friend Katinka, who used to call by from time to time. But even that soon stopped. She buzzed me from outside one night, cold night it was too, when she'd got no reply from downstairs. Thought he might be here with me. I invited her up to wait in case he was running late. But he never came. Furious, she was. And you know Katinka… doesn't mince her words."

Kagiso smiles agreement.

"Apparently, he'd stood her up a couple of times before. I tried to ease things over for him a bit – told her I had no idea where he was, that it was unlike him not to be home. Suggested that something must have happened to detain him. But really, he'd taken to going out most nights and often didn't get back till very late."

"Did he ever talk about where he'd been?"

"Never. And I didn't think it my place to ask."

In the ashtray, the cigarette has transformed itself into a long worm of ash.

'A road map into our past'

'The Report that follows tries to provide a windowonthisincredibleresource, offering a road map to those who wish to travel into our past.'

Archbishop Desmond Tutu
October 1998

KAGISO DUSTED ON THE DAY HE ARRIVED. Not that he enjoys housework, only wanted something to do. Decided to start by eliminating the gloomy layer of grime that had settled between him and the flat, as Issa would have known it. The wardrobe was empty, the bathroom and kitchen were left spotless, the small bar fridge was washed, turned off and the door left ajar. Disconsolate relief, everything had been done, nothing to do...

Except pack the bookcase.

It is pleasing to look at, the handsome, commanding proportions of the solid oak, the meticulous alphabetical arrangement of the books on its shelves. Katinka has asked to keep it – she remembers helping Issa collect it from an antique dealer in gentrified Crouch End over the hill. Couldn't believe what he'd paid for it, couldn't understand why he wouldn't make do with something from IKEA. Its contents will be shipped back to Johannesburg. But Kagiso doesn't want to dismantle it, finds it hard to get started, procrastinates, seeks distractions.

Again he handles the mementos on the shelves; the speedometer from their student banger, Issa had removed it after the car was eventually written off in a head-on collision with a drunken driver – it registers 119 251 km; the jar of sand he'd gathered from the side of the road in the Karoo – Kagiso can still see him crouching – where the car clocked 100 000 km; the poem now posted inside, scribbled on a rolled-up travel card:

The story of my life / written in the / sands of time / buried in the / warm dunes / – how many more / caravans will / move on / without noticing / the faint shadow / this ripple creates; the special edition R5 Inauguration Coin, stuck with blue tack to the front edge of the middle shelf.

He wraps the coin in the silver foil from inside his cigarette packet to distinguish it from the other coins in his wallet. Then he raises a reluctant hand to the first shelf but quickly drops it by his side with a sigh, imagining, again, the scenario: What if he comes back? Catches me? What will I say? We thought it best. Had given up on you. Decided to pack up your stuff and take it home, to your room in Ma Vasinthe's house.

His attention is drawn to a bright yellow note, which sticks out of the top of one book. He opens the book. The note is from Issa to Frances: *Found this in a bookshop on Charing Cross Road. Ahead of your trip to Canterbury, I thought you might find it interesting.* Kagiso reads the highlighted section:

> **Part Two:**
> **The Literary Heritage**
>
> Chaucer's Dame Alys, the Wife of Bath, illustrates her expertise in the art of life by quoting two proverbs. They belong to the category of sayings of Arab philosophers which are cited in the *Disciplina Clericalis* and the *Secret of Secrets*. But Dame Alys attributes them to the *Almagest* of Ptolemy:
>
> Whoso that nyl be war by othere men,
> By hym shall othere men corrected be.
> The same wordes writeth Ptholomee;
> Rede in his Almageste, and take it there.
>
> Her opinion of Ptolomy and the *Almagest* is pronounced with the authority of experience of Ptolemy:
>
> Of alle men yblessed moot he be,
> The wise astrologien, Daun Ptholome
> That seith this proverbe in his Almageste:

> "Of alle men his wisdom is the hyeste
> That rekketh nevere who hath the world in honed."

> Chaucer, in composing these passages, was following the example of the *Roman de la Rose* which gives us an important clue to the exact location of these sayings:

> [The tongue would bridled be, as Ptolemy
> Early in the *Almagest* explains
> In noble words: "Most wise is he who strives
> To hold his tongue save when he speaks to God"]

> The source "at the beginning of the Almagest," from which Chaucer and Jean de Meun drew different proverbs, is of particular importance as it confirms Chaucer's use of Ptolemy's *Syntaxis* in the translation of Cremona from the Arabic. The preface from this version was a biographical note on Ptolemy composed by "Abulguasis." It contained thirty-three sayings attributed to Ptolemy and was taken from an Arabic work, *The Choicest Maxims and Best Sayings*, by Abu al-Wafa' ("Abulguasis") al-Mubashshir ibn Fatik, a Muslim historian and philosopher who lived in Egypt. al-Mubashshir's work was composed in 1048-49. It comprises short biographies and descriptions of twenty philosophers, accompanied by a series of sayings under the heading of each, and is related to the widely read compilation of "strange sayings" of Greek philosophers by Hunain ibn Ishaq.

He boxes the book. Rising, he notices again the empty space where the postcard of home used to be. Home, he thinks, was here. And so was –

He positions himself opposite the space. Only the foundations of the towering city now remain. Undiminished, they continue to dominate the bookshelf, like five large cornerstones. His eyes move slowly over the thick black spines, the white lettering that runs down the middle – Truth and Reconciliation Commission of South Africa Report – the red volume numbers at the base of each – Vol 1, Vol 2, Vol 3, Vol 4, Vol 5.

1, 2, 3, 4, 5 / Once I caught a fish alive.

He sends out a cautious hand to the first volume and dislodges it, slowly. The gentle tug causes the shelf to creak. He hesitates, does not remove the volume entirely from its secure position, only partially, so that it balances, a little precariously, over the edge of the shelf. Cautiously, he examines the protruding cover: a collage of faces, some known (an oath-taking De Klerk, hand raised in the air, Thabo, Zuma, Tutu) others not. He leans forward to read the gravestone pictured in the centre. It is embossed with flags of the ANC and the South African Communist Party:

> The Cradock Community and the people of SA salute you in your heroic struggle for freedom, peace, justice and social emancipation. Your blood will nourish the tree that will bear the fruits of freedom. Long live the fighting spirit of our leaders.

MATTHEW GONIWE

BORN 27·12·1947

DIED 28·06·1985

REST IN PEACE

NOBLE SON OF AFRICA

He studies the faces of the two anonymous women on the cover, wondering who they are, where they're from – and about the truth they hope to find, whether they have found it, whether, if they have, they are reconciled to it? Then he notices their eyes, preoccupied, haunted.

He steps back.

"A stage-managed whitewash," his colleague, Lerato, had spat. "And Tutu wants us 'to close the chapter on our past,' with *this*? When it castrates our leaders and diminishes our suffering. And why? To assuage liberal guilt and pacify fucking bourgeois fears. Don't think for one moment that we are satisfied."

He pulls a sleeve across his brow and slides the volume back into its slot.

6, 7, 8, 9, 10 / Then I let it go again.

He studies the contents page in the second volume and flicks ahead to the fifth chapter, 'The Homelands from 1960 to 1990'. On the title page, a photograph: a young man, able bodied, black; his trousers around his ankles – made, like a boy, to stand in the corner and face the wall. In the foreground is a picture of President PW Botha. Smirking. Kagiso goes no further.

On the cover of Volume Three, a soldier takes aim, a woman is comforted, Mandela embraces Suzman and a headline reads: 'You left me blind – and I forgive you'.

He removes the volume from the shelf and sits cross-legged on the floor with it cradled in his lap, searching it, like a telephone directory, for names, names he knows – names of the tortured, the missing and the dead:

> **The case of Steve Biko 18**
>
> Black Consciousness leader Steve Biko [CT05004/ELA] was detained on 18 August 1977 in Port Elizabeth and died in custody on 12 September 1977 in Pretoria.
>
> Security police officers Major Harold Snyman [AM3918/96], Captain Daniel Petrus Siebert [AM3915/96], Warrant Officer Ruben Marx [AM3521/96], Warrant Officer Jacobus Johannes Oosthuizen Beneke [AM6367/96] and Sergeant Gideon Johannes Nieuwoudt [AM3920/96] alleged that Biko died of brain injuries sustained in a 'scuffle' with the police at the Sanlam Building, Port Elizabeth.
>
> At the inquest, magistrate Marthinus Prins ruled that Biko's death was caused by a head injury, probably sustained on 7 September during a scuffle with security police in Port Elizabeth – but that there was no proof that the death was brought about by an act or omission involving an offence by any person.

He follows a footnote to Volume 4, Chapter 5 where he finds Biko's gravestone being watched over eternally by the prayerful pose of a participant at the proceedings:

BANTU STEPHEN BIKO
HONORARY PRESIDENT
BLACK PEOPLE'S CONVENTION

BORN 18-12-1946

DIED 12-9-1977

ONE AZANIA ONE NATION

The death in detention of Mr Stephen Bantu Biko
Stephen Biko was a prominent leader of the Black Consciousness Movement in the mid-1970s. He was detained by Eastern Cape security police in August 1977 and kept at Walmer police cells in Port Elizabeth. From there, he was taken regularly to security police headquarters for interrogation. The two district surgeons responsible for his medical care were Drs Benjamin Tucker and Ivor Lang.

On 7 September 1977, Stephen Biko sustained a head injury during interrogation, after which he acted strangely and was uncooperative. The doctors who examined him (naked, lying on a mat and manacled to a metal grille) initially disregarded overt signs of neurological injury. They also failed to record his external injuries or insist that he be kept in a more humane environment (at least that he be allowed to wear clothes). When a physician was finally consulted, a lumbar puncture revealing blood-stained cerebrospinal fluid (indicating possible brain damage) was reported as being 'normal', and Biko was returned to police cells.

Finally, on 11 September 1977, Stephen Biko lapsed into semiconsciousness. Dr Tucker recommended his transfer to a hospital in Port Elizabeth, but the security police refused to allow this. Subsequently, Dr Tucker acquiesced to the police's wish to transfer Biko to Pretoria Central Prison. Stephen Biko was transported 1 200km to Pretoria on the floor of a landrover. No medical personnel or records accompanied him. A few hours after he arrived in Pretoria, he was seen by district surgeon Dr A van Zyl, who administered a vitamin injection and asked for an intravenous drip to be started.

On 12 September, Stephen Biko died on the floor of a cell in Pretoria Central Prison, naked and alone. The post mortem examination showed brain damage and necrosis, extensive head trauma, disseminated intra-vascular coagulation, renal failure and various external injuries.

Kagiso returns to the Commission's findings:

> **THE COMMISSION FINDS THAT THE DEATH IN DETENTION OF MR STEPHEN BANTU BIKO ON 12 SEPTEMBER 1977 WAS A GROSS HUMAN RIGHTS VIOLATION. [AT THE TIME] MAGISTRATE MARTHINUS PRINS FOUND THAT THE MEMBERS OF THE [SOUTH AFRICAN POLICE] WERE NOT IMPLICATED IN HIS DEATH. THE MAGISTRATE'S FINDING CONTRIBUTED TO THE CREATION OF A CULTURE OF IMPUNITY IN THE SAP.**
>
> **DESPITE THE INQUEST FINDING WHICH FOUND NO PERSON RESPONSIBLE FOR HIS DEATH, THE COMMISSION FINDS THAT, IN VIEW OF THE FACT THAT BIKO DIED IN THE CUSTODY OF LAW ENFORCEMENT OFFICIALS, THE PROBABILITIES ARE THAT HE DIED AS A RESULT OF INJURIES SUSTAINED DURING HIS DETENTION.**

IN VIEW OF OUTSTANDING AMNESTY APPLICATIONS IN RESPECT OF BIKO'S DEATH, THE COMMISSION IS UNABLE TO CONFIRM A PERPETRATOR FINDING AT THIS STAGE.

Kagiso had bought tickets for he and Issa to see *Cry Freedom*. He'd hoped that seeing the film together would help them put aside their differences, find a way forward – that in it, his love for film and Issa's commitment to the struggle would find some sort of middle ground. He'd joined the queue early. Tickets were sold out within hours.

Sweet, Issa said when he phoned to confirm their bookings. *Very cool. I'll see you in Rosebank later.*

But by the time they got to the cinema, the film had been withdrawn, confiscated by the police at the last minute, even as the first reels had started to run.

Now, sitting cross-legged in front of Issa's bookcase, it strikes him that, more than a decade later, he has still not managed to fill in all the gaps inflicted upon him by a censorious dictatorial regime. The books not read, music not heard, histories not known, have become, like the holes in the expensive smelly cheese for which he has developed a liking, a part of his truthfully reconciled and liberated life.

He has still not seen the film. To him, it remains a police seizure. That is what lives on, the film itself, a blank space, a smelly hole. He is, he thinks, a little like the front page of a national newspaper stuck in his journal; full of blank spaces:

Our lawyers tell
us we can
say almost
nothing critical
about the
Emergency
But we'll try:

PIK BOTHA, the Minister of Foreign Affairs, told US television audiences this week that the South African press remained free.
We hope that ~~not heard, histories not known have become, like the soles in the expensive smoky not heard, histories not known have become, like the holes,~~ was listening.
They considered our publication subversive.
If it is subversive to speak out against ~~the African film itself~~, we plead guilty.
If it is subversive to express concern about ~~some sort of middle ground~~ we plead guilty.
If it is subversive to believe that there are better routes to peace than the ~~search for his~~ we plead guilty.

Below it, he has scribbled: 'I am a collection of blank spaces, defined more by what I don't know, than by what I do.'

But the catalogue of crimes in his lap does not record the invisible forgettable survivable blows to the brain by the censor's axe. He starts to search for his own name: Mayoyo; Kagiso, left stupid after having been lobotomised by the South African Board of Censors in the interest of national security. He releases the pages of the fifth volume from back to front with his thumb. When the headline 'Finding on former President PW Botha' flashes past, he catches the page:

> **102** Mr Botha presided as executive head of the former South African government (the government) from 1978 to 1984 as Prime Minister, and from 1984 to 1989 as Executive State President. Given his centrality in the politics of the 1970s and 1980s, the Commission has made a finding on the role of the former State President:
> [...]

> **BY VIRTUE OF HIS POSITION AS HEAD OF STATE AND CHAIRPERSON OF THE [STATE SECURITY COUNCIL], BOTHA CONTRIBUTED TO AND FACILITATED A CLIMATE IN WHICH THE ABOVE GROSS VIOLATIONS OF HUMAN RIGHTS COULD AND DID OCCUR, AND AS SUCH IS ACCOUNTABLE FOR SUCH VIOLATIONS.**

In the front of the volume, Kagiso finds his name:

Mayoyo.

In a list of 'Victims of Gross Violations of Human Rights'.

He shudders. Seeing his own name in print, there, in black and white, in the directory of national horrors, the feeling rises, like when he saw the new gravestone his grandmother had had erected on his grandfather's grave, the first time he had associated his name – there, carved in stone – with death, the first indication of his mortality passing through him like a cold wind. The feeling rises, as in DC, when he glimpsed his reflection looking back at him from behind the names of the gratuitously dead in the polished surface of the memorial to the vainglorious Vietnam War. Angered by the audacity, he had turned around and walked away. But now he doesn't close the volume; rather, he lies down on his back and brings its weight down onto his chest.

When he wakes, his head beside the volumes, his eyes move over the open pages:

> It was not a secret march – it was in the newspapers. I remember on the 24th or the 25th Dr Boesak was still negotiating with Mr Le Grange, then Minister of Police. He sent him a telegram to say that this march would be peaceful and, to a large extent, was a symbolic march. There was no idea that we would physically go into Pollsmoor prison and break Mr Mandela out.

A breeze flows through the open window and flips a few pages.

> Lionel and Quentin were 13-year-olds and they both died. There were thousands of people, but why did the police shoot the children? Karel sat with Lionel while he was dying – now Karel is suffering because he and his brother where like twins.

Now a strong gust throws open the window. It startles him. He leaps across the small room to secure the banging pane. When he returns to the volume, he finds it open on a book-marked page. His eyes seize the heading "'Trojan Horse' killings". The words stand up like Lazarus in front of him. They don't resurrect mythological images; those have been usurped. His association, vivid, is from his youth.

Shock waves from the ambush reverberated around the country and beyond. After the attack, Athlone, at the epicentre, dropped its hands from its shell-shocked ears and looked around in dazed confusion. Then, as if in slow motion, it saw three of its boys fall to the ground, dead. The angry, speechless wave that had lapped at hearts for centuries, rose again, each time a little higher than before. In its rising it woke mythology from its age-old slumber, took its language, then sent it back to sleep.

> **The Trojan Horse and other ambush tactics**
>
> **168** The Athlone 'Trojan Horse' incident that took place in Athlone, Cape Town, on 15 October 1985 is well known: police hiding in large wooden crates on the back of a railway truck fired directly into a crowd of about a hundred people who had gathered around a Thornton Road intersection, killing Michael Cheslyn Miranda (11) [CT00478, CT00472], Shaun Magmoed (16) [CT00472] and Mr Jonathan Claasen (21) [CT00475] and injuring several others.

That night, while Cape Town of the Flats mourned its dead and young, galvanised hearts readied themselves for battle, in Johannesburg Issa lifted a rucksack onto his back and made for the front door, determined to defy Ma Vasinthe if it came to that:

"You *can't* go to Cape Town!" she asserted, barring the doorway. "What about school?"

School? I'm sorry, Ma, but if you mean that bigoted white liberal bourgeois nest you send us to every day, you can forget it.

Outside a convoy of expensive combis hooted, clenched fists and Palestinian kefiyas and V-fingers raised into the air through narrowly opened tinted windows.

Let me pass, Ma.

"No." She folded her arms.

Ma. Please. Get out of the way.

"Now you listen to me!" she commanded, waving a stern finger at him. "You're a child and you will do as I say."

Yes, Ma. I am a child. And if that makes me a legitimate target in this country then it makes me a legitimate protestor too. Now get out of my way!

"Don't you shout at me, young man."

Issa lowered his voice. He glared at his mother from under a furrowed brow. *Ma, I'd rather leave the house with your blessing, but if –*

Vasinthe dug her heels in. "I'm not negotiating with you."

Hoot hoot.

Suit yourself. Issa swung around and started running towards the back door.

"Gloria!" Vasinthe yelled. "Lock the back door!"

But Gloria did not obey. When Issa rushed through the kitchen, she looked up from the ironing. Issa paused. They exchanged glances, did not speak. A snatched wordless moment in which they understood each other perfectly.

When Vasinthe entered the room, Gloria said goodbye by glancing at the open door.

Then Kagiso was drafted in. "Go!" Vasinthe shouted, pointing up the driveway. "Stop him!"

Kagiso leapt into action and caught up with Issa at the gate. He grabbed onto the rucksack and started tugging and pulling at it.

Let me go! Issa struggled.

"Hold on to him, Kagiso. I'm coming."

One of the gleaming combis pulled up to the curve. A door slid open.

"Come, Issa!" a voice called out from the dark, shaded interior. "Drop the bag!"

Issa dumped his restraining baggage and leapt into the combi.

Go! he shouted, when he hit the floor, his legs still dangling through the door.

On the pavement, Ma Vasinthe watched as her son was carried away in an expensive motorcade of defiant resistance. As the convoy picked up speed, she saw V-fingers, kefiyas, Issa's dangling legs vanish from sight as tinted windows were sealed and solid doors slid shut. When the discreet, blacked-out fleet disappeared around the corner, Kagiso stepped forward to pick up the jettisoned rucksack.

> The day after the Trojan Horse shooting, an angry crowd gathered at the St Athans Road Mosque in Athlone. A member of the SAP was shot by the crowd, after which police opened fire, killing Mr Abdul Fridie (29) [CT00607]. On 18th October, a massive security force presence was moved into Athlone.
>
> Armed soldiers and police lined the streets and searched houses while a helicopter hovered above.

When Kagiso replaces the bookmark, he notices a quotation on its reverse side:

And why should ye not
Fight in the cause of God
And of those who, being weak,
Are ill-treated (and oppressed)? –
Men, women, and children,
Whose cry is: "Our Lord!
Rescue us from this town,
Whose people are oppressors;
And raise for us from Thee
One who will protect;
And raise for us from Thee
One who will help!"

Qur'an S.iv.75

The Monster's Name

WHEN VASINTHE TRAVELLED TO London immediately after Issa's disappearance, she brought two gifts, one of them a photograph of her and Issa, which now stands on Katinka's bedside table next to a picture of Karim. Katinka enacts a little ritual here everyday, laying a flower, sometimes just a leaf plucked in passing from a tree, or tilting perfume onto her forefinger then touching it to the frames – her altar to her missing men. At night she always lights the tea light beside it before she goes to bed.

About the picture, she remembers everything – how she had insisted they have it taken, the warmth of the night, the feeling of his strong shoulders under her hand as she pulled him towards her following the hand signals of the obliging stranger to whom she'd given her camera – the date, 11th February 1990. Her words to Issa…

"I want to tell you a story. It doesn't matter that I hardly know you. I want to tell it to somebody tonight, *now*, and then never have to talk about it again."

The previous day, Kagiso had insisted that they give the stranded girl a lift. "Bloody hell, Issa, she could be standing there for hours in this heat."

Are you mad?

"But that guy's just dumped her on the side of the road."

I'm not getting involved in their argument. He'll turn back for her. He pays the petrol attendant.

"I don't think so. He looked pretty angry to me."

Kagiso looks at the abandoned girl. She kicks her rucksack in frustration then, raising a shielding palm to her brow, turns to salute the shimmering horizon. Issa starts the engine and drives slowly out of the forecourt. When they join the main road, he accelerates.

"Issa?"

Forget it!

But Kagiso pulls up the handbrake bringing the car to a screeching stop just beyond where the girl is standing. She runs towards them.

"Cape Town?"

"Yes," says Kagiso, throwing open the back door. "Jump in."

"Thank you very much."

When she has settled down, Kagiso turns around. "What was that all about?"

The girls sighs despondently. "In this country, what else? Fucking racist doos."

Issa glances at her through the rear view mirror.

"He picked me up outside Bloemfontein. It wasn't long before I regretted ever getting into his car. But I was glad to have the lift so I just listened. But after two hours of his kak, I just couldn't keep quiet any more. So I told him why I was going to Cape Town. That's when he threw me out."

"Heavy."

"Ja well, I've seen worse. Thanks for stopping. For a moment I thought I might miss it all."

"That's all right," Kagiso says, not looking at Issa.

"You also going down for the occasion?" the girl asks.

"Yeah."

"I can't wait."

"I'm sure *he* can't either."

"I'm sure you're right."

She notices a packet of Rizla papers among the paraphernalia on the dashboard. "You guys mind if I smoke?"

"Go ahead," Kagiso says. "There's an ashtray in the door." He leans over the seat to show her.

"Woah!" he exclaims when he sees the fat hand-rolled affair cocked in her fingers. "That thing looks dangerous. Is it what I think it is?"

"Do you mind? We're in the middle of nowhere."

"Do I mind? Go ahead, please." He ignites a lighter. "I smoked my last at a party last night."

"In that case, you should go first." She holds out her offering.

"Thanks, man."

"Transvaal plates," she comments. "Jo'burg?"

"Yeah. You?"

"Ventersdorp."

Issa tightens his grip on the wheel.

"Right." Kagiso says, then holds out the joint.

"Kolskoot!" She exclaims. "That's exactly it. Ventersdorp in a word." She takes the joint. "Actually, for an even better summation of my home town, you need to prefix 'right' with 'far', or better still, 'ultra'. You get what I'm saying?"

Kagiso nods with wide stretched eyes. "That bad?"

"That bad," she raises the joint but stops short of her lips. "And my problem with it, to start with, you see," she says, screwing her eyes to shield them from the smoke, "is that I'm wired differently. As you may have noticed, I'm a left-handed nooi." She raises the illicit contents of her left hand into the air, "Cheers," and then brings it to her lips.

"I'm Katinka, by the way," she says when the music stops.

"And I'm Kagiso. He's Issa."

"And does Issa speak?"

"Not very often."

She nods. "I see."

"When you guys going back to Jo'burg?"

"Not for a while now. December probably. Maybe June. We study in Cape Town."

"You're lucky. I would have loved to study in Cape Town, under the mountains, next to the sea, but," she sighs, "it wasn't meant to be."

"What happened?"

"My father – that's what happened. He wouldn't hear about it."

"Why?"

"He wouldn't hear of his daughter going to university in liberal Cape Town. I tried to bargain. 'Stellenbosch,' I said, but he had made up his mind and when my father has made up his mind, it's because his pal, God, has had a say in the decision. So to change it again would be a sin."

"What did you do?"

"I went to Free State. What else could I do? It was that or stay on the farm. But," she says with a relieved sigh, as though dropping an unbearable weight, "I've finished my course and all that is behind me." Then she sits forward, squeezing herself between the two front seats to point at the endless open road stretched out in front of them, "and that's what lies ahead."

ꕥ

She opens the book on the back seat:

> …we had ridden far out over the rolling plains of North Syria to a ruin of the Roman period which the Arabs believed was made by a prince of the border as a desert-palace for his queen. The clay of its building was said to have been kneaded for greater richness, not with water, but with the precious essential oils of flowers. My guides, sniffing the air like dogs, led me from crumbling room to room, saying, 'This is jessamine, this violet, this rose'.
>
> But at last Dahoun drew me: 'Come and smell the very sweetest scent of all', and we went into the main lodging, to the gaping window sockets of its eastern face, and there drank with open mouths of the effortless, empty, eddyless wind of the desert, throbbing past. That slow breath had been born somewhere beyond the distant Euphrates and had dragged its way across many days and nights of dead grass, to its first obstacle, the man-made walls of our broken palace. About them it seemed to fret and linger, murmuring in baby-speech. "This," they told me,

> "is the best: it has no taste." My Arabs were turning their backs on perfumes and luxuries to choose the things in which mankind had had no share or part.

She glances at their silent driver and lays down the book, her fingers brushing the tattered flag pictured on the cover. "What is this music?" she asks of the lilting, sorrowful tune.

"It's his."

"What is this music?" she repeats. "I've never heard such music. Where's it from?"

He says his first words to her. *It's* –

She is surprised. "But that's banned."

Issa doesn't respond.

"Well, it is beautiful music. Like the desert. Like here."

It is night by the time they approach the mountains that encircle Cape Town. Scatterings of light betray the sleepy villages in the dark valleys below them, while the golden glow of the city beyond hangs over the peaks above, like a halo.

"I've not yet seen the new tunnel. I'm told it's quite impressive."

Kagiso looks at Issa.

"I believe they built it from both sides of the mountain. Apparently, when the two tunnels met, they were only millimetres off."

It's getting late and he has been driving for sixteen hours. Tomorrow will be another long day. At the fork in the motorway, the moment of choice between the tunnel and the pass, Issa makes for the tunnel.

Minutes later, they are racing down the N1 on the home run to its southernmost destination. To their left, the Cape Flats – a carpet of light stretching all the way to False Bay, glides by. Ahead, a sweeping bend brings Table Mountain slowly into the view, lit up against the night sky. There is an air of anticipation in the city.

At last the sun has set.

Dawn will usher in a long-awaited new era.

And steering the car between the flashing white lines on the freeway, a quote comes to hover in front of Issa's tired, driving eyes: "The morning freshness of the world to be intoxicated us." That is all he wishes to remember of it and tries hard to ignore the rest of it. But the passage lingers, demanding to be recalled in its entirety: "yet, when we achieved and a new world dawned, the old men came out again and took our victory to re-make in the likeness of the former world they knew."

"I wonder what he must be feeling now," she says, almost to herself.

ꕥ

The next night, when the crowd on the Grand Parade starts to disperse, they walk across town to the Underground. Inside, the atmosphere is euphoric. Issa's entrance is greeted with hoots and cheers.

"Amandla!"

"Awethu!"

"It is true, isn't it?"

"It's true."

Katinka is greeted with cautious reserve.

"Ek sê my bra," Issa's friend starts up when they are alone, "leading the way to reconciliation by example, or what? Who's the lanie nooi?"

Issa looks across the room to where Katinka has blended effortlessly into the celebrations. He felt called upon to deliver his verdict, his final interpretation of the bits of evidence she had laid before him during the course of the day. As he watched her dance, rejoice, hands high in the air, it came to him: The system imprisoned all of us.

He turned to his friend: *She's a comrade from the Free State. So don't you give her grief.*

"Nooit, my bra. If she's with you, I knew she had to be cool."

Coolest you'll meet.

"Vir seker!" his friend nods with envious admiration.

From the crowded dance floor, Katinka catches Issa's outline, crouching in a dark corner, his neck crooked as he stares into the space above her head. She follows his gaze to the ceiling above the dance floor. Being projected there, are images of the day's unimaginable events: the huge crowd that gathered outside the prison to greet him, waiting, for hours; the moment when he appeared, actually appeared, there, in front of them, walking into their midst, like the Messiah; the hush that fell, then the rising murmurs, the grappling with the most indescribable complexity of emotion, all of it, pent up, with him, for 27 years; then, the release, the catharsis, the ecstatic jubilation, here, in the city, across the country and around the world.

"Amandla!" someone shouts from the dance floor.

The whole Underground responds with a deafening chorus, which overpowers the thumping sound system: "Awethu!"

The sequence ends with the face of the man as he now is, emerging, slowly, from behind the blacked-out profile of his banned image – till today, apart from a few black and white images that predated his censure, the only image their generation had of him.

Gerry Adams at least had a face.

When she looks down from the ceiling, she finds him looking at her. He does not look away. She walks over to him.

"Wat dink jy?" she asks, crouching on the floor next to him.

Not much.

"Good."

The response surprises him. *Why good?*

"Well, if you're not thinking much," she explains "then you won't need to use too much of your daily fifty-word ration to share your thoughts."

He tries to stifle a shy smile.

She raises her head encouragingly.

I'm thinking of those who can't be here. My friends. Coline. Robert.

"Ag, forget about them," she says with a dismissive wave. "If they can't be bothered to be here, today of all days, they don't deserve your thoughts. Absconders. Forget about them." She grabs him by the hand and stands up. "Come. Dance."

But he breaks free. *And if they're dead?*

Her face falls. "Oh my God!" She slides down the wall, back into her crouching position on the floor. She buries her face in her hands. "I'm so sorry."

Katinka?

Comrade?

Hey! He takes her gently by the hand. *Don't worry about it. It's okay. Come on.*

She crawls out cautiously from behind her hands, wiping tears from her cheeks.

Hey!

"I thought – I thought you were talking about... People like..."

Like?

She sits up with a sniff. "I want to tell you a story," she says, resolutely wiping away the tears. "It doesn't matter that I hardly know you. I want to tell it to somebody tonight, *now*, and then never have to talk about it again. It must die with the old. It's only a short story. Will you listen?"

Yes.

"One day, there was a brother and a sister who grew up on a farm outside Ventersdorp. When they were naughty or when their parents wanted to force them into things like homework or going to church, which the little girl hated, they would threaten them with a monster, saying that, unless they did as they were told, the monster would come for them in the night, drag them from their beds and devour them.

It was a horrible monster, ugly and cruel, and even after years had passed and the brother and sister had grown up, the mention of the monster's name still struck fear in some part of them." She looks at him nervously. "Can you guess the monster's name?"

He thinks.

What? Not – ? He gestures to the images on the ceiling.

She nods.

Nooit!

Then looks away. "When I told my father I was coming here today, he said, 'Kies! If you go, you are not welcome in my house any more. You are not my daughter any more. What do you think the people will say? How do you expect me to face them with a daughter who runs after a communist terrorist kaffir?' And my brother, he said he'd shoot me himself if he ever saw me again."

She looks up at him with overcast eyes. "Fluit, fluit," she says with a sad smile. "My storie is uit."

The Sanctuary

KAGISO HAS FORGOTTEN HIS JOURNAL, so he unlocks the door again to fetch it from the desk. It is open at an insert, an extract he was once asked to read in an undergraduate tutorial. It seems almost innocuous now so that he snatches the journal without fully noticing the open page, but at the time the extract brought his world crashing down around him. It was what first prompted a revision of his black and white mind film:

> … Fifteen years later, in Cape Town, comes this brief glimpse of young mother, Lydia. Divorced with one child, she went back to look after her 86-year-old mother who lived with her husband in a house tied to a lime-stone processing plant whose owner forbade anyone else to stay with them. Thus, since Lydia was not allowed to stay there she has been running from the police. She and her one-year-old baby were amongst those arrested in a police raid. They spent the weekend in jail and were only allowed out because of the baby. She had to reappear in court and, at the time of the interview, did not know what the outcome would be because she did not have money to pay the R20 fine. She did not have anyone to support her. She had divorced her husband about six years previously, but although he was required to support her and the child financially she had not received a cent. "She has been in court many times for a maintenance grant but is tired of this because nothing ever materialises" (15:4). Lydia, writes MM Gonsalves, is tired of trying to make ends meet as well as running from the police. She

> states that no matter where one goes, if one does not work and 'live-in', and does not have a pass, one has to run, because of the danger of trespassing. She begs for a live-in job as she cannot stand the thought of being caught again and of being constantly on the look-out for the police (15:5).

When the tutorial was over, he returned to his room at Jan Smuts House and locked the door. He skipped classes for the rest of the day and in the evening, went to see Issa at UWC.

⁂

Kagiso roams the city – sometimes with Katinka, mostly by himself. No matter how late he goes to bed, he always wanders through the early morning streets, when security shutters on shop fronts in the neighbourhood are being lifted slowly, like sleepy lids, before the streets become crowded. While the destitute are still visible – bundles huddled in doorways, before being swept away into obscurity. Where faces are obscured, he looks to other features: ears, hands, fingernails especially – large, even and with unusually prominent half-moons – shoulders, hair, scrutinising them, not in order to classify and exclude, but to identify and embrace.

One morning, he plucks up the courage to talk to the fruit vendor, still setting up his stall. "Good morning," he says, nervously.

"Alrigh' mate? No' quite ready yet."

"That's okay. I was only wondering if…"

The vendor straightens himself.

"If…" Kagiso starts from scratch. "I believe you know my brother."

The vendor looks at him, confused. "Bruva?"

"Yes. He used to barter with you, fruit in exchange for the sports section of the paper."

The vendor throws his head back in recognition. "Oh, yes, sure I do. Yeah, 'e used to come by 'ere regular. I was only wondering abou' 'im the other day, like. 'aven't seen him for a while. He alrigh'?"

"Actually..."

The vendor leans forward.

"Actually, he's disappeared."

"Your 'aving me on! Disappeared?"

Kagiso nods.

"When? How?"

"Four months ago. In April. That's all we know."

"And you've 'eard nuffing since?"

Kagiso shakes his head. "Nothing."

"You mean to say somebody can disappear," he snaps fingers, "just like that?"

"Seems so."

"Well, I am sorry to 'ear that, mate. I really am. Nice bloke 'e was, too. Mind you, he never said very much. Came 'ere one morning, bough' a banana and gave me the sports paper. Always a banana. Same thing 'appened again the next morning, and the next, till I wouldn' take 'is money no more. 'ad to be fair, like, you know what I'm saying?"

"So he didn't say anything to you before he left?"

"Nah, he didn't say nuffing, mate. As I say, he never said much anyway." The vendor scrutinises Kagiso a little more closely. "You say you two was bruvas?"

"Yes."

"Thought so. But he was more kinda Arab looking, weren't he?"

Kagiso nods.

"Don't mean to pry, like, it's jus' that, for a moment I weren't sure, you know, if, we was talking abou' the same person, you know wha' I mean?"

"That's okay. Don't worry about it. Listen, if you hear or see anything," he hands the vendor his card, "would you get in touch?"

The vendor studies the card. "Johannesburg, 'ay?"

"Yeah."

"That where 'e was from, too?"

"Yes."

"See, I didn't even know tha' much. Aint life funny sometimes?" he asks, searching the sky. "You can see somebone every day of yer life and know nuffing abou' them, until they disappear. Tha's London for yer, mate."

Kagiso rocks back on his feet awkwardly.

"Sorry, mate, I didn't mean to upse' you, like."

"You didn't."

The vendor is not convinced. He places Kagiso's card down on a box and opens another. "'ere, take a banana."

"No, that's not –"

"Go on," the vendor insists, stuffing the banana into his pocket. "'av it."

Kagiso relents. "Thank you." He looks at the card. "You won't forget, will you?"

"Forge'?" the vendor asks.

Kagiso points at the card. "To be in touch. If you hear anything?"

"Sure, mate," the vendor assures. He slips the card into his back pocket. "Anyfing I can do, mate. Anyfing I can do."

Later in the day, the heat, inescapable, follows him like a stalker, from Issa's tiny flat, onto the tube, through the busy streets.

"I'd have thought you'd be used to it," Frances commented when he complained.

Kagiso muttered a vague, concealing response; at home he rarely has to confront the weather, his contact with it always mediated by his air-conditioned car, his modern office in a shady northern enclave of the city, his spacious, well-ventilated flat with its balcony overlooking the pool. London is a different world; he has twice had to rush off a baking stopping starting swerving turning sitting bus for fear of retching. On the tube, he tries, whenever possible, to stand by the door at the front of the carriage where he can let the window down as he has seen experienced commuters do.

With him, he carries his journal, a water bottle, a camcorder and Issa's A-Z and notebook, which he found at the bottom of the bookcase and some of the 'Missing' leaflets of Issa to distribute when the desperate compulsion to do something takes hold. He visits the places Issa mentions in the notebook, to see for himself: the new British Library, impressive inside but which from the street looked to him like a prison (he much preferred the building next door, was amazed to discover that it is, in fact, a station); Trafalgar Square, destination of protest, prestigious location of South Africa House and, to his surprise, just there, in the middle of the city, the Academy of St Martin-in-the-Fields, not at all the setting he'd imagined when their evocative soundtracks carried him on sentimental cinematic journeys to magical places, now, he doesn't even step inside; the parking lot in front of Westminster Abbey, called 'The Sanctuary', the location of a black and white photograph in Issa's notebook: a young Mandela before his eventual imprisonment and total censure.

From here, Kagiso winds his way through the narrow sunless back streets behind the abbey, past the offices of the Liberal Democrats on Cowley Street, then pausing further along to read a sign outside a house, the home of Lord Reith, first director of the BBC, before finally turning the corner into Barton Street. He is looking for number 14, so he starts to count the numbers on the front doors of the neat deserted terraced row – 10, 11, 12, 13 – odd and even next to each other on the same side of the road. Even though he knows it is next, still, in the end, after all the years, number 14 comes upon him rather suddenly, so that he has to step back a pace to study it.

Little distinguishes the house from the other near-identical houses on the quiet street, only a round blue plaque, like the one outside Lord Reith's, from the Greater London Council, reveals why Kagiso felt compelled to investigate Issa's mention of this address, also referenced in the brooding quotation above his desk, in his notebook:

TE Lawrence
"Lawrence of Arabia"
1888-1935 lived here

He finds a slight recess across the road and slips into it, looking up at the attic, willing the curtain there to twitch, expectant, remembering the soldier in blind Alfredo's story who waits 100 nights in the street beneath his true love's window. Kagiso looks left then right, up then down the quiet little street, barely registering the ding-dong ding-dong that comes rolling over the rooftops. When he moves away from the little house, he looks, one last time, over his shoulder at the attic before turning the corner. He glances at his watch just as, having struck its final stroke at four, Big Ben falls into silence.

Kagiso spends a lot of time at his destinations around the city. He is attentive to them, watches them, their other visitors, finds a good vantage point from which to sketch them, photograph them. Where possible, he always visits the restrooms before leaving, never fully aware that he is searching, always waits for the occupants of locked cubicles to emerge, before leaving.

On Grosvenor Square, he stops to film the sealed-off building on the west side of the square – the barricades, the closed road, the enormous spread-winged eagle that adorns the top of the otherwise unremarkable building. He has been recording the country's embassies whenever he visits a capital city, storing the images in a folder entitled: 'The fortressed look of freedom and democracy.' He does not linger here but retrieves Issa's notebook from his backpack before continuing down South Audley Street in search of the secluded garden with a secluded bench on which is inscribed the following dedication:

> In Memory of Derek Lane
> From a select number of friends who spent many hours
> in his company and together enjoyed the splendour of
> this city and the tranquillity of these gardens.

Issa had copied the dedication into his notebook alongside a little map of the area showing the location of the park and the bench where he wrote:

Mayfair
24th December 2000

I am sitting on Derek Lane's bench tucked away in the affluent heart of this splendid city, but, with my own accursed 'Sixth Sense', I only see the ogres – the hideous ones, the invisible ones. They roam the city, the unwanted ones, with vacant, distant stares. Absent and preoccupied, here only in unwanted, despised, brutalised, foreign body; Europe's untouchables.

From the top decks of busses, they scan the bustling pavements of the begrudging sanctuary, searching, desperately, for familiar scenes from home – the smiling face of an old school friend waving enthusiastically from the crowd; the old men at the café on the square, drinking coffee in threadbare jackets, sporting medals from wars only they can recall; the hands of the orthodox priest being kissed fervently by suppliant devotees in the market place; the teenagers with lean, healthy bodies, diving from the old pedestrian bridge – no longer there – into the warm glow of the setting sun.

Sometimes they stare at memories of torture chambers, at missing relatives, at dead friends, right there in the piece of floor between their feet on packed underground carriages, or in the unbelievably pretty shop windows at Christmas time, filled with price tags that could bring whole families to the sanctuary.

At the carwash on the corner, they catch sight of what they fear most in the polished chrome of shiny cars and buckets of dirty water; others see it in mirrors in hotel bathrooms or in the shiny cutlery they lay out before breakfast – reflections of self. Embarrassed, they look away. How could I have imagined that here, this, would be better? When they are still there? Did I leave to live with mocking reflections? Waiting on tables with an apron cut from a graduate's hood; mending shoes – my grandfather's trade – with the skilful hands of a surgeon.

> *Those who believed*
> *And those who suffered exile*
> *And fought (and strove and Struggled)*
> *In the path of God, –*
> *They have the hope*
> *Of the Mercy of God:*
> *And God is Oft-forgiving, Most Merciful*
> (Qur'an S ii, 218)

For work, they do the jobs these people no longer want to do for themselves. They washed the limousines for Saturday's wedding in the big church on the hill, tended the garden in the hotel ahead of the lavish reception, which was celebrated into the night. In the morning, they served them breakfast, and then, after everybody had set off on the journey back home, bleary-eyed and hung-over, they stripped their beds and washed their sheets stained with vomit and cum. And at the airport, they cleaned the toilets on the very plane that months earlier had brought them to the sanctuary and which would that night whisk the newly-weds off to their sun-drenched honeymoon, there.

At night they return to their lairs, where the corridors echo with anguished sobs and moans; where memories – of a carefree childhood with siblings, now dead; of frail grandparents, shell-shocked that their many years of toil and sacrifice had not made it all better; of lonely, fretful, wives, unable to escape from under the captive gaze of vigilant government gangs; of anxious parents filled with self-loathing and reproach for not having done more to prevent it all from going so horribly, horribly wrong – all come alive in vivid multicolour home cinema with surround sound on grubby walls and ceilings in the middle of the night, making sleep impossible.

Kagiso inspects the evidence around the bench – the scuffed pebbles at his feet, the recently smoked cigarette butt, the fresh match beside that may have lit it. Somebody has just left. He has arrived too late, will leave too soon, to ever know who. Whenever he leaves a place, he looks, instinctively, over his shoulder, sometimes stepping back a few paces to check.

No longer uses the expression, 'No looking back'.

ఊ

He's heard that destitute people sometimes seek shelter on the Circle Line, so he spends several hours walking the length of the trains on this line, moving, like a beggar, from one carriage to the next at stations around the never-ending line, first clockwise: Notting Hill Gate / Bayswater / Paddington / Edgware Road / Baker Street / Great Portland Street / Euston Square / King's Cross St. Pancras / Farringdon / Barbican / Moorgate / Liverpool Street

/ Aldgate / Tower Hill / Monument / Cannon Street / Mansion House / Blackfriars / Temple / Embankment / Westminster / St. James's Park / Victoria / Sloane Square / South Kensington / Gloucester Road / High Street Kensington / Notting Hill Gate, then anti-clockwise: Notting Hill Gate / High Street Kensington / Gloucester Road…

ঃ

When the singing man has disappeared into the crowd, he signs the petition then walks down the Strand. In a deserted coffee shop, he opens his journal:

> I noticed him when he stepped into the frame. I had knelt down to take a photograph of the demonstration outside Zimbabwe House. He was a big man, very tall, and the unseasonal grey tweed coat he was wearing did not restrain his free, swaying movements. I trained my lens on him for a while; he must certainly be from southern Africa, I thought. There was something in his full face, his easy disposition that was unmistakably home. How unselfconscious he was, to draw such attention to himself, to expose so much of himself to this indifferent town. I photographed him. When I lowered my camera, our eyes met. I smiled. He smiled back and started to make his way towards me. I stood up from my kneeling position.

"Boom chaka boom chaka boom chaka boom! I'm working on this tune, you see, and this is the introduction. Boom chaka boom chaka boom chaka boom! What do you think? Isn't it great?"

"It's good," I say, clicking the cap back onto the lens.

"And, remember, it's only the introduction! The song proper hasn't even started yet. And then we go a 1, a 2, a 123… Yela yela ye la la la la. Ay, my brother, now the tune carries us away, away and away! I say, my brother, what do you think of that, man?"

I tell him that I think it's a great tune, because it is. The man lets out a big roaring laugh of genuine delight, as though I had just given him the best news in the world.

"Ay, thank you my brother, man. Do you really like my music?"

I nod eagerly. "I'm sure a record company will snap you up."

"Thank you, man. Thank you."

"Are you from South Africa?" I ask, struggling to secure the worn clip on my camera case.

The man stands back, surprised. "How do you know?"

"I'm from there myself. I can hear it in your voice."

"Really! You really mean to say that, after all these years, you can still hear Africa in my voice?"

"Yebo," I say.

"Ay, come here, my brother. Come here." He throws his arms around me. "My African brother." Even though I'm a little worried about dropping my camera – I've still not managed to secure the troublesome clip – the embrace feels good. Its sincerity and spontaneity make me laugh. It is as though home has suddenly appeared on the streets of London to give me a hug. The smell of stale alcohol doesn't bother me that much. Then the man steps back to hold me at arm's length, with his enormous hands resting on my shoulders. He tilts his head apologetically. "Actually, my brother, I'm from Zimbabwe. Yes, Bulawayo, Place of Slaughter. Do you know the story of Bulawayo?"

I give up on the clip with an annoyed tut, wrap the shoulder straps tightly around the case to keep it shut and return the camera to my open bag where it is kept snug by the pile of 'Missing' leaflets, an operation the man watches intently.

"And which place are you from, my brother?" he asks when I have finished.

"Egoli."

"Ay, man! Place of Gold. Jozi! Egoli! Gauteng!" The man exclaims as if about to burst into song again with the many appellations of the city of gold. "How long are you in London for?"

"Only a few days," I say. And then I hesitate. The man notices.

"What's the matter, my friend?"

I decide that I may as well tell him. "I'm looking for my brother," I say, stooping to retrieve one of the leaflets from my bag. "Perhaps you've seen him," I ask, handing him the leaflet.

The man studies the picture of Issa intently. Then he taps it with his forefinger. "You know – " He cuts himself short.

"What?" I ask eagerly. "Do you recognise him?"

He starts nodding slowly, knowingly. "I do," he says, smiling. "Yes, I do."

I can hardly believe the good fortune of this chance encounter. "Where? When?" I ask, unable to contain my optimism.

The man looks around suspiciously then pulls me once again towards him. He whispers in my ear, conspiratorially. "I saw him just the other day," he confides, his warm breath brushing my ear.

I step back slightly to see his face, to express my delight.

"Yes. In Buck House," he continues. "I usually have dinner there with Elizabeth once a month or so. We go back a long way, you know, old Liz and I."

"Excuse me?" I blink, my heart still racing in my chest.

He pushes a dirty finger to his pouted lips. "Sshh! I don't want people to know about it. It's a discreet arrangement. You have to keep your voice down, okay?"

"Yes, okay," I agree half-heartedly, the anticipation, the hope, starting to drain anti-clockwise from my soul.

"Good," the man continues. "You have to be careful in this town... Now, when I was having dinner in the palace the other day, he was there." He studies the picture again. "Yes, it was him. I remember he was chatting to Philip – I'm not so keen on him, I must admit – about the races. And when we played cards together after dinner, he beat us all hands down." He starts to laugh and is soon shaking with hilarity. "That upset old Liz. Phil and I usually let her win, you see. Ooh, you should have seen her face."

"Really," I said to the man, feigning amusement.

But his laughter had already stopped, his face had fallen and his mind had moved on to other things. "I'm looking for my son too. He's missing you know."

"I'm sorry to hear that," I respond, zipping up my bag.

"But I know where he is, mind you. Yes, he's in jail. In Gauteng, as it happens."

"I'm sorry to hear that," I hear myself echo.

Again, he pulls me towards him. "Yes, he killed a man. A motor car accident." Then he waves his Issa-clutching hand dismissively. I start to plot my escape, make a dramatic gesture of swinging my bag onto my back, even glance at my watch, but there is a futility in that gesture, that dismissive wave, which I recognise instantly: it says yes, it's awful, thank you for your concern, but I'm sorry I can't tell you more, I'm exhausted by it because it's always on my mind and I don't know what to do, but I've been through it all too many times to go over again, here, now. I'm sorry I raised it. Sometimes it slips out. Forget I said anything. And then you put on a happy face and try to change the topic. To those who know it, that gesture spells defeat. The man is still being as generous and unselfconscious as he was when I spied him through the lens of my camera. Despite his insistence on hushed tones, he shared his joy and sorrow boisterously and in equal measure, with this indifferent town.

"How long have you been here?" I ask.

"Twenty-seven years," he answers in five flat, monotonous syllables. "Twen / ty / se / ven / years."

"That's a long time," I exclaim. "Would you like to go back home to Zimbabwe?"

He shakes his head. "Home? Zimbabwe? No. Zimbabwe is no longer home." Then he gives me a warning look. "And *not* because of Mugabe, mind you!" I follow the man's forefinger as it waves, backwards and forwards in the air, like a crazy metronome. No, not because of Mugabe."

"Why are you here, then?"

"Because of *Smith*! Remember him? You remember him?"

"I remember him a little," I say.

"Only a little! How can you only remember a little about a man like Smith?"

"I was very young," I say defensively.

"Rubbish. I'm sure you can tell me more about Hitler and you weren't even born then."

I stutter.

"Well, let me tell you. I think Mugabe's right! I think he's great. You know why?"

I shake my head.

"I was this old," he drops his hand down to his thigh with his gathered fingers, like a closed tulip, turned upwards, "when, one day, I was shepherding my grandfather's sheep. My grandfather had many, many sheep. So one day, I was shepherding the sheep when two white men came. They came up to me and said, 'Hey, whose sheep are these?' I said they belonged to my grandfather. You know what they did? They cut off their heads, like this." He chops his arms around my neck, as if in a game of oranges and lemons. "Yes, like this," the man continues. "Chop chop chop. All my grandfather's sheep. I saw it. With my own eyes. And I was this high from the ground, man. This high from the fucking ground. How can you only remember a little of Smith when I remember so fucking much?" Then the singing man starts to cry.

"Yes, I saw those things with my own eyes. That's why I'm here. That's why I'm *here* and not *there*. That's why I'm fucking *here*!" He wipes his eyes with Issa's face as though it were a handkerchief. The leaflet leaves ink stains across the man's eyes where he has wiped away his tears – and across his sweaty brow. "That's why I'm fucking here." And then he steps around me and starts staggering away with Issa's smudged image staring helplessly back at me from the man's clutched hand – like Winnie the Pooh, I think – like Winnie the Pooh dangling helplessly from the hand of Christopher Robin.

❧

And now, Kagiso is alone, high above the city. He didn't see it when he flew in; he had an aisle seat, turned away from the little window and tried to force himself back to sleep. But now he has time to survey it properly. It is the last circumference of the day. He is cocooned inside his own thoughts. Barely registers the other tourists in the glass pod.

It is vast. That is his first thought as the pod rises slowly to reveal the sprawl beyond the dense cacophony of architectural styles that jostle into a façade on the riverbank. Westminster Abbey seems at first to form part of the Houses of Parliament – the kingdom of God indistinguishable from the kingdom of man. He is surprised by the location of things. So *that* is where that is in relation to that. And from up here that doesn't seem so far away from that, when it took ages to walk it the other day.

But eventually, he concludes, all cities seem the same. From this height, at such ambiguous times of day, there is very little to distinguish one from another. He recalls some photographs Ma Vasinthe brought back of Paris, taken from high above the city at sunset; there is very little difference. The bends in the river surprise him. In his mind, it was straight.

The sun winks its last and then slips behind the horizon. A cage of metal rods comes silently into view – the structure of the thing, elegant from afar, intrusive at close proximity. He turns to the east, where night is looming. The lights have come on and now the earth is brighter than the sky. He makes a twilight wish, as they did when they were children playing cricket in the street, rushing to hug a lamppost as it flickered into life. 'Remembering games and daisy chains and laughs / Got to keep the loonies on the path.'

During his first year at UCT, he lived facing the dawn of night. He didn't like to miss it, always felt agitated when he did. He would watch its approach from his window at Jan Smuts House. From this spot, he felt in tune. He knew when the sun had sunk behind the mountain at his back; its rays would disappear from the peaks ahead. And then, like everywhere in Africa, night came quickly. It would come flooding over the blue mountains in the east, like a tide, flicking light switches in its path. He could see it rushing towards him, unstoppable. But then there would be a lull, a slight pause, a deceptive respite, as daylight hung on and darkness crept its way, out of sight, up the foot of the mountain beneath him, like a silent enemy. It was as though suddenly, everything had stopped, as though nightfall had changed its course. It was a disconcerting moment, like walking into the sea at night. It made him shiver.

In the end, the advance of night was always complete. He would throw open the windows in anticipation of azaan, a comforting sound that reminded him of home. From up there he could only hear it faintly, if at all, from the far distance below as he searched the expansive flats for Issa's college in the bush. If he did hear the faint call of the muezzins declaring God's greatness to a starry city, he would know that the sun had sunk over the mountain behind and into the ocean beyond: Allah-u-akbar, Allah-u-akbar...

Stepping out of the pod, he cannot decide which way to turn. It is easier to run down the mountainside than further up it, remember? The futility of choice leaves him empty inside. Which is the path of least resistance? What would water do? Stagnate? What are the chances that he'd choose the direction that will lead him through this sprawling city to the road and the house and the room in which he'd find Issa? What are the chances of this night's twilight wish coming true?

He has been sitting on a step by the river, watching the murky water rise, wishing for it to engulf him, suddenly, and carry him away, the water already lapping at his feet. It rises quickly up to his knees and the step he is sitting on. He lifts his backpack from the step and hooks it onto the railing above his head. The black water rises to his chest, his shoulders and then, splash splash, quickly up his nose and above his head. He feels himself becoming buoyant as the river tries to lift him from the step. And then, with a determined tug, she takes him and pulls him into her. He offers no resistance, lets the river roll him over, caress him gently and take him down to sleep. He closes his eyes and rests his head on the dark black tide.

But then, not too late, just in time, he wakes. No. He rotates himself, like Vitruvian Man in the circle, upright, arms stretched out at his sides. Then he raises his hands above his head and lurches up towards the surface. When the river grapples, trying to wrap itself around his feet, he starts to kick, raising his hands one more time above his head to lurch.

His head breaks through into the warm night above the surface; inhale.

He has not been taken far, a few strong strokes and he is back on his step, walking up out of the black river.

He slumps down against the railing, watches the water drain from his clothes onto the flagstones of the walkway beside the river. He pulls off his socks; he has lost his shoes in his struggle against the river.

Get up, he instructs himself when he is nearly dry, and walk away from this place. He rises, hitches his bag onto his back, and makes his way towards the bridge.

On the empty train, he sits, barefooted and ashamed, scanning the advertisements in the carriage – a row of bags in a police line-up under the heading: 'Guilty until proven innocent' – counting the stations to his destination again and again on the route map above the window – Leicester Square / Covent Garden / Holborn / Russell Square / King's Cross St. Pancras / Caledonian Road / Holloway Road / Arsenal / Finsbury Park – eight stops from central to north London on the Piccadilly Line, northbound, under the sanctuary, to Finsbury Park, N4

Russell Square

KATINKA HAS ONLY MET HER ONCE before, in 1995, when Vasinthe was part of a small group of distinguished female scientists invited to a special dinner, hosted in their honour by the President, at the Groote Schuur Estate. Issa accompanied his mother on the occasion and invited Katinka to join them for lunch at Hout Bay the following day. On the tube, Katinka recalls the meeting:

"So, how was dinner?" she asked excitedly, as they sat down to fresh fish caught that morning in the surrounding seas.

Issa nodded, stifling a smile. *It was fine.*

"Is that it?" She looked at Kagiso and Vasinthe in disbelief. "Can you believe this guy? He goes to dinner, at Groote Schuur, with the President, and all he can say is, 'It was fine.' Come on," she encouraged, pushing his shoulder. "Show some enthusiasm. Do you know how many people would kill for such an opportunity? It's your duty to share the experience. I want to know all about it. Everything! What did you eat? What did you...

Kagiso stretched his eyes and tensed his lips at her, but it was too late.

She finished off with a whimper, "... wear?"

The subject had been rekindled.

"Go on," Vasinthe prodded. "Tell her what you wore," her tone as sour as the lemon she was squeezing onto her fish.

Issa sat up in his seat, stretched his arms to the sky and pushed out his chest. Katinka noticed the distinctive loopy signature. "You wore *that*!" she exclaimed.

Issa reclined, smiling broadly. He threw a chip into his mouth and chewed it with big circular movements, as though it were a large piece of gum.

"Can you believe it?" Vasinthe protested. "And he hasn't taken it off since."

Katinka let out a laugh of disbelieving admiration, and then, in deference to Vasinthe, cut it. "Issa," she said with a tone attempting closure, "You've the devil in you." She unfolded her cutlery as noisily as possible from the napkin and smiled a half-smile at Kagiso from the corner of her eyes. Sorry. That wasn't too bad was it? Then waited for him to redirect the conversation.

Kagiso chased his cue, chewing quickly, with one eye on Vasinthe. It seemed as though he would either swallow the half-chewed mouthful or spit it out on the floor. Wow! Look at that yacht, he would say.

He'd missed his moment. "Absolutely!" Vasinthe agreed, turning to Katinka. "I had brought him a suit which I had had specially tailored in Johannesburg. Do you know he simply refused to wear it? Wouldn't even look at it."

I couldn't have asked him to sign my suit.

Vasinthe banged her upturned fork on the table. The impact sent a tremor through the table, which sent ripples through the ripples through the surface of their drinks and startled the table next to them. She glanced self-consciously around the restaurant, softened her stance and leaned forward to chastise Issa through clenched teeth. "I don't understand why you needed to get an autograph in the first place, as if having dinner with the man wasn't enough."

I wasn't the only one who asked.

"No, but you were the only one who stuck your chest in his face."

Katinka tried to stifle another laugh with a lip-licking smile.

What was I supposed to do? Strip?

But then it slipped out with a grunt, like a sudden, unexpected fart. She blushed.

"He's not funny," Vasinthe snapped. "Don't encourage him." She trained her sights on Issa once more. "Stop making excuses for yourself. You could have taken his biography!"

Ha! He scoffed. *That thing was ghost written. This means something!*

Vasinthe jerked her head angrily. "Why? Did Guevara weave it himself?"

Katinka buried her mouth in her palm and crossed her legs tightly.

"Ssh," Kagiso beseeched, rolling his eyes around the room. "Not so loud."

Vasinthe swivelled her eyes in his direction, inhaled deeply, then whispered rebuke at Issa. "You didn't have to *wear* the damn rag. You could have taken it in a bag! If you absolutely had to." She turns to Kagiso and Katinka in turn to make her case. "There were people there, colleagues, who had gone to great lengths, made considerable efforts, to look their best, to make a good impression. And then, lo and behold," she points an upturned palm in the direction of her errant son, "in strolls Issa Shamsuddin, wearing washed-out jeans and a faded T-shirt." She turns back to Issa, her hand now brandishing a wagging forefinger. "That's how you stir resentments, make unnecessary enemies. I just wish you would develop a sensitivity for these things."

Issa remains undeterred. *But I told you what I would be wearing.*

Exasperated, his mother raised her upturned fork once more. Kagiso cleared his throat. She laid the knife down slowly and rested her hands on the edge of the table as if to push it away. "I thought you were joking."

Have I ever joked?

Kagiso regretted glancing at Katinka; her eyes had started to water with the effort of restraint, her nostrils flared and she had turned the colour of the lobster shells on her plate. Suppressed laughter is contagious. He pushed his upper lip between his teeth as a sort of ineffectual combatant.

"Then why did you fax me your measurements?" Vasinthe demanded.

Because you insisted! In any case, they weren't even my measurements.

"What! Whose were they?"

His.

Kagiso, suddenly implicated, cleared his throat and attempted a straight face. Vasinthe turned on him. "Were you in on this?"

Laughter still twitched at the corners of his mouth. He struggled to speak. "Um..."

No, he wasn't. I figured that if you refused for me to go like this, then at least he'd be able to go with you.

Kagiso smiled, but Vasinthe was not endeared. "You stubborn, stubborn boy. And did you figure the security problems that would have caused? I'm sure that would have been very amusing indeed, absolutely hilarious."

Katinka dropped her head in awkward embarrassment.

Look, what's your problem? Issa implored with hunched shoulders and upturned palms. *I mean, he wasn't even a wearing a suit himself.*

Vasinthe pushed her untouched plate aside and pressed a napkin to her mouth. "Issa, he is the president. And you were his guest. My guest!"

Yes, Ma. The president. Not God, just the president. And I voted to make him so. Did you?

The inference landed, crash, like a dead whale in the middle of the table and drew the attention of everybody in the restaurant.

Kagiso's jaw dropped. Katinka's fork stopped in mid-air. She looked at it, contemplating whether to bring it to her mouth or put it down. Issa blinked slowly. He watched his mother's hand search the table. First, it hovered over the knife. Katinka turned her eyes to see without moving her head. She laid down the fork. Then Vasinthe's hand moved to the uneaten piece of snoek on her plate. Kagiso swallowed deeply: "Ma Vasinthe?" he whispered, as if trying to rouse her from sleep. Her hand, no longer able to restrain itself, desperate to clutch and throw, seized on the glass of red wine in front of her. Issa raised his arms in a protective gesture, exposing an autographed flank. Guevara glowered. Vasinthe, aiming at her offending son's face, flicked the glass by its stem with a deft wrist movement. Its contents travelled through the air like a red arc. Plate-balancing waiters stopped in mid-stride, other diners gasped and Kagiso and Katinka watched in horror as Vasinthe's face-seeking missile hurtled out of control and hit its unintended targets with deadly inaccuracy.

Mandela.

Guevara.

Collateral damage.
Irreplaceable.
Flapping waiters descended on the scene like aid workers at a war. "Madam, are you alright? Sir? Quick, snap snap, get some towels! And water!" Kagiso and Katinka dropped their arms limply by their sides, innocent bystanders, stunned wine-speckled targets of ricocheting shrapnel. Vasinthe slumped back in her chair. In a flash, it all came back to her, the relaxed air of the proceedings, the lack of pomp and ceremony, the way he really *does* make one feel at ease.
When the last person had had her book autographed, Issa got up from his seat and walked over to where he was seated. Neither of them had had dessert, neither of them had had alcohol. It had been clear to all that Issa, wearing only washed-out jeans and a t-shirt, had caught the president's eye.
I used to wear this T-shirt on demonstrations when you were inside, he said. *I only wear it on special occasions now* – they laughed – *because it's getting old and I'd like to keep it for posterity. It would mean a lot to me if you signed it here, please.* He pointed his finger at the space above Guevara.
"Oh, I get pride of place," the president joked.
They laughed again.
He took the pen. "My pleasure," he said, and signed his loopy signature. "You know, he is a hero of mine too." Then he leaned towards Issa and, tugging at the T-shirt, whispered loud enough for all to hear. "Maybe you could send me one of these in the post some time, so I can wear it on my next visit to the States." And then he laughed his infectious laugh as he shook Issa's hand and patted him on the shoulder.
Vasinthe brought her palm to her mouth. How to take it back? She couldn't. The shot had been fired. The war would follow its own course.
Mother looked at son, suspended in disbelief, his arms outstretched, head hung, surveying his bleeding side; the final dying pose of another Issa. She wanted to wash it all away, stop

the stain from spreading, like a flood, into Guevara's stern teetotal mouth, stop it from staining a loopy teetotal autograph, stop it sinking into the lean gashed side of her teetotal son.

He looked up at his mother. *You've killed me*, his eyes said. *It is finished.*

The clamour of the salvage operation penetrated the haze. They watched plates and glasses and bottles and silver pepper pots and pretty flowers being whisked away. Stained linen was stripped, folded and solemnly carried out. The meal was over. The deed was done.

Issa was the first to rise. He peeled the T-shirt from his body and lifted it over his head, revealing the hipbones above the belt, the hollow concave stomach, the stained red chest. He dropped the soggy T-shirt on the table, where it landed with a squelch. They watched the red liquid oozing from the lump of cloth, like blood from a bludgeoned brain – were fixed by Guevara's unblinking, lifeless eyes. Issa turned away and walked out of the restaurant, bare-chested. When they stepped out onto the pier looking left, looking right, he was already gone, wearing only washed-out jeans.

ꕥ

"This is Russell Square. The next station is Holborn. Please stand clear of the closing doors."

When Katinka arrives at Vasinthe's hotel on Russell Square, she announces herself at reception and waits on one of the comfortable sofas nearby. But she soon feels closed in by the oak panels, the marble walls and arches, the sparkling chandeliers. She moves around awkwardly in the sofa, then gets up and paces the foyer. She smiles with relief when Vasinthe descends the grand central staircase a few moments later. When they have exchanged greetings and preliminary pleasantries – Katinka compliments Vasinthe on her exquisite salwaar khamees, which, had it been presented to her in a bundle on a stick, she would have taken for candyfloss and tried to stuff in her mouth – Vasinthe inquires as to her preference: "Tea here in the hotel, or a walk and maybe something outside?"

Katinka does not hesitate. "A walk would be good," she decides. "It's a lovely day outside. Spring is in the air." She finds the hotel overbearing, too unchanged.

Vasinthe drops her key at reception then, in an unexpected gesture, takes Katinka by the arm and leads her out of the hotel. "I see they've refurbished the square," she says, as they step into the bright spring sunshine. "Do you mind if we go for an amble in there? I'm curious to see what they've done to it."

"Of course not," Katinka obliges. "I haven't seen it either." She presses the button on the traffic light and watches as the breeze lifts the scarf that is draped loosely across Vasinthe's chest, falling elegantly down her back, the weave so delicate it seems it might be unravelled in the wind.

When they step into the square, Vasinthe smiles. "This is so nice. And look," she exclaims pointing at the new cafeteria. "They've done away with the greasy spoon! That was an institution."

"You," Katinka says, cringing slightly at the crude word, "seem to know this part of London quite well." She's been anguishing over how to address her companion and wishes she could resort to the safety of an honorific pronoun, as would have been the case if they were speaking Afrikaans. She can't call her by her first name. If Vasinthe were Afrikaans she'd call her 'Tannie' or if *she* were Indian, she'd call her 'Aunty'. 'Mrs', if it were an option, would be easy, she thinks. 'Professor' seems formal and Katinka doesn't want to appear unacknowledging of her academic success, but how does one address an Emeritus Professor during a walk in the park? She decides as far as possible to avoid calling her anything.

"Yes. I studied not far from here. But that was years ago, don't ask me when!" she says jokingly. "More recently, I've been coming and going for conferences and the rest."

"And do you always stay on Russell Square?"

Vasinthe nods. "It's my corner of London. I like it. I can find my way around from here. And, of course, it reminds me of my youth, when I was young and foreign, a dangerous combination!"

Having bought drinks and two slices of pastry, they sit by the fountain in the middle of the square. Occasionally, when the jets of water rise to their full height, drowning out the city beyond, the breeze carries a cool mist from the spray in their direction against which Vasinthe shields her face. She has settled, facing Katinka, her left leg draped over her right, her right elbow resting on the backrest of the black wooden bench. The posture makes her look confident, self-assured, like an actress being interviewed, Katinka thinks. Heads turn.

When chitchat and pastry nibbling is over, Katinka makes it easy; she broaches the subject. "I'm sorry about Issa," she says.

Vasinthe's expression withers and, inside her chest, her heart sinks. The reason for their meeting has been raised and her secret hope that Katinka would know something the others didn't, something she couldn't tell her on the phone, something so significant that it was imperative she wait to tell her in person – shattered. A nervous smile takes over her face, more an embarrassed pulling of the cheeks than a smile. Then, suddenly, this poised, accomplished woman is exposed, vulnerable, like a girl. Katinka watches as she unravels a perfumed handkerchief from her pouch, releasing its delicate fragrance into the air; jessamine, violet, rose?

"Excuse me," Vasinthe says, pushing her sunglasses to the top of her head. "I'm not usually like this, and definitely not in public." She lowers her eyes gently to the perfumed cloth, first the right, then the left. "I think it's being in London."

"No need to apologise." Katinka inches her hand towards Vasinthe's shoulder, but then withdraws it, cautious of penetrating the scented bubble, which seems to mark the boundaries of her sweet-smelling silk-swathed personal space.

Vasinthe clears her throat. "The same thing happened to me yesterday when I met his supervisor," she confesses with a sniff. "You know what they say about researcher/supervisor relationships?"

Katinka shakes her head.

"That they're like marriages."

Katinka laughs nervously. "No, I didn't know that."

Encouraged by the response and wanting desperately to kindle laughter rather than tears, Vasinthe continues. "It's true. I am myself constantly engaged in polygamist commitments. At the moment I have two husbands and a wife of my own in Johannesburg. I know how close the bond can grow." She leans back to watch Katinka's enjoyment of the analogy. "So I thought that I should explain to my," she draws inverted commas in the air, "'son-in-law' in person." She tries to join in the laughter but a swarm of persistent twitches ambushes the corners of her mouth. She purses her lips and drops her head.

Katinka feels a tug. She clenches her teeth in a tight grip until it feels that they might shatter. She cannot cry too.

A few moments later, Vasinthe proceeds cautiously. "Apparently they worked very well together," she says slowly, pronouncing each word very deliberately. "He thought Issa's research was very promising. Pertinent was a word he also used. I had to admit that I knew very little of what he was writing about."

She pauses.

Katinka waits.

"Before I left, he gave me a file containing some chapters from his thesis, a few articles. When I saw his name on the front cover, in his own handwriting..."

Katinka's exhalations become staggered. She clenches her jaw again. Her ribs start to ache with the effort of restraint, so she hugs herself tightly across her chest. The embrace provides little relief.

When Vasinthe feels capable, she tries again to ease the air. She blows her nose. "What is it with me," she reproaches herself. "I seem to have you either fighting back laughter or fighting back tears."

Katinka gives vent to the sobbing laugh that had started to throb like a painful lump in her throat.

When Katinka returns with two bottles of chilled water, the glasses turned upside down over the top, she waits for Vasinthe to secure her powder puff.

"That was quick," Vasinthe says, hurrying the procedure. When she has slipped the silver case back into her pouch, she reaches for one of the bottles. "Thank you," she says with a guilty smile. They unscrew the bottles and drink thirstily.

"Issa's supervisor always sounded to me like a very nice man," Katinka says with a quenched sigh. "I would have liked to meet him."

"Yes, very nice," Vasinthe admits, sliding her sunglasses back onto her nose. "Not a great talker, like Issa." She looks into the fountain, observing its simple modern design, an almost indiscernible circular depression in the middle of a larger concentric circular space. She counts the sprays of white frothy water, like liquid stalacmites, at once shooting up and collapsing back down on themselves. Thirteen. She follows the trajectory of the tallest spray in the middle – Judas, she decides. "I got the impression they didn't actually *say* very much to each other." Her tone is distant, as though hypnotised. "That they communicated entirely in writing. Reading and writing."

She cuts short her reverie and turns to Katinka. "You two used to see each other regularly, didn't you?"

Katinka shakes her head keenly. "Once a week. At least, once a fortnight."

Reassured, Vasinthe smiles. "And what was he like? With you, I mean?"

Katinka considers her response. "Do you mind if I smoke?"

"Not at all."

She lights a cigarette hurriedly and then answers, smoke rolling from her lips. "The same way he was with everybody, I guess. Quiet, observant, never saying very much. You know what Issa was like."

"Even with you?"

"Even with me," she concedes with a shrug, then rests her smoking hand along the back of the bench.

Vasinthe is surprised. "Oh," she exclaims.

"Why? What made you think he'd be any different with me? Issa was the way he –" She revises her statement. "Issa is the way he is."

Vasinthe looks at the grassy patch beyond the fountain, as if searching the languorous bodies there for an answer. "I liked to think that there was somebody who he was normal with. At least one person he could gossip with, binge with, get drunk with, have long conversations with. Somebody he could be less lonely with." She looks at Katinka. "I always imagined that person to be you."

Katinka shakes her head. "I just can't see Issa doing any of those things. And as for being lonely, I think he was only ever lonely in company."

Vasinthe starts fidgeting with one of the silk tassels on the edge of her scarf. "But he counted you as a friend, did he not?"

"I'm sure he did. In fact, I know he did. "

She wraps the tassel around her finger "And you him?"

"Absolutely. One of my dearest."

She tosses the tassel aside impatiently. "Yet he imposed his contrary disposition on you?"

Katinka taps her cigarette. "I didn't... I didn't see it as an imposition. I didn't expect him to be any other way. I wasn't bothered by his silence. Neither, I think, was Frances."

"So what? You both endured him?"

Katinka refrains from clicking her tongue. "Not in the least," she says, attempting temperance. She looks up to where the green turrets of Vasinthe's hotel peer like a fairytale through the treetops and raises the cigarette to her lips. "Look," she says, when she has exhaled, "there are many people I can get drunk with in London. Everybody drinks here. It's the norm. An almost obligatory part of life. And there are even more people I can gossip with." She looks at Vasinthe. "But very few of them listen. Issa was different. He listened. He was the perfect audience."

When the jets of water in the fountain suddenly collapse into gurgling mushrooms bubbling in the shallow pond at the base of the fountain, the noise of the city comes rushing into the square. Open-topped buses crammed with sightseeing tourists come and go on Southampton Row – the distinctive automatic drone of the black London cabs starting and stopping in the congestion contribute to the din of the coagulated first-gear traffic on Montague Place. Huge coaches with enormous protruding antennae-like mirrors, deliver crowds of walking camcorders to the British Museum.

ꕥ

Katinka and Issa had, just a few weeks before, visited the exhibition on memory commemorating the 250th anniversary of the museum. They paused at a minute depiction of Picasso's Guernica: three months earlier, the giant replica in the United Nations building in New York had been draped in black so that its stark message would not undermine a vial-shaking Secretary of State's feeble and, till now, unsustained evidence for war. 'If there is war in Iraq,' she had read somewhere, 'there's already been the first casualty – art.'

Her favourite exhibit was the aboriginal nautical chart, the simplicity of its structure belying the intricacy of its task. After she had returned to marvel at it again a second time, she left the exhibition and went to find Issa in the magnificent circular reading room. She found him leaning back in his usual seat, A6 next to the General and Ancient History sections, staring up into the impressive domed ceiling with its azure blue panels and gold-trimmed edges. She slipped into the blue leather seat next to him and looked up too.

Ready? he enquired, some moments later.

She sat up and nodded decisively. "Yes."

I'll buy you a drink.

They left the reading room and followed its circumference clockwise to the cafeteria.

"I'll just pop in here to see if they have a copy of that nautical chart on sale," she said when they passed the museum shop.

Issa didn't stop. *They don't. I've already checked.*

They sat down to a drink at one of the long tables in the Great Court. "What did you think of the exhibition?" she asked.

Issa did not look up. *It was as much about forgetting as remembering. Not a single thought spared for how the exhibits came to be here in the first place. Chronic amnesia.*

❧

In the square, an ice cream-covered toddler on a leash leads its mother towards the fountain. The child screams with delight, stamping its feet excitedly when their dog, drawn by the thirteen rising sprays, bounds into the middle of the fountain, chasing the water jets with a wagging tongue. Vasinthe eyes the dog. The child spots a butterfly. The mother-on-a-string is soon tugged in one direction by the butterfly-chasing toddler and in another by the water-chasing dog. Arms outstretched, she looks from toddler on the left to dog on the right, momentarily perplexed at having to deny one or the other their pleasure. The toddler wins and Vasinthe breathes again when the woman reins the wet animal in with a yank of its retractable leash.

All this, Katinka thinks, in a country at war, despatching duplicitous violence to depose of dubious threat – its own routines and pleasures totally undisrupted by the destruction it is wreaking elsewhere.

Frances' words at Christmas come ringing in her ears: "As normal," she had said. "Everything as normal. War is no longer reciprocal."

Having had no appetite for the numerous excessive celebrations to which she had been invited, Katinka went instead to spend the day with Frances and Issa. She took along a dish of bobotie. When she arrived, Issa was intently studying a recipe for chocolate cake at Frances' kitchen table. She rolled a joint at one end of the table, while, at the other, he painstakingly translated words and numbers from the recipe into exact neat mounds of ingredients in mixing bowls and measuring jugs. When she'd finished, she suggested they nip downstairs to smoke it in his flat before Frances returned from Mass. He turned down the offer:

I need my wits about me for this. It's her favourite so I don't want to muck it up. You go ahead. My keys are on the fridge.

Then they heard a key turn in the door.

Issa glanced at his watch. *Already! She shouldn't be back yet. She'll see the surprise before its ready.*

The door opened and Frances stepped into the living room.

You're back early. What happened? he shouted, waving Katinka into the living room while he tried to cover up the evidence of baking with tea-towels.

Frances didn't respond. When Katinka had helped her out of her scarf and coat, she eased herself into her armchair.

"Are you okay, Frances?" Katinka asked. "Can I make you some tea?"

"In a minute. You two carry on in there. I'll join you when I'm ready."

Issa, clutching a tea-towel, kneeled on the floor beside her. *Are you sure?*

"Yes. Now go on." She patted him on the shoulder. "I'll be through in a minute."

They returned to the kitchen, closing the door behind them. She retrieved her red satin pouch.

In church that morning, Frances had started nodding off during Father Jerome's tired homily now suffering its third unedited rendition since midnight.

"We have gathered here tonight," he intoned loftily, "to remember the birth of our Lord and Saviour, Jesus Christ." Few observed the mistake. He sounded bored.

In her eye-stretching efforts to keep awake, Frances perceived a particularly well-dressed man in the pew in front of her. She observed the fine cut of his suit jacket, the neat trim of the hair at the back of his neck above the line of his shirt collar. He was poised and nodded earnestly in agreement with what Father Jerome was saying.

When the homily ended, the congregation kneeled in prayer. Frances, no longer able to assume that position, remained seated and bowed her head. Before closing her eyes, she noticed the soles of the man's expensive shoes protruding from underneath his pew. She tried to focus her mind but her efforts were futile; she had become hopelessly distracted and peeped through narrowed eyes at the shoes. They were new, the soles hardly scuffed, the white stitching around the edges still clean. She reprimanded herself and forced her eyes shut.

Throughout the Mass, Frances tried hard not to be distracted by the man. Nothing worked. When she tried to focus on the ritual at the altar, his broad shoulders got in the way. When she bowed her head to follow in her Missal, there was the smell of his cologne, or the sight of his neatly-trimmed fingernails when he held his hands behind his back.

> "Lord Jesus Christ, you said to your apostles:
> I leave you peace, my peace I give you.
> Look not on our sins, but on the faith of your
> Church,
> and grant us the peace and unity
> of your Kingdom where you live forever and ever.
> Amen."

Father Jerome looked up from his folded hands on the altar and over the congregation.

"The Peace of the Lord be with you always," he declared.

"And also with you," the congregation responded.

"Let us offer each other the sign of peace."

Frances' palms became clammy. Suddenly, she felt sure that the man had all the time been conscious of her scrutiny and that, when he turned around to offer her the sign of peace, he would stare knowingly at her. Once he had greeted those in the pew beside him, the man turned around slowly. Frances swallowed loudly and hurriedly wiped the sweat from her hands. She looked up. The shock nearly sent her to the floor.

Her jaw dropped. Her heart raged in her chest. There in front of her, with stretched-out hand and poodle coif, stood the caricature she knew from the daily newspapers: the big ears, the glassy eyes, one smaller than the other, the tufty hair, the stuck-on smile. "Peace be with you, Frances," it said, grinning broadly.

Frances woke with a fright. The homily had ended. She felt flustered and searched her bag for a tissue with which to wipe her palms and brow. She was breathless. When the congregation started to sing, she struggled to find the place in the hymn book. The lady next to her helped. "Thank you," she said, somewhat embarrassed, then tried to join in. "Sleep in heavenly peace / Sleep in heavenly peace." The words stuck in her throat. Somewhere, in a church not far from here, the man in the fine suit was probably singing along right now, wringing out these words, she frowned, hollowing out these gestures. She lowered the hymn book.

When they started on the second verse Frances wanted to shout. Shut up! Stop this sanctimonious pretence. Why don't we sing something more fitting? 'Onward Christian soldiers, marching as to war / With the cross of Jesus going on before.' Or what about, 'Bring me my bow of burning gold! / Bring me my arrows of desire! / Bring me my spear! / O clouds, unfold! / Bring me my chariots of fire!'

She sat down and dropped her head.

"Sleep in heavenly peace / Sleep in heavenly peace." The congregation fell silent. The lady next to her tapped her on her shoulder. Frances nodded that she was fine.

"Lift up your hearts," Father Jerome instructed.

"We lift them up to the Lord."

"Let us give thanks to the Lord our God."

"It is right to give him thanks and praise."

Frances looked around at the pious faces, their automated crossings, risings and fallings. Then she looked to the altar. "This is my blood. Take it all of you and drink from it." The bread raising, the chalice raising, the incense swinging, the bell ringing.

Pantomime. She thought. Repetitive, meaningless pantomime.

When the congregation rose to line up for Communion at the altar, she rose and walked to the door.

She joins them in the kitchen. Fresh flowers, a pot of tea and a plate of mince pies are waiting on the table. Frances smiles and sits down.

You were home early.

"Yes," she says vacantly. "Yes, I was. I think Father Jerome was anxious to get home to his Christmas dinner."

Katinka pours them each a cup of tea.

Frances stares into the tea bubbling up to fill the cups. "What will it take for people to notice, do you think?"

"Notice what, Frances?" Katinka asks placing a cup in front of her.

Frances doesn't answer. "They don't know what war is really like," she says, staring through the window at the low grey sky hovering above the chimneys. "They think it's all fireworks on TV." She shakes her head. "How quickly we forget."

Katinka looks enquiringly at Issa, but he is not forthcoming, just stares back at her, waiting for Francis to explain.

Frances stirs her tea, pre-occupied. "I wonder how many of the mongers would still support this war if there were the possibility of retaliation. But there isn't, so they won't have to suffer what they propagate. Everything continues as normal," she says. "As normal. Everything as normal. War is no longer reciprocal. Now the world's strongest countries bomb its poorest. Where's the honour in that?" She refuses a mince pie.

ꕥ

The square has started to fill up with lunchtime picnickers. Confident, dapper young men with loosened ties and stylised women with sitcom hairstyles in pretty frocks and strappy sandals, unfold expensive sandwiches. Most perch on unfurled newspapers in the sun. A few seek the shade of the full green trees, their crisp new leaves rustling in the spring breeze. Isn't this just lovely?

When the sun clears the trees, their positions become exposed. They rise from the bench and walk slowly towards the perimeter of the square. Their abandoned seats in the sun are quickly filled.

"I know that research is a solitary, time-consuming, at times all-consuming, endeavour," Vasinthe says, when they have reached the path that runs along the outer limits of the square. "But even my most committed students have lives beyond their work. Did he really spend most of his time at home, working on his thesis?" She grimaces at the prospect.

Katinka nods. "Although he did occasionally go to the British Library. And he also liked working in the reading room at the British Museum occasionally, but not very often. It's quite noisy with tourists coming and going all the time. I used to meet him there from time to time." She wants another cigarette but decides against it. She finds a packet of gum in her pocket and holds it out to Vasinthe.

"No thank you."

She puts a piece in her mouth. "Issa loved his work," she says, chewing. "Maybe love is the wrong word." She tries to think of a more suitable one. "Committed," she says, pleased with her selection. "I think it was when he was happiest, though he found it hard at first." Her eyes narrow as she casts her mind back. "I remember when I first came to London, he used to spend all his time reading. That was in the early days of his research.

"He always had a book with him, was always reading. He even read about reading."

Listen to this, he once told her before reading aloud from the book in front of him: *Reading is inevitably a complex, comparative process. A novel in particular, if it is not to be read reductively as an item of socio-political evidence, involves the reader with itself not only because of its writer's skill but also because of other novels. All novels belong to a family, and any reader of novels is a reader of this complex family to which they all belong.*

"I remember he was reading the first time we met in London," she continues. "I was almost an hour late; he hadn't even noticed.

And even when he eventually started writing, he was still always reading, except now he also carried a little notebook with him that he scribbled in from time to time."

Vasinthe frowns disapprovingly. "You mean you'd arrange to meet and he'd bring along a book!"

Katinka tries not to sound defensive. "He didn't bring one specially, more a case that he always had one on him. I didn't mind." She sticks her hands in her back pockets and squeezes her elbows towards each other. Only one spinal click today, she thinks. She can usually extract three or four with a tight squeeze. "We didn't meet –" she was going to say, in restaurants to have fancy dinners and sparkling conversation. Issa hated all that stuff. So do I – but then quickly rephrased her thoughts. "We'd hang out in parks, like these people here, or some evenings we'd go to our usual coffee shop on Edgware Road for a few hours. You could easily while away a whole night there, drinking mint tea, sometimes playing tawla.

"And besides, what he read was usually interesting so, if I was in the mood, I'd get him to move over so I could read with him, or I'd read the crumbled paper he always had on him somewhere, in the bottom of his bag, in his jacket pocket or tucked into the back of his jeans.

"If I didn't feel like reading or conversation, I'd play a game on my phone, or listen to the new music he'd downloaded that week.

"We were very easy. Anyway, I knew that if I wanted to talk he'd close the book immediately and then I would have his undivided attention. That was enough."

For a while they walk in silence, looking down at their feet. When Vasinthe looks up, she sees a man approaching from the opposite direction leading a panting dog on a leash. Observing the animal's pink, dripping jowls, she gathers her flowing khamees and scarf to her and steps behind Katinka to the other side of the path. When he passes them the man shoots her a disdainful glance, which, leaving go of her garments, she deflects with a slow blink and a slight elevation of her nose.

"You don't like dogs, I take it," Katinka concludes when the man is out of range.

Vasinthe tenses her neck and shakes her head stiffly. "I can't bear them. It's the one thing about London, England, I really dislike; dogs." She says the word with a scowl, as though she were talking about vermin. "They're everywhere. And their owners seem invariably to assume that every one adores their blubbering smelly mutts as much as they do." She feels a sudden urge to wash her hands and, even though she has not actually touched the animal, she nevertheless reaches for the anti-bacterial waterless handwash, which she always carries with her.

"So that's where Issa gets it from," Katinka observes pointing at the tube.

Vasinthe, as though caught shoplifting, opens her palm guiltily to reveals its disinfecting contents.

"He used to use that too," she says. "Mind you, it didn't stop him from washing his hands constantly. He was always washing his hands."

"He was?" She squeezes a blob of gel into her palm then secures the cap.

"Yes, whenever he came to my house, it's the first thing he'd do. I never understood why he needed to."

She returns the tube to her pouch. "Why was that?"

"Because Issa never actually touched anything when he was out in public. Not unless he absolutely had to."

Vasinthe is taken aback. "Really," she says, tilting her head in interest. "Did he say this much to you?"

"No, but it was impossible not to notice, especially as he grew more and more obsessive about avoiding contact. The more preoccupied he became, the more elaborate his methods."

Vasinthe rubs the gel vigorously into her hands, as though she is scrubbing up for surgery. "Like?"

Katinka immediately recognises the astringent smell, its familiar freshness crashing into her like a tidal wave from a distant sea. She stops to look at her feet while half forgotten memories, like foamy bubbles on a sandy beach, come swirling all around. "Like," she recalls, breathing in the smell, "he wouldn't open a door with his bare hands, he'd always pull his sleeve down to cover it. Or if he were wearing short sleeves, he'd use his handkerchief to clutch the handle. And at cash points, or in lifts, he never pressed the buttons with the tip of his finger, he always used the knuckles of his clenched fist. He never held onto handrails in buses or on the tube; he'd always find somewhere to lean instead. That was why he sprained his wrist that one time. He wouldn't grab onto the handrail, so he went flying down the aisle. I asked him once why he still needed to wash his hands if he never touched anything."

You never know. I might have touched something.

"And if you had, why would that be such a bad thing?"

Drop it. You wouldn't understand.

Vasinthe pats her hands dry. Her meticulously manicured fingers spread from facing palms like the wings of a perfumed butterfly. She points to a secluded bench in the shade. When they sit down, Katinka gives in to the craving and lights another cigarette.

"According to Frances," Vasinthe whispers urgently, leaning forward, her body taught with intensity, "he washed all the time. Is this true?"

Katinka shrugs her shoulders. "I wouldn't know Issa's daily bathroom habits in the way that she does – that conversion is like a house of cards." She frowns dismissively. "Why? Does it matter? In any case, a lot of people here still see a daily bath as excessive."

Still, Vasinthe thinks, a word not used very often in relation to western habits. She leans forward. "I mean more than hands," she says. "I'm talking about ritualised washing. That's the impression I got from what Frances described."

Katinka looks puzzled. "I'm sorry, I don't understand."

Vasinthe straightens herself. "Look," she says, "our family is of diverse faiths. Diversity is our normality. It's what we take for granted. It's what we nurtured. In fact, homogeny has always been anathema to us."

Katinka screws her eyes and nods attentively in response to the urgency in Vasinthe's tone.

"You see, when the boys were growing up, home was always, still is, a secular place. It's what held us together, gave us a future, brought us to where we are now. School on the other hand," she shrugs, "that was different. I wanted them to be educated together; in those days that meant Christian and private. It wasn't perfect. In fact, sometimes it was seriously lacking, but back then there simply was no other choice." Katinka continues her urgent nodding, trying hard to resist memories of her own, very different, upbringing.

Vasinthe resumes her probing. "At what times of day did you meet Issa? Was he as obsessed with time as he was with washing?"

"No, no, not in the least." Katinka protests. "We met at all times. Different times. It just depended."

"On what?"

"On what we were both doing; on what suited us both. Why?"

Vasinthe hesitates.

"Tell me," Katinka insists. "Why?"

A woman approaches, struggling along the path against the weight of an enormous, elaborate pram. Does one need to take a test to push that thing, Vasinthe wonders. She waits for a woman to pass. "Katinka," she says anxiously, "I need to know. Had Issa become religious?"

Katinka is stunned. "Issa!" she exclaims. "Religious? God, no."

"You sound certain."

"Absolutely," Katinka insists. "Without a doubt." She takes a quick distracted puff before elaborating eagerly on her rebuttal. "Look," she says, chopping the air in a decisive gesture, "I admit that it wasn't always possible to tell what Issa was thinking, but it was always obvious what he thought and, I can assure you, he thought very little of those whose principles are governed by a religious creed."

Vasinthe appears unconvinced.

"Believe me," Katinka implores. "I can still hear him now."

Like some Tory MPs, the religious would quite happily drag us all back to the 15th century if they're really honest.

After lunch, Vasinthe invites Katinka to her room, "Just for a few minutes," she says, puckering her nose encouragingly. When they enter the room, Vasinthe gestures to the armchair by the window. "Please, take a seat."

Katinka sits neatly on the chair, aware of the smell of tobacco on her clothes.

"I hope you don't mind," Vasinthe says, perching herself on the corner of the bed nearest to Katinka. She holds out a package with both hands. "This is for you."

Katinka's face lights up with surprise at the unexpected gift. She rarely receives gifts and, apart from her conservative education, most of which she has had to unlearn and revise, none, ever, from her family. "For me? You shouldn't have."

She feels around inside the bag, like a child exploring a Christmas stocking. She retrieves the bigger of the two objects first and brings her hand to her chest in exclamation at the ornate box.

"What is it?" she asks with heightened curiosity. Slowly, she opens the box. And gasps. Carefully, she sets the crystal bottle on the table beside its lavish ornamental box. Sunlight strikes the crystal and a rainbow of colour explodes into the room. Katinka leans back admiringly. "Pragtig," she says. "Can I try some?" she asks, unable to contain her excitement. Without waiting for a response, she removes the elaborate gold cap and rubs a drop of the rich amber liquid onto her wrist, releasing its perfume into the air like a flock of fragrant flapping wings.

"I hope you like it?" Vasinthe smiles enquiringly.

"Like it?" Katinka exclaims with delight. "It's wonderful. I've never smelt anything like it. Thank you very much."

When she has secured the bottle and returned it carefully to its tabernacle, she removes the smaller object from the bag. She carefully undoes the wrapping to reveal another box, this one shallow, blue and rectangular. Again she smiles expectantly. She opens the box to reveal the rich velvet rear casing of a picture frame. Intrigued, she turns the box upside down on her palm and lifts it carefully off the frame, like a lid. When she registers the photograph, she raises her free hand to her gasping mouth.

"Oh my God!" she exclaims, "I'd forgotten about this."

There, cradled in her hand, encased in pure silver, is the Grand Parade on the balmy late summer's night of February 11th 1990. The moment comes flooding back. She runs her hand affectionately around the frame. "I only knew him for a day, then. I remember asking the guy next to us to take it. How young we both look," she sighs, scrutinising their ecstatic faces in the foreground. She brings the picture closer. "And see," she says, pointing at the tiny figure waving from the balcony in the distant background. "He *did* come out, even if only we know who he is." She looks to Vasinthe. "Thank you very much," she says. "I'll keep it where I can see it everyday. I miss him."

Vasinthe smiles a nodding clenched-lipped smile.

At the door, Katinka hesitates. Vasinthe looks expectantly at her.

"I never had the opportunity to congratulate you," Katinka says.

"Congratulate me? What for?"

"Well, it's been two years, so it's a bit late, but our country's past is longer than that, so I want to say it, to acknowledge it." She becomes flustered, her palms sweaty, fiddling with the bag of gifts like a nervous schoolgirl. Then stops fidgeting, raises her head and looks Vasinthe resolutely in the eye. "I wanted to congratulate you on your Emeritus Professorship. I hope you don't mind."

Vasinthe laughs. "Oh that," she exclaims, waving her hand. "There's no need."

Katinka straightens herself. "Yes, there is. I don't know why, I can't explain it, but when Issa told me, it made me very proud. And he was proud too, I know it."

"Well, I didn't know it meant so much. I had no idea.

Thank you very much."

Katinka turns to leave, then turns around again. "One more thing, if you don't mind?"

"Of course."

"I was wondering, how does one address an Emeritus Professor?"

Vasinthe laughed. "Well, just call me Vasinthe."

"No, officially I mean?"

"I prefer Ms, but most people call me Mrs."

Katinka was surprised. "Mrs, is that it? After all the years of – ? But why?"

Vasinthe shrugged. "To be honest, I don't really know."

Then Katinka raises her eye browse and nods knowingly. "So, beyond title then."

Vasinthe smiles and adjusts her scarf modestly.

"But no ordinary Mrs," Katinka continues, still nodding.

Vasinthe laughs. No ordinary Mrs. She likes the sound of that.

alif, dál, dhal...

SHE HAS FLED HER SUNNY KITCHEN for the cooler recesses of her bedroom where she is perched on her bed, surrounded by sheets of paper covered in elegant calligraphy. All that remains for her to learn are those letters that can be joined to the preceding letter but not to the letter following: alif, dál, dhal ا د ذ.

Then she reaches for the card she has bought specially. It is of a little boy in a village school practising the alphabet on a hand-held writing board. She opens the card and writes down the entire alphabet with her best pen, neatly and without mistakes. When she is done, she holds it at arm's length, then smiles. She adds a sentence at the bottom: I miss you.

After she has sealed and addressed the envelope, she sends him a text message: I no da alfabet ☺

Setting aside her work, she turns to the pictures on her bedside table, Karim's striking greyblue eyes – "Alexander left them to me" – looking straight into the lens. Issa's look over the photographer's shoulder into the distance. She opens her tabernacle of smell, then anoints the pictures with the luxurious precious essence.

The Verses

KAGISO FLIPS ONTO HIS BACK. The buses, noise from the pub, his foolishness by the river, thoughts of work, all conspire into a cocktail of insomnia. He is especially anxious about the final order of sequences: history, he realises, can't always be told in a straight line. The documentary is not being broadcast till next March, to coincide with the 10th anniversary of Mangope's fall, but a lot remains to be done; he has a big meeting with the SABC scheduled for when he gets back to Johannesburg.

He turns on the bedside lamp to reveal the story of Mafikeng and Mmabatho spread out on the floor like an intricately woven carpet. He knows it all, from siege to siege, by heart. And when he closes his eyes, he can see the cities' story, from the oldest haunted sepia images to the vivid contemporary depictions, unfold in front of him, accompanied by the rattle of an antiquated projector. He does not like the narrator's voice, here, in his film, telling his story. He regrets having signed the compromise:

"Well, he is an accomplished narrator. His voice will bring authority and a dignified stature to your film. Without him, we'll have to reconsider our participation."

"In that case," Lerato replied decisively, "I think we should leave." He rose from his seat and looked to Kagiso to follow him.

But Kagiso saw years of work and energy, months of research – the starting point, Issa's revisionist bibliography – go anti-clockwise down the drain. He thought it his responsibility to be less petulant, more accommodating – so he compromised.

Lerato's face fell. And so did his regard for Kagiso. He sat down again, defeated.

Kagiso gets up from the mattress, frustrated. Suddenly, he feels trapped. My bloody broom cupboard in Johannesburg is bigger than this whole flat, he thinks. So is my grandmother's simple little house. There is nowhere to go, no other room to go into.

He is not like Issa. When he works, he likes to spread out. Already he has turned the whole floor into a workspace. Soon he will have to spread out onto the walls. He stretches his arms out beside him, as if to push out the walls.

They haven't decided on a name yet, either. He wants something like, *'Anglo Boer War to Afrikaaner Weerstand Beweging: The Sieges of Mafikeng and Mmabatho'.*

"We can be inventive with acronyms of the war and the organisation," he suggested.

"What!" Lerato argued. "ABW / AWB? That sounds like something a ref would shout out at a cricket match." He wants to call the film, *'The Three-Second War: The Fall of Lucas Mangope'.*

"Why don't you just accept that it *was* a fucking war, man. The fucking AWB had invaded the homeland to suppress the uprising by force," Lerato insisted, cracking open a Castle. "It was a war with an army of one against an army of three, the last of the frontier wars, and in the end, that policeman was the lone, victorious impi." He put the can to his mouth and swallowed deeply.

But Kagiso was uncomfortable with the word 'war'. "I think it's disrespectful to those who have seen *real* war. Yes, we can apply the metaphor of war, and we do use it in the voiceover, but to be true, it was more of a coup."

"It wasn't even a coup," Farida interjected. "It had the effects of a coup, but when he pulled the trigger, that policeman had no way of knowing that his actions were going to topple the government. Why don't we just call it, *'The Gang Bang of Mafikeng and Mmabatho: Baden-Powel and Mangope'*, finish and kla'? Enough of all this psuedo nonsense."

They agreed to disagree and marked the tape: *ABW – AWB / The Three Second War / Gang Bang: The Fall of Lucas Mangope.* They will make a final decision on the title when Kagiso returns from London. When they had wished him well and left, Kagiso rolled a joint and rewound the tape to the section of raw archival footage shot on the day at the scene – a dusty road outside Mmabatho, Northwest Province. Capital of the former Republic of Bophuthatswana.

He'd first heard about it from his grandmother:

"Have you heard the news!" she shouted down the phone.

"No," he said, rubbing his eyes. "What's happening?"

"Hey batu!" She exclaimed. "You're sleeping and meanwhile the sky has fallen on Mangope's head! Turn on your TV."

Sequence 1 A convoy of heavily armed khaki-clad AWB paramilitaries enters the shaky frame. At the back of the convoy is an old green Mercedes. Its three occupants aim guns into the crowd.

Sequence 2 Shots ring out from the armed convoy. The crowd disperses. A frightened youth runs up to the camera: "Mangope has sold us to the AWB and now he has gone."

Sequence 3 More shots ring out. The camera tries to locate their source. In the background, armoured vehicles from the Bophuthatswana Defence Force enter the scene. The crowd cheers. "AWB out!"

Sequence 4 The camera settles on the green Mercedes, now isolated from the rest of the fleeing convoy. Two of its passengers seem injured. "Black bastards," one of them shouts, slumped against the rear tyre. Another crouches between the open doors. A jeering crowd surrounds them.

Sequence 5 The camera zooms in on the crouching man. "Please, God help us," he pleads.

Sequence 6 Shots ring out. The footage becomes shaky. A Bophuthatswanan policeman executes the three men with a series of shots fired at point blank range.

Sequence 7 The camera settles on the bodies of the three executed men lying in the dust beside their car.

The phone rang.

"Kagiso?"

"Yebo."

"Your cab is waiting to take you to the airport."

"Thanks. I won't be long."

He put the tape in the safe, grabbed his bag and left the studio.

ﷲ

He tiptoes around the storyboard on the floor, pulls a beer from the fridge and lights a cigarette. Lazily, he turns to the half-packed bookshelf. He takes down a book, another of those enduring blank spaces and, in view of his uncritical support for it – "As a matter of principle" – perhaps the smelliest unfilled hole of them all. A friend had given it to Issa after he'd smuggled it into the country in the dustcover of *The Complete Works*.

Shakespeare?! Issa grimaced. *Enough already.*

"Don't judge a book by its cover," the smuggler cautioned.

Issa uncovered the contraband. *Woah.*

Kagiso opens the book. Under the dedication is scribbled:

Proceed with caution. This book can change lives. Don't condemn without reading, don't support without reading. Always read. It was that imperative that started the iman.

He flicks through the pages. Nearly all are annotated, with underlining and comments added on all the unprinted areas of nearly every page. The third chapter catches his attention. The annotations are in red:

20/11/01

I was at immigration. Despite my student visa, perhaps because of it, I was stopped. My luggage was searched. Even sealed packages were opened. Then I was taken to a small windowless room. 'Where are you from?' one of the other detainees asked me. I told him. 'Then why have they stopped you?' I don't know. 'What's your name?' I tell him. 'That's why. In here, we all have such names.'

Yes, but I'm different, I want to shout. I notice the guard at the door. Let me out of here, I want to shout. Yes, you! I'm shouting at you, with the toned muscles and limp brain.

I wait. That's when I hear the voices.

I am suspect. I am being observed. I am being described. I am being investigated. My story about myself is being verified. The voices get louder.

An hour later, the immigration official comes back for me. I will be interviewed.

Oh no! I succumb. I grow horns and hooves. Halitosis. When I open my mouth, my interrogator pulls grimaces and covers his nose. His colleague at the door laughs in disgust. My interrogator writes down every word I say. The same questions, over and over again. I lose patience.

Write this in that little book of yours, I say.

He looks surprised.

Write this: First, don't you look at me with that air of condescending suspicion, as if you know something about me that I couldn't possibly know about myself.

Sir?

Write it! Then write this.

Sir, I really must insist…

And so must I. Write this: Inaugural.

I beg your pardon!

Yes, inaugural. Do you need me to spell it for you?

Sir, may I remind you that I am in charge…

No, you're not. You're a minion, and you have no charge over me. Have you written it? Inaugural? When you've done so, write this: Inaugural lecture. Because that is where I've been. My mother's fucking inaugural lecture for her Emeritus Professorship: on the finer points of cornea transplants. I'm afraid I won't be able to recite the details for your intelligence records; I struggled to keep awake, airport to lecture, you see.

I need to ask you to co-operate, Sir.

And I need you to write this: PhD Yes, Big P, small h, stop. Then big D. Because that's what I am doing here. Now let me out of this fucking place before I start reciting my thesis for you to write in that fucking little book of yours. You might find it interesting. Bits of it have to do with islands of interrogation, a little like this one.

When I get back here, I have to verify the voices. I rush to the bookshelf. I feel violated. I feel sick. I want to puke. I flick through these pages...

Yes. It's me. I am Salahuddin.

ꕥ

Kagiso looks at the time: 4am. South Africa is one hour ahead. He has made up his mind. "We'll deal with the consequences," he says to himself. He wants to communicate his decision, to make it real.

"Call a little later...? Fuck it." He switches on his phone. "I'll give the bully a wakeup call. He'll be annoyed, but he'll like the news."

"Hello."

"Lerato, it's Kagiso."

"Hey, man. You back?"

"No. Not yet."

"How's it going up there? Any... um... news?"

"No... Listen, I'm sorry to wake you, but I wanted to say, you were right. We should have left. I'm sorry."

"Ja well, it's done now."

"No. No, it's not done. I've decided. When I get back, we'll pull out of the agreement."

"Hey man, that's gonna cause shit. We've already signed."

"It would have caused shit if we hadn't."

"That's true. So what we gonna do?"

"Find another narrator."

"Who?"

"Lindiwe. You think she'll reconsider us?"

"I don't know about that, hey. You want me to call her?"

"Yes. And tell Farida too."

"Sure. But what if Lindiwe won't come back?"

"Then we'll have to sort out something, because you were right. Why should we be bullied into having our history narrated by old white men?"

Missing Persons

"MARGARET WILL BE WITH YOU in just a moment," the receptionist says. "Please, take a seat."

On the table in the reception area is a pile of brochures. Vasinthe is familiar with them; she'd received a copy in the post that morning. "Read this," she says to Katinka, pointing at an inside page:

- About 210,000 people are reported missing in the UK each year. The vast majority return safe and sound within 72 hours, but thousands do not.
- Males in their late twenties are more likely to disappear than any other group of adults.
- Adults are more likely to go missing if they are going through a crisis or a difficult transition, or if they are vulnerable due to chronic difficulties.
- State agencies such as the police are sometimes unable to help, leaving the National Missing Persons Helpline to fill the gap.

Katinka, forgetting her reserve, instinctively takes Vasinthe by the hand. Vasinthe doesn't object; she re-establishes the contact once they are seated in an intimate cluster of three chairs in Margaret's office.

"Thank you for seeing us in person, and at such short notice," Vasinthe starts bowing her head. The gesture surprises Katinka, and Vasinthe too; she does not know where it came from, feels suddenly taken over by body language more akin to her half-remembered grandmother. "I do appreciate it," she continues, "am aware that it's not your normal procedure.

Margaret, touched by the elegant gesture, finds herself bowing too. "You're welcome," she smiles. "Some cases require exception. Issa is foreign and you are returning to South Africa tomorrow. Under the circumstances, we felt this the most conducive way of proceeding. And we hope it will make your journey back to Johannesburg a little easier." She reaches for an already open file close at hand. "We've started compiling a preliminary profile for Issa based on the telephone conversation we had yesterday. Once we've finalised it, we can start publicising. I'll also need to get the specifics from you to complete this poster for circulation." She lays the incomplete poster out in front of them:

MISSING

Can you help?

South African student missing from Finsbury Park, North-London-since April 2003

Age at disappearance: 32

Height:

Weight:

Eyes:

Hair:

If you have seen Issa, please call the confidential National Missing Persons Helpline on-Freephone 0500 700 700.

National Missing Persons Helpline

www.missingpersons.org

"It's our standard poster," Margaret explains. Our contact details are at the bottom and," pointing at the empty rectangle, "his picture will go here. Did you bring the photographs?"

"Yes," Katinka says, sitting up in her seat. Vasinthe lets go of her hand while she retrieves the envelope.

"A good-looking lad, isn't he?" Margaret acknowledges, looking up at Vasinthe.

Vasinthe's mouth smiles to acknowledge the compliment, but her eyes, fixed on the upside-down image of her son, remain void.

Margaret looks at Katinka. "When were these taken?" she asks.

"In December. Just before Christmas."

"So," she looks up to the ceiling and counts the months quickly on her fingers, "nearly five months ago?"

"Yes," Katinka replies.

Margaret makes a note of the date on the back of the photographs, then gathers them neatly so that the corners are aligned. "Let's hope they do the trick. People always tend to notice a pretty face, don't they?" she says optimistically.

Margaret does not close the file, only sets it aside, Issa's photogenic image looming, like an invigilator, in the room. "We'll return to the details in a moment. Do you have any questions, any more information, before we do?"

Vasinthe does not hesitate. "It doesn't look good, does it?"

Margaret changes her seating position. "Well," she starts, her eyes moving from Vasinthe to Katinka to Issa's face staring up at the ceiling.

Vasinthe interrupts. "Before we continue," she says. "Maybe it would help if I told you that I'm often in the position you're in now, of having to put a bad scenario to anxious loved ones."

Margaret leans back in her chair. Her shoulders drop.

"Straight talk isn't easy," Vasinthe continues, "and it sounds cruel. But I think false hope is even more so. Please, be frank."

Margaret releases a nervous laugh. "Thank you, that certainly does help." She crosses her legs the other way. "Obviously, as

I explained on the phone, we don't anticipate outcomes on the basis of statistics and although there are patterns, we treat each case as individual and unique. But," she turns her palms to face the ceiling, "Issa's case, even with the little we know, is consistent with the majority of cases involving young men of his age. They are by far the most prone to going missing and, I should add, are usually only found when they wish to be. Now," she leans forward to tap the photographs of Issa on the table, "if we add to this scenario the fact that he is a foreigner, then his circumstances become more urgent."

"And why is that?" Vasinthe asks, sternly.

Margaret sits back and clasps her hands in her lap. "Simply put, xenophobia. Immigrant communities, especially young men, often experience a sense of social isolation and exclusion, which can be very traumatic."

"But Issa wasn't destitute," Vasinthe protests. Margaret listens patiently while Vasinthe elaborates on her son's academic success, her eyes moving discreetly over the fine clothes, the expensive shoes, the earrings – diamonds, surely – the meticulous manicure. "It's not as though he didn't have options," she hears Vasinthe say in her commanding tone. She does not sound to Margaret, typically South African.

When Vasinthe has finished, Margaret responds, finding it necessary to address her by title and name. "Mrs Kumar," she says, but then immediately doubts herself. Her only encounter with the name is a sitcom and a quick glance at Issa's details confirms that he is Shamsuddin. She cringes at her potentially embarrassing slip. "I'm sorry," she says, blushing. "It is Kumar, isn't it?"

"Yes," Vasinthe nods, bracing herself for the stock response: 'Like the sitcom?' She cannot bear the programme, the grotesquely stereotypical family, the dirty little grandmother, the annoyingly marriageable son; she cannot recognise herself in any of them. 'No,' she usually retorts, whenever the reference arises, 'Not at all like the sitcom. Not all Indians are clowns and I rarely make people laugh.' "Shamsuddin," she explains to Margaret, "is his father's name. But please call me Vasinthe."

"I see," Margaret nods, relieved. "Vasinthe, we strive to be a non-judgemental organisation and in our experience, professional attainment does not always act as surety against vulnerability. We have solicitors, teachers, people like yourselves," she says, gesturing to the two women, "bankers, judges, successful people, who, for whatever reason, have walked out of their lives. And a small minority of them will probably never return."

Vasinthe looks perplexed. "So you mean that this drastic action on Issa's part may have been prompted by some sense of social alienation. Would that explain it?"

Margaret shakes her head pleadingly. "I only raise social isolation as a possible motive." Then she leans forward, elbows on knees, to appeal to Vasinthe. "You know, straight talk and honest assessment is laudable, but as Issa's case worker, I don't want us to obsess about the negatives and lose sight of the possibility of a positive outcome. As a charity, we have a seventy percent success rate in reuniting missing persons with their families, most often, within a short period of time. But even in more rare long-term cases, we always believe that there is hope. That is why we are here. And until the day of reunion, however near or far, our role is to plough every available resource ceaselessly into making that reunion possible, and into offering unconditional support for as long and as often as it is required until that day comes." She turns to include Katinka. "Now it's still early days with Issa, and hopefully, he will be found soon, but in the meantime, we cannot allow ourselves to become defeatist. The hardest thing to come to terms with in cases like Issa's is that we just don't know. Only Issa can explain. We, unfortunately, are left with the agonising uncertainty, the self-reproach. Some people leave notes. Others, sometimes months, sometimes years later, communicate with their families in person or via this organisation. Issa hasn't yet done any of these things, as we hope he will. In the meantime, who knows what may have motivated him? To speculate and dwell on worst-case scenarios is counter-productive and very wearying in these early days." She looks to both women for a response before continuing.

Nothing.

"Now, about the possible political motivations which you raised on the phone." They rejuvenate their attention. "We see instances of politically motivated disappearances all the time, many with far more evidence as to motive than Issa's. It is true that young Muslim and Asian men feel singled out at the moment and the area of London where Issa was resident has been particularly targeted and affected by a range of worrying manifestations, but to conclude that that is what motivated Issa, is speculation. And we cannot judge. We simply don't know what may have motivated him to leave, and it would be dangerous, both for Issa and ourselves, to construct hypothetical reasons, reasons that might stick or possibly pre-empt any future outcomes. The truth lies with Issa."

Vasinthe looks down at her feet. "If he was so unhappy," she says, her voice quavering, "why didn't he just come home?"

Margaret starts to respond but Vasinthe releases her hand hurriedly from Katinka's. She makes tentative eye contact with Margaret: "I'm sorry. Would you excuse me for a moment please?" She makes to rise.

"No, please." Margaret jumps up from her seat and gestures to her to remain seated. "You stay. I'll get us something to drink. Then we'll finalise his profile and I'll talk you through the support structures we provide for family and friends. Tea? Coffee?"

ঌ

She has been sitting on a secluded step by the river, watching its murky water rise and rise. She came to sit for a while in the evening, but it is night now; the sun has long since set and the walkway beside the river is deserted. She wants to leave, has wanted to for several hours, but feels too weighed down to get up. So she sits.

If she does not move away, the river will soon engulf her, the water already at her feet. It will rise quickly to her waist, her chest, her shoulders, then, splash splash, up her nose and above her head.

For a while she will panic, but not for long. Soon she will be overcome by calm. She will feel herself becoming buoyant as the river tries to pluck her barnacled sorrow from the sunken step.

And then, with a tug, the river will take her and pull her down. She will offer no resistance, let the river roll her over, caress her gently.

When she closes her eyes and rests her head on the dark black tide, the river will take her gently down to sleep.

Finsbury Park Mosque

"Of course, you may," Frances says, offering him the packet.

When he has settled back into the deck chair, she continues. "The last vivid memory I have of him is out here on the roof, standing by the wall over there, and staring over at the mosque. It was during the early hours of Monday morning, January 20th. There's nothing particular or distinctive after that – just a slow turning down of the volume over the dark weeks and months that followed. Until one day there was only silence.

"I'd had neither sight nor sound of him all weekend, so I had no idea whether he was down there or not. I'd seen him only once the previous week when he brought me back some milk – I had become a bit embarrassed to knock twice and only did so when I was really desperate. But I thought it best to keep up some form of contact from time to time.

"In the wee hours of that Monday morning, I was woken up in the middle of the night by helicopters, flying really low. It sounded as though they were flying right above my roof. I got out of bed and walked over to the window, but I couldn't see anything from that angle. So I came out here. That was when I saw them, two police helicopters flying directly over the mosque, with spotlights trained on the building, just there. The noise was deafening.

"It was obvious that something serious must have happened, so I went downstairs to see if he was there. I had to knock a few times..."

"Come to the roof, quick," she orders, when he opens the door.

He rolls his eyes up to the ceiling, cocks his ears, then looks at her. She steps aside. He doesn't turn back for clothes, but scales the staircase ahead of her.

She follows him to the roof. He seems oblivious to the cold. She has brought a blanket to wrap around his nakedness, but he doesn't notice. He just stares through the helicopters hovering threateningly above, and into flashes of the past, a Trojan horse, a university corridor...

ꕥ

It was the first day of Ramadan. When the shots rang out, most turned to run. He was at the head of the demonstration with the other organisers. They hadn't taken the shots seriously. Nor the initial advance from their usual positions across Modderdam Road and up to the gates. Scare tactics, they thought. Didn't imagine that they would actually cross the boundary and enter the campus. So they stood their ground. But then the casspirs revved and roared, and rolled in.

It was Robbie and Coline who grabbed him by the arms, turned him round, thrust him forward and forced him to run. "Admin!" they shouted. "Run for Admin!"

They leap and duck and dive through the mayhem left in the wake of the retreating protestors. They reach the square outside the overcrowded administration building just in time to see its doors being forced shut against the swelling crowd. The library, to the right, has already been sealed. They get caught up in the desperate crush into the Union.

The throng inside rolls in cascades of mayhem and confusion. He loses the others. *Think! Think!* But he can't think. Just can't think. Behind him, furious batons start to rise and fall, rise and fall. *Can't get beaten. Won't be dragged away.* But what to do? If not that, then what? *Get to the grass patch outside. The car's not far. Can hide in the car.* He clamours over shouting heads and tables and shoulders and pool tables. Outside. *Now, breathe! Then find the car.*

The grass patch fills in seconds with the overflow from the Union. And then, the unmistakable sound of propellers. *But where?* They search the clear blue sky. *Where?*

And then – *Fucking hell* – Hollywood Vietnam descends into view from over the Union building. A blind spot, disorienting approach from behind; police hang out of helicopter, balanced on the landing rail, but not to lift them all to safety, guns at the ready, aimed at the crowd. Most fall to the ground in fear, covering their heads with flailing arms.

"En in die heilige pwasa!" the girl next to him exclaims. She pulls her scarf across her face, collapses to her knees and gives up.

History! He grabs the panicked girl and runs through the parking lot towards English. *Not!* They're already beating and dragging away from outside the building. Quick u-turn. Round the other way. *There are trees in the back, and the little herb garden.* They crouch.

Is jy ok?

"Ja. Waan toe nou?"

History. Jy nog met my?

"Ja. Together we stand!"

Gereed?

"Ja."

He peers over the fragrant shrubs. She adjusts her scarf. The path seems clear.

Kom.

They break through the hedge, and run. He knows the route well. He can't be distracted. Can't be panicked. *Blind trust.* He closes his eyes, tightens his grip on the girl's hand and increases their pace.

Should be nearly there, nearly there now. In five, leap, four, leap, three, leap, two, leap, one. Open eyes.

They slam through the glass doors and into History.

"Alhamdullilah!"

Jy okay?

"Ja."

He looks around. *You're on my turf now, you fuckers. Catch me if you can. Not far now. Just down here. Kom.*

They run down the deserted corridor, and then down the next. The senior reading room is just at the end. He has a key. Once inside, they'll be safe. There are doors, and there are doors, and shelves and shelves, and books and books, and he knows them all, well. He can run rings around them in there. Get them lost. Drive them crazy. But then he hears. They stop to listen. *Fuck.* The unmistakable sound of boots has entered the building.

Sister. Take off your shoes. This is it.

He kicks off his own and gets the key from his pocket. It usually catches and niggles in the lock, but not if you get it just so. They slide on socks towards the door. The boots get louder. He replays the just so technique in his head. *Issa, you miss, you lose. You miss, she loses. What the fuck were you thinking about anyway when you dragged her into this? Out there she may have stood a chance of getting lost in the crowd. In here, with you, she'll be taken with a prime suspect. So you don't miss. You owe it to her.* He holds the key to the lock. In a few more paces the boots will turn the corner. The girl breathes heavily. She looks nervously down the corridor. He slides the key into the lock. First notch, slot. Boots. Second notch, slot. Boots. Third notch, slot. Boots. *Now, turn!* His eyes squint in concentration. The girl holds her breath. Boots. His whole body turns with the key. Click click. Boots. *Khulja Simsim? Open Sesame?*

Click click click.

Just so.

"Alhamdullilah!"

A gust of wind lifts his hair and drops the loosely draped blanket to the ground. She sees his eyes fill with all the resentment and rage she had first seen in them a few months back.

And all for what? For this? All over again?

"Issa! Wait! Where are you going?"

He doesn't turn around. Just says, as he crouches through the open window:

To stop them.

"I sat up to wait. In the morning, I woke to the normal sounds of the buses in the terminus. For a while I didn't know where I was; I never sleep in my armchair. The TV was still on. It was just before six. I got up to turn on the kettle. And then, slowly, it all started coming back… But what had become of him? Was he back? Perhaps he'd knocked. Perhaps I'd slept through. And then.

"When I came back in here, there it was, all over the TV, the mosque, the police in riot gear, the motorcycles, the helicopters.

I turned up the volume. They had shut down the whole area, more than a hundred, hundred and fifty of them. From up here I had no idea all that was taking place down there. And for what? A toy gun and a couple of gas canisters? More enemies made than caught, if you ask me.

"But whether they had sealed off the area before or after Issa got down there –" She shrugs her shoulders. "Several men were arrested. All foreigners. At the time I thought he might have been one of them; the rage he was in when he left here, there was no telling what he might do."

sifir wahed athnaan

NEXT SHE LEARNS THE NUMBERS, Arabic numerals, starting with the number they invented, zero, sifr: ٠ .

"The sum total of Arab contribution to modern culture," a fellow diner at a dinner party had quipped, raising his thumb and forefinger into a circle: "Zero."

When the laughter subsided, she turned to the man. "You might want to get it right," she said. "In Arabic, zero is indicated by a dot, not a circle and, just off the top of my head, I can think of at least two more things," she said.

The man dropped his hand and looked indignantly at her.

"Plato and Aristotle."

"My dear," he said with an air of vindication. "*They* were Greek."

"So they were," she conceded. "But I would have expected one who has clearly had the benefit of an expensive education to also know that, when Europeans deemed it best to *burn* the pagan thoughts of their Greek forebears, their ideas would have been lost for eternity, had their survival not been ensured by the translations of Arab scholars kept safe in the libraries of Baghdad.

"With such glaring gaps," she said, filling her glass, "I suppose you also believe that the Renaissance was an entirely Italian affair. More wine?"

٠	١	٢	٣	٤	٥	٦	٧	٨	٩	١٠
صفر	واحد	إثنان	ثلاثة	أربعة	خمسة	ستة	سبعة	ثمانية	تسعة	عشرة
ṣifr	waḥid	ithnān	thalātha	'arba'a	khamsa	sitta	sab'a	thamānya	tis'a	'ashara
0	1	2	3	4	5	6	7	8	9	10

She decides to make a list, in Arabic, of all the names and telephone numbers stored in her telephone. In future, as an ongoing exercise, she will consult this list when she wants to make a call rather than select and dial the number automatically from her phone. In her list, names, where possible, take their Arab equivalents: Peter becomes Boutros, John Yahya, Mary Miriam, Paul Boulos. And because Arabic has no p or v sounds, Paul becomes Baul and Vivian, Fifian. She loved the way Karim said please, 'Blease,' as if spelt with a b. When it is finished, the list, at first sight still little more than a collection of elegant unintelligible strokes and loops, undecipherable to everybody on it, becomes to her access to her life.

And when she goes about the city, she pays special attention to its many Arabic signs, reading them slowly, letter by letter, until the vowel-less string clicks into meaning:

حلال	h l a l	halaal	
مطعم	m T ' m	maT'am	restaurant
فندق	f n d q	funduq	hotel

She particularly enjoys deciphering the registration plates on luxury cars from the Middle East that glide through affluent parts of the city. It thrills her that she is able to pierce the 'exotic' surface of the image and identify the real country, the very city beyond:

دمشق	d m sh q	damashq	Damascus
الكويت	k w y t		Al-Kuwait
بيروت	b y r w t		Al-Beirut

One day, a Jeep darts by flashing a registration plate, which she is certain read as 'mSr'. But this makes no sense to her and Maseru is all she can come up with. But with an Arabic registration plate? Surely not. So she looks up the entry in her dictionary:

مصر	m S r	miSr	Egypt

A veil is being lifted and slowly, a whole world – its symbols, its rules, its logic – is beginning to reveal itself to her, right here, in London. Where once she was blind, she can now do so much more than see. She can read.

III
The Café

'When the Reagan Administration began its war with Nicaragua, I recognised a deeper affinity with that small country in a continent upon which I had never set foot. I grew daily more interested in its affairs, because, after all, I was myself the child of a successful revolt against a great power, my consciousness the product of the triumph of the Indian Revolution. It was perhaps also true that those of us who did not have our origins in the countries of the mighty West, or North, have some things in common – not, certainly, anything simplistic as a unified "Third World" outlook – but at least some knowledge of what weakness was like, some awareness of the view from underneath, and of how it felt to be there, at the bottom, looking up at the descending heel.'

Salman Rushdie
Jaguar Smile
1987

Vasinthe's Letter

IN JOHANNESBURG, VASINTHE HAS BEEN agonising over it for days. Not about whether to write it – she does not dispute his right to know, or, for that matter, hers to tell him – but about how and what to write. That was what bothered her. She hasn't heard from him since that near-fatal morning when he stormed out of the house, leaving her –

She shuts out the memory.

He must know of the son that was born minutes later. She'd given him the name they'd agreed upon, the name he had wanted. She had written to him at his parents' to tell him.

Faced with a silence of more than 30 years, she could not decide on what to say, what to leave unsaid.

Not even on how to begin.

But now it is written. Short, she decided, was best. She reads the letter one last time:

Johannesburg
30th August 2003

Muhsin

I regret that I have been unable to make direct contact with you at this time. I would have preferred to speak with you in person. I wasn't aware that you no longer live in South Africa – though where, your sister would not say. But she assured me that, if I wrote, she would see to it that my letter reached you. She may in fact already have told you my news; I am pleased that they seem to have reconciled with you.

I feel it incumbent on me to let you know that Issa has disappeared from London where he was studying. I have always been certain that, whatever our past, yours and mine, I would inform you if anything happened to your son. And now it has.

My first instinct was that he might have gone in search of you. I cling to the possibility that this is the case – although, as the weeks and months pass, it seems less likely. It has been four months now. But I trust that you will let me know if he does turn up on your doorstep. I assume he is not already with you; whatever has happened between us, I think you would at least have let me know?

You've never seen Issa, so I am enclosing the most recent photograph we have of him, taken by a friend of his in London a few months before he went missing. I think you'll agree that I may as well have sent you a picture of yourself at that age.

Vasinthe

She joins the queue at the small campus post office. While she waits, she retrieves the photograph discreetly from the unsealed envelope. It is a bright picture, taken in Katinka's sunny flat; one of the pictures they left with Margaret. Issa is leaning against a doorframe, smiling, as he does, has always done, only slightly, head at an angle, arms folded casually across his chest. His thick black hair is swept back from the high forehead and falls in sleek waves on his shoulders. Muhsin, she thinks again: running a trembling finger down the strong nose and along the jaw, wiping the deep eyes gently with a tender thumb. The resemblance only struck her recently.

She has been unable to recall her son's face; is kept awake at night by faceless memories of him. She can conjure countless images of him as a child: following the trauma of his birth, the relief, when Gloria handed him to her, of holding him, bloody and blue, in her arms for the first time; the way he'd sit, legs crossed on the floor in front of the television, engrossed by the adventures of Lawrence, crossing the Empty Quarter with him, tensing himself, rocking anxiously backwards and forwards, when Daud falls into the quicksand, sitting up on his knees as the struggle to save him grows more and more desperate, rewinding his favourite scenes over and over again until he could recite whole stretches of dialogue.

She can still hear him now: "What is it, Major Lawrence, that attracts you to the desert?" / "It's clean." The confused expression on his face when, chasing Kagiso at a picnic, he stepped onto something concealed in the long grass. The terror when he sat down, lifted his bare foot and saw a broken bottle neck stabbed into his sole. Kagiso's question, asked sheepishly on the backseat during the rush to hospital: "Does it hurt?" Issa's response, recited in a swoon: *The trick, William Potter, is not minding that it hurts.* The giant teardrop that welled up in his right eye, like Pharaoh in Tadema's 'Death of the first born' she always thought – suspended in that throat-clenching moment of utter devastation, the teardrop welling up slowly, first in one eye, later in the other, before breaking free of the lid, then rolling down to where it dangled, for just a moment, from the tip of one of the long lashes before its gathering pear-shaped weight sent it falling, down and down till it landed, plop, on the official advice of his Matric results.

Vasinthe can recall all this detail over and over again, but she has almost no recollection of the young man he'd turned into in Cape Town, the man in London. She now keeps a copy of this photograph in a silver frame – a gift from Katinka – by her bedside and one on her desk, the first personal memento to encroach on her professional domain. The queue inches forward. She becomes aware of the cold. She has come out without her jacket.

She recalls an incident some years earlier when a colleague lost his son in a motorcar accident. A few weeks after the funeral, he came into her office:

"They've found a cornea for Mrs –"

"At last!"

"But can *you* do it?"

"What do you mean? We've been preparing this one for months. And you're the ophthalmologist. This is *your* case. I don't understand?"

He stepped forward, "Please?" She could smell that he'd been drinking.

"Bloody hell, Peter! How much have you had? We can't postpone. How long will it take to –"

"Too much. Too long. Look, we've worked on this one together. This was your referral."

"I know I can, but that's not the point, Peter," Vasinthe shouted. "I haven't had time to –"

Peter interrupted her. "I've got the file here. We have time. Let's sit down with it. And then we can go to inform her."

"Of what? That her surgeon can't operate because he's bloody drunk."

"Vasinthe, she knows you. She was your patient too."

"You sneaky shit! You knew that all along, didn't you? That the team would cover for you. That's why you went and got yourself bladdered."

"Look! I know I'm out of order –"

"But remember that old adage, Peter, the one about strong chains and weak links."

He looked pleadingly at her. "Vasinthe, this isn't helping."

She exhaled deeply.

He watched her for a response.

"Okay," she sighed. "I don't have much of a choice, do I? But we'll have to inform the super. It's very late to be swapping the lead surgeons."

"But you're the Head of –"

"Yes, and I'll deal with you in that capacity on Monday. For the moment, talk me through the latest progress. Where's that file? Who's assisting?"

He flopped into her armchair, despondent relief hanging over him.

"I'm sorry Peter, I don't mean to be harsh, but we'll have to play this one by the book. *You* know what's at stake here."

He dropped his head.

"Look, is there anything I can do?"

He looked up at her, his red eyes welling with tears. "It was only when I went to identify his body, when I saw him lying there, lifeless on a tray in front of me, that I realised…"

Her expression softened.

"That I realised what a beautiful son I had. Even with all those fatal injuries. He looked like a god, fallen in battle." He swivelled the chair round to face the window. "Too busy making medical history here to even have noticed."

❧

In the queue, Vasinthe shudders. She'd registered the words as he spoke them and made private little pledges to herself, but her progression to a JME appointment, the celebrated success of the difficult transplant, the flurry of invitations to overseas lecture-tours, Peter's disappearance into an obscure early retirement on his remote ancestral farm somewhere in the Eastern Cape – it was easy to forget about his regrets when work was so rewarding. She'd forgotten about the pledge until asked by Margaret in London during their preliminary telephone conversation for a description of Issa. She fumbled. Margaret suggested they finalise the description when she came to the office the following day.

"Can I –" She started hesitantly. "Can I bring along his friend? She knew him very well."

"Of course you can," Margaret said, reassuringly. "Our role is to support family and friends alike."

"After you, Professor."

Vasinthe looks up, startled by the familiar voice. She hadn't noticed her student ahead of her in the queue. She quickly slips the picture back into the envelope.

"Are you sure?"

"Yes, please. You go first."

Vasinthe smiles thanks. She steps forward and places the sealed envelope on the scales. "Special delivery, please."

"Where to?" the cashier asked.

"Durban, please."

Walking back to her office, she tries to recall the picture. She remembers that it is bright. She can recall folded arms, a leaning posture, a slight smile – but that is all. She becomes agitated. Muhsin, she thinks, as she tries to reconstruct the son through memories of the father. But all she gets are crazed blood-shot eyes, flaring nostrils, clenched fists, a kick in –

When she reaches the department, she increases her pace into a doctor's determined stride: "See their white coats flapping, Sinth. See their stethoscopes." If you stop me now, someone will die. She can't remember where she'd heard the comment, but she cringed in recognition.

Normally she makes a conscious effort to be less hurried around the office. This is a different space, and though busy, it doesn't demand the urgency that accompanies her life-or-death role in the hospital up the road. Here, she is Professor Kumar, the teacher, the researcher, the scholar. She makes herself amenable, approachable. She smiles and, from time to time, stops in the corridors to exchange pleasantries with colleagues and students.

But not now.

She does not enter her office as she usually does, via that of her assistant, but slips in through the private, back entrance. At her desk, she reaches for the framed photograph of Issa hidden beside her monitor and slides it into the centre of the desk in front of her. She doesn't hear the students streaming out of the adjoining lecture theatre and into the sunny quad behind her. She runs her forefinger slowly around the edges of the frame, then rocks it gently from corner to corner.

Like a cradle.

She picks up the receiver:

"Yes, Professor?"

"Susan, can you get Professor Godfrey on the line for me."

Susan hesitates. "Professor *Peter* Godfrey, Professor?"

"That's right."

"Certainly, Professor."

"And Susan –"

"Yes, Professor?"

"Hold my calls."

"Yes, Professor."

Another Brick in Another Wall

KATINKA AND KARIM WOULD LIE in a knot and talk through the night, of London and of home. Not sleeping, sinking into each other's stories like water into sun-cracked earth, like salve into raw wounds.

One night, he tells her about the wall that is being built across his family's property. It will separate their house from their decimated olive-grove, their last remaining trickle of income. The wall surrounds their town on three sides. Most of the businesses in the town have shut down. "It is eight metres high. We never see the sun. Our house is always in its shadow. When I look through my bedroom window that is all I can see. The Wall. It does what it was designed to do; make us feel small."

Another night, he tells her about Wafa Idris. "It's not what I would do, but I understand why she did it. Here, in the free world, even the prime minister's wife was not free enough to say that, but I can. You know: 'When this life makes you mad enough to kill / When you want something bad enough to steal.'" They laugh at his imitation of the rap.

"I understand why she did what she did. And those who tell you otherwise, let them spend one day in the life of Wafa and others like her – my father." He raises a solitary finger into the night, then lets it rise and fall three times, once for each word: "Just one day."

One night, she comes to hear of her mother's death. Despite all the years, the news, the indirect route by which it reached her, months later, leaves her devastated. She goes to find him but he isn't there. She can't think of what to do. She doesn't want to go back to her empty flat. She doesn't want to see Issa. She only wants him. So she sits down on the pavement outside his building because it's *his* pavement, it's the pavement outside *his* building. She barely notices the cold, barely notices the two hours before he returns.

When he gets home, he sees her huddled in the shelter between two cars. "My God," he exclaims and scoops her up in his arms. "Why didn't you come to the café?"

But she is unable to speak. She just lies face down on the bed, crying – not the inhibited sobs of earlier, but a terrifying, howling lament that she is only brave enough to release because he is now with her.

When she wakes in the middle of the night, thick-eyed and dry-throated, she finds him watching over her:

"*What's* the matter, habibti?" he asks, tilting his head pleadingly to one side, running his fingers through her hair.

She tells him.

"So you will be going home soon?"

"No."

He doesn't understand. He offers to lend her money – money he himself will borrow, if money is the problem.

"It's not money," she says. "It's history." He is the only person to whom she repeats the story about the monster's name.

On their last night together before he returned home – "Hell on Earth, but hey, apart from you, this is not that great either. I don't know what I'll do. Home is like a ghost town now, I'm told. But I'll have my family and my friends, and they'll have me. They need me" – he gave her an inexpensive watch with Arabic numerals. She put it on immediately.

"Now you'll never confuse seven and eight... And, insha'allah, you won't forget me."

"I won't forget you."

He sniffed. "That's what they all say."

"I'm not like that."

"Then maybe you'll visit, one day?"

She lifts herself onto her elbow and lays her hand on his shoulder: "'Except for thy haven, there is no refuge for me in this world other than here / There is no place for my head.' I'll come visit, I promise." Then she snuggles back into him.

He smiles a fading smile. "Come soon," he says. "Before we're completely walled in. While we're still there."

On her first night without him, she compiles an indulgent playlist, which she names 'Melancholy'. Some of the songs on the list, she hasn't heard for years. When the selection is complete, she puts it on continuous play and goes to bed:

die
'Every time we say goodbye, I a
li
ttle…'

In the middle of the night, 'They're dancing with the missing' – a tune she once used in a teaching practice lesson when she was a student in the Free State – 'They're dancing with the dead' – a way, she thought, of alluding tangentially to the horrors of apartheid. 'They dance with the invisible ones'. She failed the lesson. 'Their anguish is unsaid'. Her subject was South African history. 'They're dancing with their fathers'. Not Chilean. 'They're dancing with their sons'. She sees herself in a vigil of veiled women. 'They're dancing with their husbands'. Around their necks are draped photographs, pictures of the dead. Some women have so many photographs around their necks that other women have to help them, like bridesmaids attending to a bride. 'They dance alone'.

One of the women steps forward and walks towards the police barrier. 'It's the only form of protest they're allowed.' When the woman reaches the barrier, the police step forward to block her way. She removes the veil from her face. Decades of sadness bursts from under her veil, causing the police to shield their eyes and step aside. 'I've seen their silent faces scream so loud'. When the unveiled woman reaches the main gates, she turns around to signal to the other women. They follow her up the short street and through the already-open shiny black door. 'If they were to speak these words they'd go missing too'. One by one, the women enter the house. 'Another woman on a torture table what else can they do'. One by one, they place their photographs next to those of the happy family on the mantle piece. 'They're dancing with the missing.' One by one, they lay down the pictures of their missing and their dead. 'They're dancing with the dead…'

When she enters the house, she realises that she too has a picture draped around her neck. She enters the room and moves to the photograph of the woman on the mantelpiece. 'Can you think of your own mother / Dancin' with her invisible son'. She lifts her photograph from her neck and places it on the mantelpiece next to the smiling woman.

'They're dancing with the missing
They're dancing with the dead
They dance with the invisible ones
Their anguish is unsaid
They're dancing with their fathers
They're dancing with their sons'

When she sees the photograph she has placed, she wakes and shouts his name into the night.

'They're dancing with their husbands'

It is a picture of…

'They dance alone'.

"Karim!"

One day, she will be on a train, looking out through the window, only half-conscious of the story a mother next to her is reading to her daughter. When the train enters a tunnel, her ears will take over from her eyes: "…but Salim had fallen in love with the court dancer. When Akbar heard of this, he warned his son to give her up, but the prince refused. And so the Emperor ordered his masons to bind the girl and then build her into a wall while she was still alive."

When she gets to school, she will resign her thankless post. Her superiors will try to dissuade her. "I'm sorry," she will say. "This isn't education. It's crowd control."

A week later, she will land in Tel Aviv, from where she will travel by land to Qalqilia. By the time she reaches her destination, she will have spent five hours flying from London to Tel Aviv, and a disproportionate eighteen hours travelling the short distance from Tel Aviv to Qalqilia. To Karim. Karim behind The Wall.

Baghdad Café

"This is Bond Street. The next station is Marble Arch. Please allow passengers to get off the train first. Please move right down inside the carriage. Please take up all available space inside the carriages. This train is now ready to depart. Please stand clear of the closing doors."

On the tube, Kagiso notices a picture of a family strolling on an idyllic private beach. It is an advertisement for a credit card company offering an exotic holiday on an exclusive island for a lucky winner and nine people of their choice. On the golden sands of the beach, someone has scribbled:

> 'The world is *not* your private holiday destination. People *live* here and *they* probably don't have access to this beach.'

"This is Marble Arch. The next station is Lancaster Gate. Please stand clear of the closing doors."

They exit the station and step out onto the throng of Edgware Road on a Saturday night, four lanes of traffic, a huge crowd waiting to enter the cinema complex, bustling pavements, busy restaurants.

"Many Londons," Katinka says, "and if Brick Lane is like the Meghna flowing through its east, then this is the like the Euphrates, or the Tigris, or the Nile flowing through its west."

A little way up the road, Kagiso follows her into an elaborately decorated café, filled with scented smoke and intoxicating music.

"Woah!" he exclaims as the waiter leads them to the alcove in the corner behind a mashrabeya screen. "What is this place? Are we still in London?"

"Do you like it?"

"It's... It's like I stepped through the glass doors and into *The Thousand and One Nights*. How did you come by this place?"

"Issa's hangout. And the last place I saw him." A waiter approaches their table. "I'll tell you later."

She places their order in Arabic. "A pot of mint tea and two shisha... Apple, please."

"I'm impressed," Kagiso nods when the waiter has left.

"Don't be. That's the only sentence I'm fluent in, because I say it all the time. The rest of my Arabic is still pretty dire."

"I'm sure it isn't."

"All conversations I have, whether it's about the past or the future, they all still happen in the present tense. I find the conjugation of the verb in Arabic incredibly difficult."

"And people understand?"

"Mostly, but I could do better," she admits. "Of course, I prefix the past with yesterday, even if I'm talking about ten years ago, and the future with tomorrow, even if I'm talking about next year; not very sophisticated, I know, but mostly people appreciate the effort."

"And can you read and write?"

"I've just about cracked the alphabet," she says, smiling broadly. "I'm still at the c-a-t, cat stage. So let's say that I can decipher rather than read."

"So what does this say?" he says, pointing at the menu.

"That says Baghdad."

"Well, *that* was pretty fluent."

"I've had a lot of practice with that one too. It's been on there constantly these last few months," she says, pointing a finger over her shoulder at the giant screen behind her.

He introduces another round of the game they have been playing randomly during the course of their ambling afternoon – the game he taught her during that first shared drive to Cape Town, all those Februarys ago, with Issa's deep, reticent silence driving them through the hot Karoo.

"Marianne Sagebracht, Jack Palance and CCH Pounder? *That's* a hard one." She raps her fingers on the table and screws up her eyes as she tries to guess the film in which the three actors appeared.

Pleased with his challenge, he reclines in the plush sofa and smiles, blowing out large plumes of apple-scented smoke.

"Is it recent?" she asks.

"No."

"Marianne Sagebracht?"

"Sexy woman. Fat *is* beautiful."

She shakes her head. "Don't know."

"Clue?"

"Clue... You're sitting in one."

"An arabesque sofa?"

"Not the sofa, the place."

"An Arabic coffee shop?"

"Warm."

She repeats the information he has given her, "Jack Palance, not recent, Arabic coffee shop," and then opens her eyes wide with excitement, as a child would, to indicate she's hit on the answer: "Lawrence of Arabia!"

Kagiso chokes on a lungful of smoky laughter. "Still as crap as ever. You haven't got one right so far!"

"That's because you keep coming up with the most obscure films."

"You give up, then?"

"Ja, tell me."

"*Bagdad Café!*"

"*Bagdad Café?*"

"Yes, *Bagdad Café*."

She remembers. "Café in the bundus?"

He nods.

"Gosh, that takes me back. Surreal film? Really haunting theme tune? I can almost hear it now."

"Callin U," he says.

"That's right." She struggles to hum the tune.

He helps her out.

"Anyway," she says, slapping his wrist, "how was Arabic coffee shop supposed to be a clue?"

"Katinka!" he sighs, with a tone of mock exasperation, and points to the same menu in front of her.

She sucks her teeth and slaps her palm to her forehead. "Baghdad Café... Very good!"

❧

"Baghdad, we used to call it. Meet you in Baghdad. Sometimes I'd get texts from him – 'Comrad! Smokin in bagdad. Wair r u? Join me!' Once, he texted me in the middle of the night, oblivious of the time. I was really pissed off, and sent a text back saying – 'In bed! Iv got 2 teach 30 bastad brats in da am.' But, being Issa, he had to push it even further:

'An on fone means u not ntyly unavlbl.'

'Im vlbl 4 emgncis only! Now Fuk off!'

He didn't.

'In bagdad dis is an emgncy. Fuk da bastad brats. Kids r dying here. Get u gat ova here asap. & Fuk lemonde – we r all afghanarabs now!'"

"What was he doing here in the middle of the night?"

Again she points over her shoulder at the enormous screen. "Watching the war on that."

"What did you do?"

"I couldn't get back to sleep, so I thought, fuck it, and jumped in the car. By the time I got here, everybody was gripped. The place was packed out, with thick fumes of smoke hanging in the air. It felt as though I had driven across London and into Baghdad itself. The waiters were all standing in a group facing the screen, their backs towards the door. They didn't turn around to meet me when I walked in. That one," she says pointing discreetly, "held an empty tray to his chest."

"Issa wasn't in our usual seat, so I had to search among the dazed observers to find him. It was a strange feeling. The whole room was caught up in the screen – the shock and awe of the bombs, the explosions reverberating around the world, all the way here, into this room. It felt as though I was walking through a war, looking for my friend amongst the dazed and stunned.

"I found him over there, at that table behind the banister, pipe in mouth, chin to chest, staring at the screen. On his T-shirt was written: 'I am a standing civil war.'"

Sit down. Come see the view from underneath. This is what the descending heel looks like – the soles of George and Tony's feet.

"I squeezed in next to him."

These bombers left Britain as people here were sitting down to tea.

"He gave me the mouthpiece." She puffed her pipe. "Have you ever seen a real war projected live onto a screen the size of a fucking Piccadilly Circus billboard?"

They stare through the window at the pavements now crowded with late night strollers. The waiter replenishes their drinks, the sabby stokes their pipes.

"It was here, in Baghdad, that we first met when he came to London. He was sitting in his favourite seat, where you are now, smoking a shisha pipe. I was quite nervous, but of course I pretended not to be."

He frowns. "Why were you nervous?"

"I was intimidated by where we were meeting. Jy moet onthou, ek is 'n plaasnooi. I thought it a strange place for him to suggest. And when the waiter brought the damn pipe he'd ordered for me to the table, carried high through the air, and then set it down beside me in an elegant bow, like a ceremonial offering, I had no idea what to do with the damn thing, so I just puffed it like you would a cigarette. Of course once Issa told me to, 'trek soos 'n bottle kop,' I was away and never looked back."

"Why were you intimidated by this place?"

"I'd never been out on Edgware Road. I guess, like a lot of people, I saw it as rich Arab turf. It would never have occurred to me to socialise here – I didn't know what that entailed. But look at me now; a regular who can't get enough. When I told a friend that this is where I was coming, she warned me to be careful, said I might get rolled up in a carpet and smuggled into sexual slavery."

He smiles.

"I said I wouldn't be that lucky."

His smile turns into a laugh.

"Yes, I laughed too. But I don't think it's funny anymore."

He moves around awkwardly in his seat. "Why?"

She shrugs. "Now it makes me cringe to think that I, an Afrikaner, the victim of so much stereotyping, could have done the same to others. It makes me think of Afrikaaners and Arabs as brethren. The last of the Mohicans. The two tribes it is still acceptable to denigrate and berate." Her thoughts fly to Karim, and to her friend; she never told her about him, knew she'd never understand, didn't want to hear her sexually-charged references, doesn't see that friend anymore. She drinks a deep inhalation causing the water in the pipe to gurgle and boil as in an agitated teapot. When she has filled her lungs, she releases a huge cloud of smoke, like a dragon, into the air, thick and fragrant and white, dense enough to hide her face and, for a moment, to cover her sorrow.

She reaches for her phone – "The next day I got a text from him" – and hands it to Kagiso. 'Tnx 4 cumin last nite. Wen we achievd & da new world dawnd da old men came out again & took our victry to remake in da liknes of da 4mer world dey new. Read Anil's Ghost, the last sntnc on pg 43.'

Kagiso puts down the phone.

"That was the last I heard from him," she says. "I never saw him again."

London N4

WHEN KAGISO FIRST SAW ISSA'S address, he took N4 to be the postcode for London: Finsbury Park, N4, Piccadilly Circus N4, Covent Garden N4, Buckingham Palace N4. London N4. Now, walking around the area, at the end of his stay, he shies away from the memory. How little I knew.

He moves in and out of the station, as if exploring a maze. That was what it seemed like when he first arrived. He was sure he would never find his way and expected to get terribly lost.

"Customer information. Please do not leave your baggage unattended. Customers are reminded that smoking is not permitted on any London Underground train or platform."

Now he sees the tunnels as they are – simple, like a T with staircases descending down from the vertical branch to each of the platforms. Right for the Piccadilly Line which, tomorrow, he will take, westbound, to Heathrow. (Katinka is insistent that she will drive him as it is a Saturday, but he would prefer to slip out of London, quietly.) Left for the Victoria Line to Brixton – the name reminds him of the Brixton Murder and Robbery Squad near downtown Johannesburg – the Brixton Murderers and Robbers Squad, as they used to call it. Detainees would end up at John Vorster Square slipping accidentally and falling through open windows to their pavement deaths far below. Oops.

"That shit still happens here," Katinka had said. "And Brixton Police Station is notorious for it."

The perpendicular tunnel leads to the bus terminus and Issa's flat in one direction, and in the other to the mosque, with the silent minaret. A phone booth at this exit is covered with stickers: 'Read Chomsky'.

Frances was right. It is all boarded up, all the ground floor windows and the door covered up with corrugated iron. It strikes him that this is the only time he has seen corrugated iron in London – the metal out of which nearly all South African shanties are built, the metal of his grandmother's shack before Ma Gloria had the walls bricked.

He imagines the dark emptiness inside the mosque, the deserted corridors, the quiet prayer hall full of unsaid supplications, the dusty, moth-eaten carpets.

He hears just the ends of sounds, the silence after shoes have been kicked off, the last drip from a tap in the ablution fountain – plop – the hush that follows bending bodies and folding cloth when the straight lines of worshippers have fallen to their knees, foreheads to the ground.

Like at Issa's flat, when he first opened the door. He was sure he'd heard the shower being turned off. He paused in the doorway, thrilled. Plop. He's back!

"Issa!" he shouted, dropping his bag. He ran into the bathroom. But there was nothing, just a dusty cobweb dangling silently from the dry showerhead.

The excitement had lasted only a moment, but the disappointment was crushing, ultimate, like Vasinthe's sinking feeling in the park when she realised that Katinka, in fact, knew nothing.

He slid down the wall, sank into his knees, and wept.

"You're back!" an old voice exclaimed in the doorway.

He looked up and saw the anticipation fall from her face like a mask and crash into pieces on the floor, like it did from Ma Vasinthe's at the airport, when she realised the missed call wasn't from Issa.

"Oh," the old lady said, not able to conceal her disappointment.

He rose to his feet. "I'm Kagiso. I'm here to pack up his things."

"Come with me," she called, turning away from the door. "I'll get you some breakfast. There's nothing in there."

He raises his camera to the disused building. Through his lens, he sees a sticker on the padlock by the gate. When he has taken the photographs – the windows covered in corrugated iron, the silent minaret, the locked gate – he crosses the road to read:

To those against whom
War is made, permission
Is given (to fight), because
They are wronged; – and verily,
God is Most Powerful
For their aid; –

(They are) those who have
Been expelled from their homes
In defiance of right, –
(For no cause) except
That they say, "Our Lord
Is God."

Qur'an S. xxii, 40

Vasinthe and Gloria

ONE SPRING MORNING IN EARLY September, when Vasinthe gets home, she finds that Gloria has moved her seat, as she has done for three decades, from its winter position next to the stove to its summer position by the door. A new season has been ushered in. Comforted by the continuance of this small tradition, Vasinthe smiles. Soon – always at otherwise unobserved Diwali – they will spend a weekend cleaning the house. Cupboards, wardrobes and bookshelves will be unpacked and scrubbed – old clothes and utensils set aside for delivery to a destitute women's shelter in Braamfontein – curtains changed, windows cleaned, carpets steamed. The operation will commence on a Friday afternoon. They will work late into the night and start again early the next morning.

When the boys were at home, they each had their allotted roles – men's hands can clean as well as women's. Issa always participated fully, almost with relish, offering help elsewhere when he had finished his own chores. Kagiso had to be goaded. All weekend, they'd eat convenience food: fish and chips, microwave dinners. By Sunday afternoon, they'd start rushing towards completion, like the fast forward sequences that come towards the end of makeover programmes. On Sunday evening, Vasinthe would drive them to a roadhouse for burgers and milkshakes. When they returned home, they would collapse into bed, exhausted, in their spotless house.

But this year, Vasinthe and Gloria will be less efficient. They will call an end to Friday without having completed half their usual tasks. On Saturday, they will start late, half-hearted and listless. By the middle of the morning, Gloria will mention two young girls who are in the neighbourhood in search of work. Vasinthe recruits them without question. She leaves Gloria to supervise them while she retreats to her study. She starts to unpack her bookshelves, but slowly works her way towards the wooden Thai box in which she keeps their old report cards, some childhood drawings, some of her favourite hideous souvenirs from school trips. She spends the rest of the afternoon going through the mementos in the box.

"I don't understand," she recalls saying to Peter during a recent visit to him on his remote farm. "I don't understand why he just disappeared. That is just cruel. Why couldn't he talk to me, to us? Why had he become so alienated, from his own family?"

Peter didn't look at her. Instead, he lit a cigarette and stared into the rolling green hills of the Eastern Cape. "Distance is a powerful thing," he said, softly. "It changes people... When I went into exile, all those years ago, I promised myself that wherever I went, my journey would not be over until I returned home, to South Africa. I spent the next fifteen years wishing away my life, Harare, Lusaka, Lagos, London, my fifteen years across the Styx.

"'Ha, banishment? Be merciful, say death for exile hath more terror in his look, much more than death. Do not say banishment.' Romeo knew whereof he spoke.

"I don't think I had a lucid moment during any one of those interminable years. The day after the ANC was unbanned, I finally boarded a plane at Heathrow, bound for home. I couldn't wait. Only Jacob was there to meet me. He held a sign that said 'Peter Godfrey' – in case. His mother was waiting in the car. I walked past the sign. Everything had changed, the airport building, the atmosphere, Jacob – but most of all, me. I couldn't even recognise myself in the name plate held up by my own son."

"But Issa wasn't in exile."

"No, but he is a child of the struggle."

"The struggle's *over*, Peter."

He looked at her. "No Vasinthe, the struggle's never over," and then turned away. "There is a lot in Britain to alienate a young idealist. 'Inglan is a bitch', Vasinthe." He leaned forward, rested his elbows on his knees and brought the cigarette slowly to his mouth.

"When Jacob was killed, my first reaction was to phone my parents. I picked up the receiver, but I couldn't remember the dialling code for Port Elizabeth. Couldn't even remember their home number, so I dialled the only number I've ever been able to remember: 0181 926 0215."

"Who's was it?" Vasinthe asked.

"Cheb's – the exiled Algerian journalist who lived in the flat next to mine. We met in the pub on the corner. We both worked nights. Nights were the worst. We both worked them, then stopped for a pint on our way home, to help us forget the night and sleep through the day." He drops the butt into his empty beer can then reaches into his top pocket. "On the day I left London, he gave me this." He passes Vasinthe the note folded inside a small plastic sleeve:

> Goodbye Peter and good luck. This is what you've been waiting for. When a new society dawns in South Africa, as I'm sure it will, spare a thought for those whose struggle continues. Maybe the land of the vast African continent will prove to be a better conductor of democracy than the water of the narrow Mediterranean Sea.
>
> Your brother, Cheb

When she handed him back the note, he returned it to his top pocket, and tapped his heart.

On Sunday, she repacks the books she'd taken down the day before – no dusting, no culling, no alphabetising. In the afternoon, she gives Gloria the cash to pay the girls and suggests that she recruit the more diligent of the two for full-time work, under Gloria's supervision, starting Monday.

❧

On the table is a bunch of fresh flowers with a little card. In her summer seat by the open doorway, Gloria sets aside the newspaper and watches as Vasinthe opens the envelope:

Fish River

12th September 2003

Good to see you again, Vasinthe. Don't think I can do the big city anymore, but you're welcome back here anytime. Thinking of you today. Hope the boy shows up/gets in touch/is found soon. Please keep me informed. Not knowing is killing, but be gentle with yourself...

"They're from Peter," she says, laying down the card. "Aren't they lovely?"

Gloria nods. "It was a huge bunch. I've put some in the living room as well."

"Thank you. I'll have a look at them later." She sits down while Gloria pours them each a cup of tea; a ritual that Gloria has insisted upon ever since the boys left for university.

"You have to take a break," she chided. "You can't keep going on like this. There's no need for it any more. Time to take it easy now that they are gone."

"But –" Vasinthe tried to protest.

"No buts! That university won't collapse, not one of your patients will die, not one of your students will fail if you have a cup of tea when you get home."

When they have had their tea, Gloria will chop onions and tomatoes while Vasinthe has a shower. When she returns to the kitchen in a fresh kaftan which Gloria will have chosen, ironed and laid out at the foot of the bed, she will cook the dish that has always accompanied whatever main meal Gloria has already prepared – dhal. "The staple food of India," her uncle used to say. She loved it as a child and, as an adult, after so much had been forgotten, revised, deliberately abandoned, this simple dish remains her one unbroken link to her convoluted, inaccessible past. It is often all she eats when she is alone and, for all of them, no meal is complete without it.

Before she says goodnight, Gloria asks what she already knows the answer to – if the answer were any different, she'd be the first to know. Still, she has to ask her obsolete question. To ask is to demonstrate hope, articulate possibility. Not to, would be unthinkable.

Vasinthe knows when the question is coming. She could pre-empt, but she waits to hear it. Gloria is now the only one who asks daily, here, in the privacy of their home. She prefers it that way. In the early days, she found the constant questions everywhere she went, invasive. By the time she got home, she felt prodded, tugged at. Every day she wishes that she didn't have to release her unchanging answer, like a poisoned bow into the air, deadly accurate, slowly fatal. But she accepts Gloria's acknowledgement and waits to acknowledge it in return.

Having wiped away every last drop of water from the shining kitchen sink, Gloria will wring the cloth tightly and wipe the sink again. Then she will drape the cloth over the draining board, slowly, carefully, as if to defer the moment. She will wipe her hands on her apron and look up at her reflection in the kitchen window – the window through which she peeped, terrified, from the outside, more than thirty years ago. With her back to Vasinthe and her hands tightly clutched in her apron, she will utter her simultaneous question-statement, gently, cautiously:

"No news today."

Vasinthe will lay down the newspaper and take off her glasses. "Sorry Gloria. No news today."

This exchange marks the end of their day, like turning out the light.

But, not tonight. "Thirty-three years today," Gloria adds, still staring at her reflection in the window.

"Yes. Thirty-three years today."

Gloria turns around. "I've made a cake."

Comforted by the continuance of another small tradition, Vasinthe smiles.

Gloria smiles too. "Would you like a piece?" she asks, puckering her nose encouragingly.

Somewhere and Nowhere

KAGISO WAKES UP IN A BLACK VELVET SKY. The stars hang around him like diamonds, the full moon hovers overhead like a huge pearl. He doesn't move his head; just stares out through his small oval window at the majesty.

Lethargically, one by one, his senses rekindle and he becomes aware of a gentle, lilting, slightly sorrowful tune in his ear. Katinka knew it. How Frances smiled when she heard the exhumed piece of music earlier that afternoon.

"Would you like me to play it again?" Katinka asked when the tape stopped.

"No, no. I'll listen to it later. You two had better be off now. This young man has a plane to catch."

They descended the staircase. When they reached the landing outside Issa's flat, Kagiso stopped. "I'll just pick up my bag," he said nervously to Katinka.

"Need help?"

"No. I'll manage."

"Okay." She tapped him on the shoulder. "I'll wait in the car."

He stepped into the room. An amplified silence bounced around its emptiness like a crazed ball in a squash court. The exposed corner where the bookcase used to stand cowered, trying to cover its nakedness like a shy girl. On the bedstead lay the mattress, awkwardly restored, like a shamed adulteress. Only the quotations remained on the walls. For a moment, he thought of just leaving them, but only for a moment. He walked from one to another, picking them off the wall. Like truths from a fortune cookie, reading them, then slipping them into his bulging journal.

Upstairs, Frances listened to the echo of his footsteps ricochet around the empty room. The daunting sound was all she could hear; it crowded out even the sound of the buses in the terminus. She reached for the solace of her red satin pouch.

When he had removed the last quotation – 'History includes the present' – Kagiso left the key on the desk as the agent had requested and walked towards the door. He picked up his bag and cast his eyes around the stark room, surveying a disappearance that had now been made complete (everything, he thought, consigned to Alexandria, memory house of the world).

When Frances heard the door close, she turned up the volume on the gentle lilting tune and started a prayer to St Christopher, the patron saint of travellers.

His throat is dry.

When he got into the car, Katinka smiled at him. "Okay?"

"Ja. Let's go."

"Nie so haastig nie," she said mischievously and opened her palm. "See what I made."

He gawked. "Three!"

"Padkos mos. One for the North Circular, one for the M4 and one for the car after you've checked in. Smoke and fly. Vestaan jy?" she joked, laying the spliffs in the recess by the gear stick then stroking them gently with a maternal touch.

He laughed.

"But wait. That's not all!" she exclaimed, reaching behind her ear. "Here's one I made earlier, to get us on our way. After all, we have to get from here to the North Circular, you know, en die vader weet, ek is daai desperate vroumens."

At Heathrow, when it was time to say goodbye, she walked him back into the terminal building. At the entrance to the departure gates, she pulled him back. "I can't go any further," she winked. "I'm a sharp object, you know!"

He laughed, and then, when she threw her arms around him, he cried.

"My engel," she whispered, pulling him tightly towards her. "Kom hier!"

"I'll be fine," he said, trying to straighten himself. But it was too late. The floodgates had already opened and all that could be done was to step aside while the months of tears and sobs and snot came gushing out.

She stroked his hair gently and started singing that strange rhyme from home:

"Siembamba mama se kindjie
Siembamba mama se kindjie
Draai sy nek om
Gooi hom in die sloot
Trap op sy kop
Dan is hy dood."

"I've never understood," he sniffed, "how that was supposed to console a child. I mean, how is anybody supposed to take comfort from being strangled, thrown in the gutter and, how do you say trap in English, stepped on the head?"

"It's a poem – Langenhoven – from the Boer War," she said distantly, staring at the huge gun draped around a security guard at the far end of the departure hall. "About Boer children in British camps."

"Is that so?"

"Yeah. But I guess the comfort's in the tune, not the words." She sat up and tapped his head. "Anyway, it worked, didn't it?"

"Yeah," he conceded, nodding forlornly. "It worked. Thanks."

ꕥ

He tries to swallow, but his tongue gets stuck to his palate. He lifts his head above his headrest to look around. The cabin is dim and quiet, just the drone of jet engines propelling them through the night sky. The darkness is pierced here and there by the occasional beam of vertical light from overhead reading lamps. I must have slept through dinner, he thinks, looking down at the book in his lap. He recognised the girl balancing on a stick from Frances' description of the cover and had set it aside for the journey:

> '... Just when things are improving?'
>
> 'All the more reason,' said Ishvar. 'In case things become worse again.'

'They are bound to. Whether Om marries or not,' said Maneck. 'Everything ends badly. It's the law of the universe.'

He lays the book aside and moves slowly up the inclined aisle towards the galley. He wants to hold an upturned bottle to his mouth and drain it in a quick succession of deep quenching gulps. But satisfaction is to be staggered. On the counter are small glasses of water and orange juice, neatly laid out in rows. He knocks back several of the glasses of water. He wants another, but decides on an orange juice in mid-reach. Then he steps aside to peep through the small window in the thick door.

From this angle, moonlight bouncing off the front edge of the enormous wing, transforming it into a long blade of silver light, evokes an image Frances conjured: "a laser beaming across the Sahara. I often sit here at night and try to imagine what that must look like, a green laser beaming across a clear desert sky."

Where are we, he wonders? If we've crossed the equator, I've slept halfway down the world.

A steward comes to replenish the drinks. "Where are we?" Kagiso asks.

"Just above Kano, Sir," the steward says, pointing at the monitor.

Kagiso looks up dozily. "Thanks, I didn't see that there." He focuses, follows the red route of their flight path from London as it snakes its way, like a river of blood, through the African continent in the dead of night: France / across the Mediterranean / Algeria / Chad / Niger…

"I always feel it should be announced."

Kagiso looks at him questioningly.

"Kano, I mean. It's exactly half-way. Only another six hours to go. But our passengers wouldn't appreciate the interruption. You must be hungry, Sir? You slept through dinner. Would you like something to eat?"

"No, thank you. Just another orange juice, please."

Back in his seat Jimmy Cliff makes him smile. "Any self-respecting traveller should have this track," Katinka said emphatically as she downloaded it onto his music player. He glances at his watch – 2am, then turns to look out through the window again. At 34 000 feet, the past steps forward into his present.

Muhsin.

He has never actually *said* the name. He wonders what it will be like if he meets another Muhsin. Would he ever let a Muhsin into his life? He can't imagine picking up the phone and saying, "Oh, hi Muhsin," or, "I saw Muhsin for lunch today." He can't imagine saying the name with a neutral or loving tone.

One day he was day-dreaming into the kitchen floor when Issa crossed his gaze. He looked up.

"Stop!" he ordered.

Issa stopped out of surprise rather than obedience, a scarred bare foot suspended hesitantly in mid-stride. *What?*

He sat up in his seat and cleared his throat. "You were born on that very spot."

Issa looked back at him in disbelief.

"Don't you get it? You can stand on that spot and say, 'I was born here.' How many people can do that?"

Issa looked down at the floor. For a while he just stood there, looking at his feet.

Kagiso couldn't tell what he was thinking. Then Issa looked up at him – *I haven't looked at it like that* – and smiled.

ஃ

In his window seat, tucked away under a blanket, both somewhere and nowhere, he remembers the first time he got stoned. It was a summer's night in Cape Town – the best. They were lying on Issa's mattress, listening to Rodriguez and Pink Floyd:

'For long you live and high you fly
And smiles you'll give and tears you'll cry
And all you'll touch and all you'll see
Is all your life will ever be…'

Clearly delighted at the impromptu visit, Issa laughed and joked, even let him in on a few secrets. They talked through the night, but in the morning returned to their separate lives.

After showing him the new library building, Issa walked him to the main gates on Modderdam Road. They sat on the curb, strangers once more, and waited in silence for a taxi that would take him back to the lush southern suburbs – back to the idyll of Rondebosch with its book shops, wine bars and frozen yoghurt parlours – back to UCT with its occasional vogue demonstration, but otherwise mostly undisrupted academic routine.

Please don't resent me, Issa, he wanted to say. You had a choice and I'm glad you came here. You would have hated it up there. But I didn't have that choice. You must know that. And I can't afford to screw this up.

Issa was scratching around with a stick in the sand that had gathered by the curb. *Don't go back*, he wanted to say. *We can have another skyf and go back to bed for the rest of the morning. This afternoon we can hang out at the pool. And then I'll drive you back to Rondebosch. We can have fish and chips at Seaforth – best in town, you're right – and maybe I can stay over. Tomorrow's Friday, I only have one lecture.*

But neither said a thing. They just sat there on the curb with their heads lolling between their knees, seeking shelter from the already scorching 10 o'clock sun.

When the taxi came, they got up reluctantly – Kagiso dusting his bottom, Issa sticking his hands deep into his pockets and hunching his shoulders around his ears.

Sweet, he said.

"Ja, sweet," Kagiso echoed.

When he had squeezed into the crammed taxi, the gaatjie, still dangling nonchalantly through the open door, pointed at the horizon in an exaggerated gesture and shouted the command for the driver to continue: "Kap aan, driver. Driver, kap aan!"

Before the taxi disappeared over the brow of the bridge ahead, it occurred to Kagiso to turn around and wave, perhaps gesture a phone call, or, with tweezed thumb and forefinger to puckered lips, a joint. But he was too late; all he saw was Issa swing around on his heel and start walking lazily back towards the main gate.

Kagiso readjusts his neck pillow. Despite all the years before, and all the iconic events that were to follow, that arbitrary, insignificant moment has endured to become his most vivid memory of Issa, perhaps because it is also his most lasting qualm. Issa must have stood there on the pavement while the taxi drove away, watching it recede, waiting for him to turn round. Kagiso still shies away from the memory. It is his trifling tragedy. It was the sudden unexpected recollection of this moment – his enduring petty regret – that had distressed him at Heathrow.

The previous morning he had returned to Jan Smuts House following a sociology tutorial. 'The lunatic is in the hall.' The cleaning ladies had taken over the place: trolleys, stacked high with clean bedding, were parked in the corridors, wastepaper baskets were being emptied into huge black bags, everywhere the smell of disinfectant. He couldn't decide whether the handsome old residence reminded him of a hotel or a hospital; in the lofty ceilings, the stone pillars, the ivy and courtyards – grandeur, in the fittings, functional simplicity in the furniture. When he got to his room, he locked out the cleaning ladies and skipped classes for the rest of the day. That evening he would jump into a taxi to UWC to see Issa.

In the tutorial, Dr Johnson had presented them with an article from a prescribed text and asked him to read. For the first time, that morning – as he read out loud about the effects of the calculated, rational brutality of the homeland system, Kagiso contemplated the circumstances by which privilege had come to be a part of his life. Later, sitting in his window seat at Jan Smuts House overlooking the Cape Flats, the raw details of life in the Bantustans – his grandmother's life – meticulously set out in his lap, he felt hollowed out, as though Dr Johnson had held his life up to the class and torn it into a thousand pieces before flinging it across the desk.

The grainy black and white sequence and the noise of the antiquated projector fill his head as he considers his mother as a young rural woman, walking from house to house in search of work in an affluent 'coloured' suburb in Johannesburg.

As the sequence progresses, it turns slowly into colour. She knocks at closed doors, like the insistent cleaning lady in the corridor outside. Eventually, she knocks at Ma Vasinthe's door. He tries to reconstruct the sort of conversation they would have had.

The noise of the projector fades and he can hear his mother's voice speaking from the past, but only faintly, a bubbly underwater sort of voice, like the Highlander's at the bottom of the lake when he realises that he is immortal. He can't imagine his mother saying the word, but she *must* have, at least on that first day, said it:

"*Madam*, I'm looking for work."

He tries to say the sentence, but it feels as though his tongue will explode. It sticks in his throat, this unutterable sentence, yet, it is certainly what his mother must have said upon first meeting Vasinthe.

Knock knock. "Cleaning." Knock knock.

–

Knock knock. "Kagiso?" Knock knock. "I need to clean your room." Knock knock... The game would start with a knock at the door. Ma Vasinthe would look at Gloria who would rush the boys into hiding, while Ma Vasinthe counted slowly and went to answer the door. With each game, their hiding places grew more and more elaborate: in Ma Vasinthe's secret bathroom behind the built-in wardrobes in her bedroom, behind the geyser in the roof. Once Ma Gloria even took them to hide in the neighbour's kitchen, where they ate cakes and biscuits, Issa refusing his place at the table, refusing the glass tumbler and plate that had been set out for him, joining Ma Gloria and Kagiso on the step outside the kitchen, drinking from the dented tin mug given to Ma Gloria, waiting for Ma Vasinthe to find them. Ma Gloria had thrown them over the back wall, before jumping over the wall herself and spraining her ankle. Once, when they didn't have enough time to find a good hiding place, they scrambled under Ma Vasinthe's bed and waited. That was an eerie round and they didn't enjoy it very much. It frightened them and, even though Ma Vasinthe said that they were imagining things, they *knew* that from under the bed they *had* seen boots. "Lydia," writes MM Gonsalves, "is tired of trying to make ends meet as well as running from the police. She hates that no matter where one goes, if one does not work and 'live in', and does not have a pass, one has to run, because of the danger of trespassing. She begs for a live-in job as she cannot stand the thought of being caught again and of being constantly on the look-out for police." After that they enjoyed the game less and less... Knock knock. "You won't have clean bedding if you don't open the door, Kagiso," the cleaning lady shouts.

"Kagiso?"

"Please," he begs in Setswana, "leave me alone. Please."

'You lock the door
And throw away the key
There's someone in my head but it's not me.'

When he wakes, darkness is creeping up the foot of the mountain below him. For a while he doesn't know who he is and, in this strange twilight, can't figure out where he is. He is gripped by fear and sits up, looking around, like a hostage waking for the first time in his cell.

Bit by bit, the details of his room emerge from the fading light. I'm Kagiso. I'm in my window seat.

He yawns and lifts his arms above his head. But in mid-stretch he sees the article on the sill beside him. His yawn stops, leaving just a gaping mouth, the pleasure of the stretch drains from his muscles, leaving just a contorted body.

He remembers who he is. I am Kagiso Mayoyo. I grew up in Johannesburg but I was born in Taung, a small village in Bophuthatswana, a small village in the Republic of Bophuthatswana, the homeland of Bophuthatswana, the Bantustan, Bophuthatswana. The reserve, Bophuthatswana.

'The lunatic is in my head
You rise the blade, you make the change
You re-arrange me 'till I'm sane.'

And then, while the far-off muezzin calls the faithful to the last prayer of the day, the reconsidered snippets, the re-interpreted half-truths, the unfathomable whispers, the edited histories, the received ideas all start to fit neatly into orbit around the morning's reading, piece by recast piece, like blocks in a well-played game of Tetris, until, a new picture emerges, boom, like a kick in the – Along with the hollow relief of the realisation that his mother never would have uttered that underwater sort of sentence.

At least not to Ma Vasinthe.

From his window at Jan Smuts House, it is not the Cape Flats lit up against the night sky he sees, but a spring morning in Johannesburg, 1970, now replaying itself in vivid cinematic colour with deafening sound.

He sees Ma Gloria walking down the road. He is himself only two months old, the bundle strapped in a blanket to her back. He sees the houses on their road, and, for the first time, the neighbours who would have turned her away.

He sees her eventually walking down Ma Vasinthe's driveway. The new film now deviates from the minimalist black and white version of his childhood because Ma Gloria, he now knows, first entered Ma Vasinthe's house by the back door. But the back door is not visible from the driveway and, on her first visit to the property, she would have had no way of knowing where it was. Not unless something happened that drew her attention there. A noise? A shout? A crash?

He sits up, draws together, finally, the words of the eternal, never-formulated riddle, asks them of the approaching night: how does it happen that a woman like Ma Vasinthe, a doctor, obsessive about schedules, comes to give birth on a kitchen floor?

In his revised film he sees Ma Gloria cautiously approaching the back door. But Ma Vasinthe doesn't open the door. She isn't even standing in the doorway. Where is she? Ma Gloria puts her face towards the kitchen window, her hands at her eyes like blinkers to shut out the light. He shuts his eyes against the sight.

The woman falls to the floor. The man looks up and sees the witness in the kitchen window. He turns away and runs. The woman calls his name. Kagiso hears the name, not called out as a plea for help, but as Ma Gloria has always said it, with a hiss of contempt: Muhsin.

Like a kick in the –

Guts.

He jumps from his seat and runs out of the building and into the car park. Once outside he doesn't know where to go, except that it is easier to run down the mountain than further up it. So, like water, he follows the path of least resistance, leaping down the stairs at the war memorial, then tearing across the rugby field and through the underpass under the M3.

When he trips on the landscaped lawns outside The Woolsack, he doesn't try to stop his fall – just allows himself to tumble and roll down the mountainside all the way to Lover's Walk, where, landing on his feet, like a cat, he continues his sprint. Hares across Main Road without stopping to look for traffic and, at the Mowbray taxi rank on the lower slopes of Devil's Peak, he dives into a departing taxi, heading east down Klipfontein Road – white in the west, black in the east, Coloured and Indian in between – across the Cape Flats, bound for Bellville: Athlone / Gatesville / Vanguard Estate / Surrey Estate / Manenburg Police Station / Heideweld / over the bridge onto Modderdam Road – coloured in the west, white at the east / Valhala Park / Bishop Lavis / Elsies River / Little House on the Prairie / the graveyard / Belhar Station / UWC.

"Kap aan, driver. Driver, kap aan!"

In the taxi some factory girls natter ceaselessly in Afrikaans over a bag of shared chips, the smell of vinegar mixing noxiously with the heady scent of cheap perfume:

"They say mos that she's sleeping with the manager."

"Really?"

"So I hear."

"I don't believe it. Who told you?"

"Rashieda, and if *she* say so then it *must* be true because she mos know everything that happen in the factory."

"Ja, you can say that again."

When his heart has stopped pounding and he has caught his breath, he starts to regret his impulsive decision to visit Issa. What if he isn't there? It's been weeks since they even spoke. What will he say? Why has he come to visit? What story will he tell?

"But with *him*? What does she see in him?"

"Money, baby. Money."

"Hoer."

"And white skin, don't forget."

"Jagse slet."

"Ja. Just you wait, I'm gonna ask her tomorrow how do white piel taste."

"Why you want to know? You want some?"

"Who? Me? Sies!"

He decides that he can't go through with it, that when he gets to UWC, he will cross the road and immediately get a taxi back to Mowbray.

"Wait, let me tell you this before I get off. My ouma darem ma made us laugh last night, hey! We was watching that police raid of that hostel in Guguletu, so she shouted at the TV, 'Ja, catch the trouble makers, but it's that ringleader, Amandla Awethu, that take over our children's heads so and make them act like kaffirs that I wish they will also catch and put in jail.'"

The girls laugh raucously, but muffle their hilarity when one among them sneakily draws attention to Kagiso.

At the main entrance to the university, he squeezes out of the taxi and crosses the road to wait for a taxi heading back to Mowbray. But he immediately becomes aware of the casspirs lurking in the shadows under the tall trees and, not wanting to appear suspect, proceeds casually across Modderdam Road and into the campus.

Inside, he asks for directions to Ruth First. As he approaches the hostel, he sees Issa standing outside the entrance hall with a group of friends. His gestures are loose and generous, frequently punctuated with hand-clapping, finger-snapping and air-punching. From time to time, agile bodies double over in laughter.

Kagiso doesn't approach them but waits on the low wall beside the pathway, mesmerised by the sight of an Issa he does not know.

When Issa breaks away from the group, Kagiso gets up and, with a deep breath, follows him, at a distance, to his room. He watches the carefree, relaxed saunter. Everybody he passes, knows his name:

"Ek sê, Issa, my bra!" they exclaim, knotting hands and arms in elaborate handshakes. "Hoesit, my broe?"

Kagiso decides not to say anything. It is not his place. Besides, Ma Vasinthe may already have told him herself. That would explain Issa's unending devotion to Ma Gloria, and hers to him. It will be up to Issa – if he knows, if he wants to – to raise it.

Take a seat, Issa says, pointing at the mattress on the floor. Kagiso kicks off his shoes and sits down, knees raised, his back against the wall.

Issa retrieves a small wooden box from the drawer in his desk and throws himself down on the mattress beside Kagiso. *What's up?*

"Not much," Kagiso shrugs, awkwardly. "Just wanted to say hi." He watches Issa empty some of the contents from the box onto a vinyl album cover, purple. He shakes the cover so that the tiny seeds go tumbling back into the box. He transfers the dry leaves carefully into his hand, drops the album cover between them on the bed and gathers the leaves, gently, into a neat line in his cupped palm. Then, in a deft movement, he transfers them from his hand to a blade of thin white paper, which he rolls and licks and lights.

Kagiso picks up the album cover while he thinks of something to say. On it, a pyramid refracts a single beam of white light into a rainbow of colour. "Nice cover," he says, laying it down.

Brilliant album. Want to hear it?

"Yeah, okay."

Here, hold this. Issa gives him the joint, takes the vinyl record from the sleeve and walks over to the turntable.

Kagiso holds the joint in his hand, its thick, pungent smoke, swirling in front of him like a charmer's snake.

Issa turns around and, with outstretched arms, starts to sing to him:

Breathe, breathe in the air
Don't be afraid to care
Leave but don't leave me
Look around and choose your own ground
For long you live and high you fly
And smiles you'll give and tears you'll cry
And all you'll touch and all you'll see
Is all your life will ever be

Issa flops back onto the bed. Before handing him back the joint, Kagiso brings it to his lips and inhales.

The Last Night

KATINKA IS IN BAGHDAD CAFÉ, drinking mint tea, smoking shisha. She has driven here from Heathrow, taking the M4 back into central London, driving against the flight path on her right, a queue of planes waiting to land hangs for miles into the distance. On the dreaded elevated section of the motorway, as she approached the top of the steeple, the bulk of the church out of view below, she tightened her grip on the wheel and divided her concentration between the stream of traffic in front and behind, the lorry passing on her right, the steeple-marked edge on her left; whenever she hears the expression 'going over the edge', it is this short, congested strip of elevated motorway that always come to mind. When the traffic came to a halt with the approach to the Hogarth Roundabout, she released her grip, stretched her fingers and lit a cigarette. She continued east along the Great West Road, through Hammersmith, Kensington, Knightsbridge. At Hyde Park Corner, she turned left and headed up Park Lane towards Marble Arch. That was when she heard the boisterous singing coming from Hyde Park:

...The nations not so blest as thee,
Shall in their turns to tyrants fall;
While thou shalt flourish great and free,
The dread and envy of them all...

She can't think of a time when she didn't know the anthem; like *Die Stem*, it has been there all her life, all her history, relishing exclusion, celebrating subjugation. The tune sparks tangential, flash-by memories; a dislike of it and a continued reverence, a persistent tenderness, for a little corner of her past which she cannot – despite the protestation, the spurning and the never-to-return walking away – bring herself to surrender:

At school, she loathed excursions, which always included long, solemn visits to national monuments around the country –

Die Taalmonument (the world's only monument to a language) in Paarl, Die Vroue Monument in Bloemfontein, Die Voortrekker Monument in Pretoria, Die Groote Kerk in Cape Town. She'd feigned sickness whenever one of them loomed, or deliberately ambled to school so that she would miss the bus.

Except when the opportunity arose of a trip to Kimberley. She had just read *The Diary of Anne Frank* and tagged along as they visited the Mine Museum – "This is the biggest man-made hole on earth. Work here ceased on 14 August 1914, by which time 22,5 tons of excavated earth had yielded just 2 722 kilograms of diamonds" – Magersfontein – "It was in this battle that trenches were first used in modern warfare" – the McGregor Museum – "this grand building was once the residence of Cecil John Rhodes."

But it was at the nondescript site on Long Street, in front of the big church, that she took up her place in the front row, the Diary tightly clutched in her hand. "This is the site of the first concentration camp on earth, designed by Lord Kitchener for the imprisonment of Boer women and children during the Anglo-Boer War, the first war of the 20th century, the first modern war. A total of 26 000 women and children died in these camps. In the single month of October 1901, when the camps held 113 606 people, there were 3 156 deaths. Let's have a minute's silence to remember their sacrifice."

"Is that it?" she wanted to call out as they boarded the bus. "Come back! This place is not just about your tribe and the cruel indignity it suffered at the hands of the British. It's not just about the hundreds of black people who, by the way, also died in the camps.

"It's about the world, because on this spot, on this very spot, the British initiated a system of incarceration which, fifty years later, would be refined with deadly efficiency on the other side of the world – a system of extermination in which ultimately millions would be led to their gasping gassy deaths and for which this site, this very spot, provided the blueprint, the prototype, the inspiration.

"Don't you see?" she wanted to plead, "Our people, the 'Volk', weren't the *only* victims here, they were *only* the first."

⁂

'... To thee belongs the rural reign;
Thy cities shall with commerce shine;
All thine shall be the subject main,
And every shore it circles thine...'

Frances mutters her usual irritation as she always does at this point. It annoys her that so many reasonable people will sing along, flushing proudly, without any sense of irony or reflection, teaching their children to sing along too. Not just the blatantly supremacist, but ordinary, likeable people, informed people, liberal people. Catholics.

"But there have to be limits, Frances," Father Jerome once insisted. "Countries have to set limits on the number of immigrants they can accept, otherwise they'd lose their national character."

What was the use, Frances thought, of countering the priest? He had orthodoxy on his side. But she persisted: "And what about this country's national character, Father. Was it lost when you and your order came here from France, or me from Ireland?"

"Have you ever thought, Father, about what would happen if the anti-immigration bigots had their way? For instance, would the Holy Family be given asylum in Britain now on the evidence of Joseph's bad dream?"

The priest shut himself off with arms folded tightly across his chest.

"I'll tell you what would happen, Father. Next, it would be the Catholics, the Jews, the –"

"Well that's just absurd," the priest spluttered.

"Is it, Father? Is it really? I've been around long enough to know that there is no end to their malice. The more you pander, the more they'll take. With the blacks out of the way, we'll be next, Father – you," she said, pointing a finger at the priest, before turning it on herself, "and I. Once again, we'll be at the bottom of the pile. Remember what that was like, Father?"

ꕥ

When she decided on this route, Katinka had forgotten that this year, for the first time, the last concert of the season is being relayed to Hyde Park from the Royal Albert Hall up the road. This anthem means it must be nearing its end. She doesn't want to get caught up in the flag-waving crowd when it leaves the park, so she increases her speed up Park Lane.

'… Thee haughty tyrants ne'er shall tame,
All their attempts to bend thee down
Will but arouse thy generous flame;
But work their woe, and thy renown…'

She recalls the moment when the old flag came down on the old country – to her, a sublime, 'at last' moment, everybody suspended between the eternity that had passed and promise of what was yet to come. She looked at the expectant faces around her, unknown faces in a sea of faces that had gathered on the Grand Parade, the very spot where once a castle, without consultation, had been built. Three hundred and forty-two years, she counted, finally draw to a close – wrong years, dark years, evil years, driven by the philosophy behind songs like these, all of them now, finally, behind. She felt the uniformed, straight lined, saluting little girl she once was step out of line, throw off her badges and run towards this stateless moment: no flag to wave, no anthem to echo, no eternal enemy against which to perpetually defend, no God-chosen nation for which to die in gory glory. She looked up at the empty flagpole, the muted brass band, not wanting the stateless moment to end. If she had to spend an eternity anywhere, it would be right here, now, in this moment.

In the park, the bellicose crowd has started the final verse. Katinka turns up the volume on her stereo to try and shut out the sound: 'So here's a toast to all the folks that live in Palestine, Afghanistan, Iraq, El Salvador / Here's a toast to all the folks living on the Pine Ridge Reservation under the stone cold gaze of Mount Rushmore…'

But her sound system cannot compete with the patriots now in full swing. Even when she has rolled up the windows, she can still hear the final chorus:

'Rule, Britannia! Britannia, rules – '

Frances switches off the TV. The flags, she thinks, seem to grow more numerous every year, the singing more triumphalist. And this year, after everything that has happened. She shakes her head. The arrogance of it all, the hankering. The embarrassing self-deception.

She steps out into the night and settles into the driver's seat. Not many more of these remain, she thinks. At this time of year, she always believes that the summer will linger. It is still too much in evidence – the trees are green, the beer garden in the pub downstairs is still in use, there is laughter in the street – to imagine that in only a few weeks, everything will have changed: the evenings will start to draw in, the leaves will turn, the clocks will go back, initiating the long, dark winter months when the streets will be filled with the soulless trudge of coated bodies and booted feet. The thought makes her shudder and she quickly tries to un-think it.

She looks up to the sky. It is a clear night.

'And dost thou not see that the stars in the heavens are without number, and yet none of them but the sun and the moon are subject to eclipse.'

It doesn't take her very long to locate the North Star. She's been practising with the help of the book Kagiso gave her. She can identify all the main constellations and, just to the right of the North Star and slightly above, the location of a new comer. She cannot see it, but she knows it's there. She has even given it a name.

It did, of course, end – the sublime, stateless moment. When the new flag was raised and the new anthem sung and thousands, millions, cheered, Katinka wiped away a tear; the moment had ended. By the time the new flag reached the top of the flagpole (where the interim quickly – just one patriotic puff, one nationalistic sniff – became the addictively permanent) the endless, limitless, possibilities of the stateless moment had already been diminished.

ꕥ

The waiter delivers another pot of mint tea to her table, while the sabby with his basket of coal diligently stokes her pipe, first scraping away the burnt-out embers then replacing them with five glowing coals arranged neatly in a circle on the tobacco.

"Shukran," she says.

"You speak Arabic?"

"No," she says, not wanting conversation.

"How you know this word?"

"We're all Arabs now," she says.

"Pardon?"

"Nothing," she waves. "Just something a friend once said. We're all Arabs now," before obscuring her face with a cloud of thick, fragrant smoke.

Closed Chapters

> 'My appeal is ultimately directed to us all, black and white together, to close the chapter on our past and to strive together for this beautiful and blessed land as the rainbow people of God.'
>
> *Archbishop Desmond Tutu*

'WE'VE GOT STARS DIRECTING OUR FATE.' The song prompts a name – Robbie – that wakes him. The sky is changing, a familiar African dawn nudging at the horizon, the red trail of their flight path lengthening: DRC / Angola / Botswana... Home isn't far away. In the half-light, Kagiso starts to feel his way carefully around the past, like a blind man identifying a corpse.

The date comes to him; 22 July 1989. His nineteenth birthday. The day Issa broke his leg. And a few days later, made the courtesy call (intended, Kagiso now speculates, to throw him off the scent). Then disappeared for weeks. Turning them into strangers.

But there was another name, Kagiso thinks. Robbie and... Candice? No.

In December, at the end of another academic year, they set off once again on the long drive from Cape Town to Johannesburg. He recalls following the route on a map, tracing its path from its starting point at the foot of Table Mountain, as far as he could, to Alexandria.

Memory house of the world.

Cathy? No.

Now the monitor in front of him traces the red path of their journey from London across the English Channel to France then Spain and across the Mediterranean to Algeria then Niger / Nigeria / Cameroon / DRC / Angola / Botswana / then South Africa.

To celebrate his birthday that year, he'd been out with Richard and Sophie and the other bright young things from upper campus.

The past grudgingly yields the other name – Coline!

He removes his earphones and retrieves his satchel from the overhead compartment.

Issa had refused to send the volumes by post or even to check them in when he flew to London. He had insisted on carrying them in his hand luggage. Kagiso, his shoulders aching under the weight of the five cumbersome, heavy volumes, had felt obliged to accord them their owner's respect.

He turns on his overhead reading light.

> **Resurgence of public protest:**
> **the Defiance Campaign, 1989**
> **130** After the 1986 declaration of the state of emergency, the Peninsula experienced only isolated clashes between protestors and security forces. Of particular note were the large high-profile burials of MK operatives such as the 'Gugulethu Seven', Mr Ashley Kriel, Mr Robert Waterwitch and Ms Coline Williams.

Cape Town burned.

'We will not forget?'

'Steve Biko!'

'Long live?'

'Nelson Mandela, long live!'

'We Shall Overcome!'

'Liberation before?'

'Education!'

'The People Shall?'

'Govern!'

'We will not forget?'

'Matthew Goniwe!'

'We will not forget?'

'Hector Pieterson!'

'Viva?'

'Oliver Tambo, viva!'

'Long live?'
'Govan Mbeki, long live!'
'We will not forget?'
'Ashley Kriel!'
'We will not forget?'
'Robert Waterwitch!'
'We will not forget?'
'Coline Williams!'
'Amandla!'
'Awethu!'
'Senzenina...'

> The Kriel funeral in 1987, attended by thousands of mourners, was marked by uproar as police failed to stick to undertakings not to interfere in the event. Major Dolf Odendal marched into the funeral procession and attempted to seize the ANC flag off Kriel's coffin. With such incidents sustaining the political tension, the Peninsula took the lead in spearheading public protest, defiance actions and mass action in 1989.

The celebrations had started with a bottle of champagne at Rhodes 'Mem' – Sophie's choice. "Will Izzy be joining us?" she asked.

"Maybe later," Kagiso said, not knowing how he would negotiate the ancient hostilities between Issa and Richard.

"Isn't this just lovely?" Sophie said, exhaling admiringly over the view, before passing the joint to Kagiso. "Happy Birthday, Kaggy," she said when he took it, and kissed him cheek to cheek.

131 The Defiance Campaign against apartheid laws was launched as a national initiative by the Mass Democratic Movement (MDM), but the Western Cape was to play a leading role. By March 1989, protest actions resulting in arrests had begun in Cape Town. There followed a proliferation of defiance activities targeting a range of apartheid laws, peaking in opposition to the 'whites-only' election of 6 September 1989.

From Rhodes Memorial they drove to Sea Point, taking the longer scenic route along De Waal Drive, up over Kloof Nek, then down to Camps Bay and along the coast to the Hard Rock Café, spectacularly located on a rocky outcrop in the sea, waves crashing all around.

"The *Constantia*, please," Richard said emphatically when the waiter came to take their order and then, as soon as the waiter had turned, finished his sentence, "What else?"

Now, his glass is raised in his hand. "Looks like Shamsuddin's running late. Probably out saving the world."

"So that we can enjoy it! Ha ha ha."

"May as well get started then. Cheers! And *Happy Birthday.*"

"Yes. Happy Birthday, Kaggy. Cheers."

Throughout dinner, Kagiso kept an expectant eye on the door.

132 On 6 August 1989, sixteen restricted activists announced their defiance of their restriction orders at an Athlone church service, sparking off a cycle of arrests and continued defiance. On 8 August, defiance rallies were held at schools and campuses in the Peninsula, and the United Democratic Front was declared 'unbanned' by a mass meeting in St George's Cathedral followed by a march under banners of banned organisations. On 12 August, restricted activists

> again publicly defied their restriction orders at a National Women's Day rally in Hanover Park, which was then teargassed. Many were detained under the emergency regulations.

As they were leaving the restaurant, Sophie pointed at a sign above the door which read: 'Ssh. People sleep out there.' "Cute," she said, and lifted her leg like Marilyn Monroe.

They walked down to the rocks where they smoked another joint. Kagiso positioned himself with a view of the parking lot.

"Have you guys heard this one?" Richard started when he'd passed on the joint. "There was once a colony of ants whose ant heaps were being repeatedly stamped into the ground by a herd of elephants.

"One day, a feisty little ant, Pietie, decided that enough was enough, so he called a mass meeting to rally the ants into opposition.

"He jumped onto an ant heap and made a fiery speech about David and Goliath and strong chains with weak links. When he finished, the ants cheered and shouted, 'Viva Pietie! Viva Pietie!'

"And then they heard the rumble of the elephants approaching...

"The ants scattered to hide behind ant heaps and trees.

"Only Pietie stood his ground. When the leader of the elephants stepped forward flapping his ears angrily, Pietie started marching towards him.

'Go Pietie, go!' the other ants shouted. 'Go Pietie, go!'

"When Pietie got to the elephant's foot, he jumped up and started climbing up the elephants front leg.

"The ants were beside themselves: 'Go Pietie go! Go Pietie go!' they chanted.

"Pietie marched up and up and up. 'Go Pietie, go. Go, Pietie go!'

"When Pietie got to the elephant's neck he stopped to consider his next move. He turned to look to the ants for advice.

"You know what the ants shouted?

They shake their heads.

"Choke him, Pietie! Pietie, choke him!"

"Isn't this just lovely?" Sophie sighed when they had caught their breath and wiped away their tears of hilarity.

> **133** On 19 August, thousands of people set off to defy 'whites only' beaches at Strand and Bloubergstrand in a high-profile act of "beach apartheid defiance'. Some groups were shot at with birdshot, others were *sjambokked*. There were multiple public protests in the following weeks. On 23 August church leaders, including Archbishop Desmond Tutu, were teargassed on a march in Guguletu, and a week later 170 women were arrested while kneeling during a women's mass march in town. In a climax of the defiance campaign, thousands of protestors participated in a three-pronged march to Parliament on 2 September. The march was dispersed with batons and a water canon loaded with purple dye, and more than 500 people were arrested. Altogether, over 1 000 people were arrested during these activities.

Then they drove to a club that played Richard's favourite music: Duran Duran, Orchestral Manoeuvres in the Dark, Sting. They danced in a circle, showering Kagiso with visible displays of liberal affection, and screeched with delight when the DJ played 'Englishman in New York'. Kagiso glanced at his watch.

> **Election day, 6 September 1989**
>
> **134** Election day itself saw an explosion of resistance and police repression in which at least 23 people were killed and hundreds injured. Statements were received regarding the following fatalities: Ms Liziwe Masokanye (23), Stellenbosch [CT00829]; Mr Patrick

> Muller (13), Bellville South [CT00322]; Mr Joseph Michael Makoma (25), Kalksteenfontein [CT00300]; Mr Leonard Rass (13), Kleinvlei [CT00637]; Mr Pedro Page (18), Grassy Park [CT00416]; Mr Ricardo Levy (11), Kalksteenfontein [CT00313]; Ms Yvette Otto (16), pregnant [CT00300]; Ms Elsie Chemfene [CT008605]; Mr Thembinkosi Tekana, Khayelitsha [CT01535] and Mr Lubalo Mtirara (20), Khayelitsha [CT00217].

When the song finished, Kagiso stepped out of the circle.

"You can't go yet, Kaggy!"

"I'm going to check on Issa."

"No, Kaggy. I refuse to let you go." She threw her arms around him.

When she stepped back, he smiled. "Really, I should go and say hello."

"But it's your birthday. He should come to you. Besides, how will you get there at this time of night?"

"I'll get a taxi from Mowbray."

"At this time of night! Are you mad?"

Kagiso starts to move around the crowd of bright young things, slapping shoulders, saying thank you.

"Richard will drive you, won't you Richard?"

Richard doesn't respond.

"Really, that's not necessary."

"No. It's decided. We'll all go."

> **135** The public horror at the extent of the violence reached into sectors of the western Cape not previously drawn into oppositional activity. This sense of outrage culminated in one of the largest mass marches ever seen in the Western Cape on 13 September, the so-called 'Peace March'. The march, led by a range

of religious, community and political leaders including the mayor and members of the city council, brought Cape Town to a standstill.

They chase down the N2 bound for UWC: smoke, music and laughter.

"Isn't this an adventure? I've never been to UWC. I can't wait to tell the others about it tomorrow! Is Issa still such a hunk? I haven't seen him since we left school."

Richard turns up the music. Somebody passes around another joint. Kagiso declines.

The river of blood has run its course. Kagiso traces its red route on the tiny monitor in front of him with a slender finger, 9 074km from London, across France and the Mediterranean, then over Algeria / Chad / Niger / DRC / Angola / Botswana / South Africa.

"Ladies and gentlemen, we have started our descent for Johannesburg International Airport. In preparation for the landing, please make sure that your seats are in the upright position and your seatbelts fastened, that your tray tables are folded away and that your hand luggage has been safely stowed."

> **136** Simultaneously, a senior policeman 'broke ranks' and publicly criticised the actions of the police. Lieutenant Gregory Rockman described police action in his area, Mitchell's Plain, as "brutal", saying that the riot squad had "stormed the kids like wild dogs. You can see the killer instinct in their eyes". The SAP was forced to initiate an inquiry into the behaviour of the Riot Squad in these incidents as well as the election night violence.

"Thank you *very* much," Kagiso says when Richard stops the car outside Issa's hostel. He squeezes through a knot of legs and limbs on the back seat and opens the door.

"Who is Ruth First?" somebody asks.

"She was Joe Slovo's wife," Kagiso replies.

"Didn't know he was married."

"She's dead. Killed. Blown apart by a letter bomb in Mozambique."

"Oh. What a morbid name to give a residence."

Kagiso shuts the door.

"Wait! I want to say hello to Izzy. Wait for me, Kaggy! Come Richy."

Richard follows, exasperated.

Kagiso knocks nervously on Issa's door. Sophie taps her toes. "Ooohh!"

"Yes?" a voice calls from inside the room.

"It's Kagiso."

"Who?"

"Kagiso."

"What do you want?"

"Is Issa there?"

Returning to the report, Kagiso reads the date; Sunday 23rd July, the day after his 18th birthday, the day after Issa broke his leg... The words on the page add to his growing sense of unease and he wants to shrink away from the emerging realisation.

> Four limpet mine attacks in the Peninsula were planned for the evening of Sunday 23 July 1989 as part of an anti-election bombing campaign by MK. Magistrate's courts were targeted as they were to be used for election nominations the following day. Mines exploded at a police station in Mitchells Plain and at Somerset West magistrate's court. At the Bellville magistrate's court security forces intervened to prevent the blast.

Issa steps out into the corridor through a door which closes behind him.

"Ooohh, such a long time, Izzy!" Sophie shouts, before throwing her arms around him. "So nice to see you again. And even more handsome now." She turns to Richard. "Say hello, Richy."

Richard nods awkwardly: "Shamsuddin."

Issa reciprocates: *McKenna*, and then turns to Kagiso. *Hey. Happy Birthday you.* He taps him on the back.

Kagiso beams. "Thank you."

Issa starts leading them down the corridor, away from his room. *Sorry I couldn't make it. You have a good time?*

"Yes. Very nice."

Sophie squeezes herself between the two of them. "We missed you, Izzy. You should have come. We had such fun, didn't we Kaggy?"

Kagiso nods.

"We went to Rhodes Mem and then the Hard Rock in Sea Point and then – Oops!" She stumbles on the first step of the staircase.

Issa, who has been watching with attentive disinterest, reaches out to stop her fall but loses his own footing and is unable to counterbalance her drunken flailing.

Sophie lands astride Issa at the bottom of the stairs. "Ooohh, Izzy," she says sitting up, her head in a spin, "Is this a dream or am I really –" Richard pulls her off Issa. "Oh, Richy," she exclaims, dangling loosely off his shoulder, "you're such a spoilsport."

Kagiso bends down to pick Issa up.

But Issa stops him. *I think,* he groans, straining to look at his twisted leg. *I think my leg is broken.*

Fuck!

"Ek sê my bra, it's kak timing for sure, ek sê," Issa's friend says, shaking his hand reassuringly when the paramedics load him into the back of the ambulance, "but Mr B will go with them."

I told you. Issa protested, banging his hand on the stretcher. *I don't trust that guy.*

"Who, Mr *B*?"

His friend sucks his teeth. "Don't you stress about Mr B. He's ntszaa, ek sê."

You tell them to watch out for him.

"Shap."

And tell them I'll see them soon, for sure.

Kagiso squeezed into the back of the ambulance and crouched apologetically next to Issa. The paramedics shut the doors and the ambulance drove away.

"Issa, I'm sorry."

Sorry. Issa snorted. *You're sorry? You have no idea how – Anyway, what the fuck were you doing bringing those stupid fucking naaiers to my room?*

Kagiso tried to explain but Issa turned his head to look away.

His leg was badly broken. Struggling against the anaesthetic, he muttered the two names which tonight have woken Kagiso from his somewhere and nowhere, black velvet sleep.

> The fourth mine, intended for the Athlone magistrate's court, detonated behind public toilets opposite the court. The bodies of MK operatives and youth activists Ms Coline Williams (22) and Mr Robert Waterwich of the Ashley Kriel unit were found at the scene.

Kagiso feels trapped. His palms leave a wet smudge when he rubs them on his trousers. Nausea starts to turn his stomach.

> Subsequent inquests found that they had died as a result of an explosion. While initial impressions suggested that the operation had simply gone awry, a number of questions have remained concerning the circumstances of their deaths. Suspicions existed that the explosives had been 'zero timed' for immediate detonation.

The steward won't allow him to go to the toilet. "Sir, we're coming in to land."

In desperation, Kagiso grabs the bag from the seat pocket in front him as the aircraft strikes the runway with an unnerving high-speed jolt.

"Ladies and gentlemen, welcome to Johannesburg International Airport. Please remain seated until the aircraft has come to a complete stop. We trust that you've enjoyed your flight with us. On behalf of the captain and all the crew, we wish you a pleasant stay and look forward to seeing you again in the future. Thank you for flying South African Airways and goodbye."

'The summer is over, Theresa'

LIKE STATELESS MOMENTS, summer, in the end, never lingers either. Huddled in her armchair, Frances hears the stacking and the carrying away of furniture from the beer garden, the taking down of floral hanging baskets, the shutting and the locking of the garden gate. She finds herself humming that autumnal tune which it feels like only she still remembers: 'The summer is over, Theresa.'

One day, while stooping to turn on the gas fire, she looses her balance: crack, snap, crash. When she eventually comes round, she does not know how long she's been lying there in the numbing cold. She bangs on the floor but perhaps her banging is too feeble, perhaps the music downstairs too loud. Whatever it is, her new neighbour does not respond. Exhausted, she gives up. What else to do now, Frances, but lie and wait?

Suddenly, she is gripped by fear: Wait – but for whom, Frances? Then she starts to hear sounds, little taunting sounds: bumps on the roof, taps on the window, scratches on the door. And she starts to see things: the porcelain doll on the mantelpiece – it grimaced, she is sure. On the carpet, depressions, like footprints in sand, except more like claws, pace, slowly, up and down. Sometimes they come to stand by her head and she can feel the air change and a putrid smell descend and wrap itself around her, like a shroud. Sometimes the depressions move over to her armchair and she can hear the chair creak, and see the cushions sink in. She reaches slowly into her pocket but her pocket is empty. Then her armchair creaks and again the claws cross the room and come to stand by her head. And then she hears the words, but not in her ears, in her nose, she smells their meaning in her nose, in the putrid smell when it descends: They're on your smoking table. Frances closes her eyes. There are no on-holiday relatives. I lie and wait, for nobody...

One dark afternoon, she confides in the young lady from Church who has been visiting her regularly since her fall. She can only manage a slow murmur now and her visitor has to lean over her to hear her. "In this envelope," she gestures limply towards her bedside table, "are the details of his star."

The young woman nods, turning her head slightly to read the careful, old-fashioned writing on the envelope:

To:

Professor V Kumar

Frances stares into a faraway place beyond the ceiling: "I wrote my will across the sky in stars." Her sunken eyes turn slowly in their sockets. "Can you please send it recorded delivery?"

"Of course," her companion smiles, reassuringly.

Frances nods in gratitude. "The money is in the little pot beside."

Father Jerome arrives with his portable altar in the middle of the night. Frances watches him unpack the last rites from his bag, then drape a purple stole around his neck. She squeezes the young lady's hand beckoningly: "I want this with me, like this," she requests, then clutches the red satin pouch and folds her hands across her chest.

"Behold the angel said:
O Mary! God hath chosen thee
And purified thee – chosen thee
Above the women of all nations.
And she conceived of the Holy Spirit
Hail Mary,
Full of grace,
The Lord is with thee
Blessed art thou amongst women
And blessed is the fruit of thy womb,
Jesus."

Katinka's Text Message

WHEN SHE HAS BEEN THERE A WHILE, Katinka writes to Kagiso.

Katinka Du Plessis

Subject: Elke liewe dag

Date: Friday August 6 2004

From: katinka@thewall.com

To: kagiso@mayoyo.net

... And I've never felt as many emotions in one day, as I have here. Every night I try to count them, but I always fall asleep before I'm through. Sunrise over these ancient hills is simply breathtaking. Crushing too; nothing here is simple.

Because I live in the shadow of The Wall, I have to get up early and walk far if I want to see it; even sunrise is denied, and the beauty of daybreak is filled with the promise of further oppression.

But spirits lift like the mist and throughout the day there is the infectious joy of the children and in everybody a willingness to laugh. Remember the irony of the townships? How they were also the happiest places you could visit? Have you heard this one?

A young man in Jenin finds a lamp in the ruins at Ground Zero. He takes the lamp to his cramped room in his in-laws' house. When he is eventually alone, he rubs the lamp. A grumpy genie appears:

"What do you want?" the genie barks.

The man is surprised. This is not how a genie is supposed to behave. But he continues with his request all the same. "Please, genie," he begs. "First, I would like a flat for my wife and my children. Then," he takes a deep breath before rattling off the rest of his wishes, "I would like –"

"Stop just there," the genie interrupts. "I'm afraid I can't help you."

The man shakes his head. "But you're a genie!" He exclaims.

"Now listen here," the genie says, irritated. "If I could find a flat in Jenin, or anywhere else on the West bank, do you really think I would be living in this poxy lamp?"

I've been reminded of why I became a teacher – to teach, not fill out forms. I have rediscovered the joy of the classroom. I earn very little, but the strength of mind, the will to succeed in kids who have to travel for hours around The Wall to get to school (and who can draw helicopter gun-ships with their eyes closed) makes me rich.

The small things: the comfort in routine, the distress when, at a whim, it is disrupted. The calm solitude of a walk in the hills, the nostalgic melancholy in a landscape in parts indistinguishable from the Karoo.

Death is everywhere; every day an anniversary, every day a future one assured. Despair is a sitting tenant.

Last month our neighbour went into labour while waiting at a checkpoint. Still, the soldiers wouldn't let her through. The baby, a girl, died with her mother by the roadside.

The crime? To go into labour in a queue.

The punishment? Death.

I teach the dead woman's daughter. She's ten. The hot chill when I found a picture of Wafa Idris in her exercise book the other day.

The joy of a new life. My sister-in-law had a baby girl last week. They've named her Kulsoum, after our neighbour; the dead in the living, the old in the new, the past in the present.

The present in the future? Most probably. The sinking feeling that today will be like yesterday, and tomorrow will be like today. There is a refugee camp four stories high. It's not allowed to expand outward, so it rises into the sky: four stories, four generations, four decades.

The phenomenal hospitality. The humility that comes with being made the guest of honour at a meal where the family can barely afford to feed themselves. Poor here (tap your pocket). Rich here (tap your heart). How often the converse is true in England.

The inescapable helplessness. Go find an eight-metre high wall. Walk up to it. Stand next to it. Imagine it stretching on and on, for 710 kilometres – longer than the length of our first shared journey through the Karoo all those Februarys ago. It will make you feel diminished.

The sheer determination. Remember, 'Ons dak nie. Ons polla hier!'? The absolute refusal to give up. I'm attaching a photograph of a piece of graffiti on the wall not far from our house:

كشجرة الزيتون كنا هنا قبل ان ينبني هذا الحائط.
وكشجرة الزيتون سنبقى هناحتى يسقط الحائط.

It reads: like the olive tree, we were here before this went up. Like the olive tree, we'll be here when it comes down. 'Ons polla hier!'

The poetry of the language:
Good morning! It's the morning of light!
Response. It's the morning of roses.
The etiquette. The manners.
It's not trendy to be rude.

All the time the frustration that, every day, the world chooses to buy the propaganda, the misinformation, the lies, the crude racism, the blatant stereotypes. Every day, the world watches the horror here that it so readily and continuously and honourably challenged and disputed back home. Why? Because? Oh really! Is that so? Well then, why don't you come here for a day? Just one day and then tell me again.

And amidst it all, after all the years of searching in unlikely places, there is the contentment of being at home, in the most unlikely place. Yes. Loved – and at home.

So, Mr 'Best Documentary Film Maker 2004', when you've lapped up the praise and feel ready for your next assignment, why not bring your cameras here? But be warned. It's far more horrendous than anything you've seen in the homelands…

ঌ

One day, Katinka is reminded of something Issa wrote. At the time she thought it might be overstated, but he wouldn't change it. Now she thinks he was right and sends a text message to his mobile number, as she still does from time to time:

> Im by da wal@qalqilia. Wen jan landd @cape he plantd a hedj 2 sepr8 setlaz frm locls. Da histry of erly urpean setlmnt @da cape is unversly&eternly pertnt x

Acknowledgements

Black and White
The lyrics 'We don't need no education' are from the song Another Brick in the Wall (Part 2), by Pink Floyd on the album *The Wall*, EMI, 1979.

The Summer of 2003
'London ceases to be London,' is from Virginia Woolf's, *The London Scene*, Snowbooks, 2004.
'Summertime' is by Irvin Berlin, performed by Nina Simone, Mastersong, 2004.
The lyrics 'We're lovin' it', are from the song Do You Really Like It? by DJ Pied Piper, Ministry, 2000.

Homelands
The term 'Imaginary Homelands', is from Salman Rushdie, *Imaginary Homelands: Essays & Criticism, 1981-1991*, Penguin Books/Granta, 1992.

Disappeared
Kagiso looks up the words 'disappear' and 'disappearance' in the *Oxford English Dictionary.*

The Karoo
'Freedom is taken, never given', is by Salman Rushdie, in defence of *Satanic Verses.*
The Song 'Summer Holiday' was written by Bruce Welch and Roy Bennett (1962) and preformed by Cliff Richard & The Shadows, on the album *Summer Holiday*, 1963, re-released by EMI in 2001.
The dialogue between Bentley and Lawrence and Issa's response that "the desert is an ocean in which no oar is dipped" are from the Sam Spiegel David Lean production of "Lawrence of Arabia", Columbia Pictures, 1962.
Issa recalls an extract from TE Lawrence's *Seven Pillars of Wisdom*, The complete 1922 text, Castle Hill Press, 2003.

Violent Night
'I am a standing civil war', is by TE Lawrence. See also 'A Standing Civil War', Edward Said, *Reflection on Exile and Other Essays,* Harvard University Press, 2000.

Man's Most Dangerous Myth: The Fallacy of Race, is by Ashley Montagu, Columbia University Press, New York, 1942.

"I Just Don't Give a –"

Transcript for Talking Point is from www.bbc.co.uk/ talkingpoint.

The song, which Issa listens to is Eminem's, 'Just Don't Give a Fuck', *The Slim Shady*, Interscope, 1999.

'A road map into our past.'

Quotations are from the transcripts of the South African Truth and Reconciliation Commission (TRC) set up by the Government of National Unity to help deal with the violence and human rights abuses that took place under apartheid.

The poem scribbled on a rolled-up travel card is by Satish Gupta.

Kagiso reads from Dorothee Metlitzk's *The Matter of Araby in Medieval England*, Yale University Press, 1977:7.

Issa's note to Frances refers to an extract from Dorothee Metlitzki's *The Matter of Araby in Medieval England*, 1977: 111 – 112.

The self-censored front page stuck in Kagiso's journal is from *The Weekly Mail* of Friday June 20 to Thursday June 26, 1986.

The Monster's Name

Katinka Reads from TE Lawrence's *Seven Pillars of Wisdom, op cit.*

The Sanctuary

The extract in Kagiso's journal is from the archives of the Black Sash as quoted in Francis Wilson & Mamphela Ramphele *Uprooting Poverty: The South African challenge*, David Philip, 1989: 211.
Blind Alfredo's story is from Giuseppe Tornatore's *Cinema Paradiso*, Italy, 1988.

'Remembering games and daisy chains and laughs / Got to keep the loonies on the path' is from Pink Floyd's song 'Brain damage' on the album *The Dark Side of the Moon*, originally released in 1973, re-released by EMI Records Ltd, 2003.

Russell Square

"If there is war with Iraq, there's already been the first casualty – art." Peter Goddard, *The Toronto Star.*

The extract which Issa reads to Katinka is from Edward Said, 'Arabic Prose and Fiction After 1948', in *Reflections on Exile: and Other Literary and Cultural Essays*, Granta, 2001.

The Verses
Quotations in the raw archival footage of the roadside executions in Bophuthatswana are as quoted in *The Star*, March 12-13, 1994.

Kagiso reads Issa's annotations in Salman Rushdie's *The Satanic Verses*, Viking Penguin Inc., New York, 1988.

Missing Persons
Information in the leaflet, which Vasinthe gives Katinka to read, is from the National Missing Persons Helpline, registered charity No. 1020419.

The song in Katinka's dream is Sting's 'They Dance Alone', from the album *Fields of Gold: The Best of Sting 1984 – 1994*, A&M Records, 1994.

Vasinthe's Letter
Issa's words to Kagiso, "The trick, William Potter, is not minding that it hurts," are from the Sam Spiegel David Lean production of *Lawrence of Arabia*, Columbia Pictures, 1962.

Another Brick in Another Wall
The rap which Karim imitates is from Eminem's, 'Rock Bottom', *The Slim Shady*, Interscope, 1999.
The line which Katinka quotes in her promise to Karim is an extract from Hafiz embroidered in the Arbadil Carpet on display in the Islamic Gallery at the Victoria and Albert Museum, London.

'Everytime we say goodbye' is by Nina Simone, *The Best of Nina Simone – the Colpix Years*, Blue Note Records, 1993.
The story Katinka overhears on the train is from the film *Mughal-E-Azam*, directed by K. Asif, India 1960.

Baghdad Café
Issa's text message to Katinka includes a quote from TE Lawrence's *The Seven Pillars of Wisdom* and an instruction to read Michael Ondaatje's *Anil's Ghost.*

Vasinthe & Gloria
'Ha, banishment? Be merciful, say 'death'
For exile hath more terror in his
Look, much more than death.
Do not say banishment.' William Shakespeare; *Romeo & Juliet* 3·3·12–14

'Inglan is a bitch,' was a rap song written by Linton Kwesi Johnson in 1980.

Somewhere & Nowhere
The book in Kagiso's lap is Rohinton Mistry's; *A Fine Balance*, London, Faber and Faber, 1995.
All song lyrics in this chapter are by Pink Floyd.

The Last Night
'Rule Brittania' is by James Thomson, set to music by Thomas Augustine Arne in 1740.

Statistics of fatalities in the British Concentration Camps are from John Fisher's *The Afrikaners*, London, Cassell, 1969: 181.

The song on Katinka's stereo is 'Self Evident' by Ani Di Franco, from the album *So Much Shouting, So Much Laughter*, Righteous Babe Records, 2002.

'And dost thou not see that the stars in the heavens are without number...', as quoted in Dorothee Metlitzki's *The Matter of Araby in Medieval England*, Yale University Press, 1977: 16.

Frances' thought, 'I wrote my will across the sky in stars', is from Lawrence's dedication in *Seven Pillars of Wisdom*.

A later chapter entitled 'The Muslim Prisoner.'

Closed Chapters
'We've got stars directing our fate,' is from the song Millennium by Robbie Williams, on the album *I've Been Expecting You*, Chrysalis, 2002.

The Summer is Over, Theresa
Frances quotes from the Qur'an S.iii, 42.
The following works and sources were central to the writing of this book:

A critical biography of Shaykh Yusuf, Suleman Essop Dangor (Centre for Research in Islamic Studies University of Durban-Westville, 1982); *A history of South Africa*, Leonard Thompson (Yale University Press, 1995); *A History of South Africa*, Frank Welsh (Harper Collins, 2000); *BBC News*, *BBC World Service*, *BBC Online*; *Factfile: Five Hundred Years: A History of South Africa*, ed. CFJ Miller (Academica, 1984); *Frontiers*, Noël Mostert (Jonathan Cape, 1992); *Islam in South Africa: Mosques, Imams, and Sermons*, Abdulkader Tayob, (University Press of Florida, 1999); *Islands*, Dan Sleigh (Tafelberg, 2002); *Krotoa, called 'Eva': A Women Between*, VC Malherbe (1990); *Krotoa-Eva:*

The Woman from Robben Island, Trudie Bloem (Kwela Books, 1999); *Lawrence of Arabia*,
Sam Spiegel David & Lean, (Columbia Pictures, 1962); *Monuments of Syria: An Historical Guide*, Ross Burns (IB Tarus, 1992); *Palestine is still the issue*, John Pilger, 1977; *Reflections on Exile: and Other Literary and Cultural Essays*, Edward Said (Granta, 2001); *Seven Pillars of Wisdom*, TE Lawrence (Penguin Books, 1962); *South Africa: An Historical Introduction*, Freda Troup (Eyre Methuen, 1972); *Sowetan*, South Africa; *The Afrikaaners*, John Fisher, (Cassell, 1969); *The Holy Qur'an*, translated by Abdullah Yusuf Ali, (Islamic Propagation Centre International, 1946); *The Guardian*, UK; *The Guardian Year: 2003*, ed. Luke Dodd (Atlantic Books, 1985); *The Independent*, UK; *The National Missing Persons Helpline Factfile*, (NMPH, 2004); *The Matter of Araby in Medieval England*, Dorothee Metlitzki (Yale University Press, 1977); *The Mosques of Bo-Kaap: A Social History of Islam at the Cape*, Achmat Davids (The South African Institute of Arabic and Islamic Research, Athlone, 1980); *The Muslim Jesus: Sayings And Stories In Islamic Literature*, edited and translated by Tarif Khalidi (Harvard University Press, 2001); *The Palestinian People: a history*, Baruch Kimmerling & Joel S Migdal (Harvard University Press, 2003);
The Rough Guide: South Africa, Lesotho & Swaziland, (The Rough Guides, 1997); *The Star*, South Africa; *The Sunday Times*, South Africa; *The Truth and Reconciliation Commission Report of South Africa*, (Juta, 1998); *The Weekly Mail*, South Africa; *Uprooting Poverty: The South African challenge*; Francis Wilson & Mampele Rampele (David Philip, 1989).

Thanks

I would like to thank my teachers,
Pamela Nichols and William Radice,
researchers, Mbongisi Dyantyi and Gila Carter,
and readers, Munizha Ahmad, Colette Fearon,
Anne Harte, Rafiek Mammon and Shaun Viljoen.

I would also like to thank Cadi Fester,
Deborah Hooper, Barry Willis, Michael Chackal,
Zahra Mackouie, Jane Mitchell, Razzaq Moosajee,
Roya Shahr-Yazdi, Eric Stobbaerts,
Maureen Cantwell, Alan Fransman, Vikram Malhotra,
Somana Sachin, Andrew Cooke, Bridget Maclou and
Hassan Ramadan at Al Saqi Books, London.

My special thanks to everybody at the
National Missing Persons Helpline UK
(www.missingpersons.org),
especially Ross Miller.

I would also like to thank everybody at Jacana Media
and their partners in the EU Literary Award,
as well as my editor, Alex Dodd.

As thank-you is forbidden, I hope that Shobha
Bohra and Pratibha Pathak will not mind me saying:
"Dhanyavaad."

And to all my family and friends, shukran.